865/0407

The BlackGuard of

~~ The Glen Highland Romance ~~

Book 8

Michelle Deerwester-Dalrymple

The BlackGuard of the Glen

Copyright 2021 Michelle Deerwester-Dalrymple All rights reserved
ISBN: 9798470994769
Imprint: Independently published
Cover art/model: Period Images
Michelle Deerwester-Dalrymple

All rights reserved. In accordance with the U.S. Copyright Act of 1976, the scanning, uploading, distribution, or electronic sharing of any part of this book without the permission of the author constitutes unlawful piracy of the author's intellectual property. If you would like to use the material from this book, other than for review purposes, prior authorization from the author must be obtained. Copies of this text can be made for personal use only. No mass distribution of copies of this text is permitted.

This book is a work of fiction. Names, dates, places, and events are products of the author's imagination or used factiously. Any similarity or resemblance to any person living or dead, place, or event is purely coincidental.

If you love this book, be sure to leave a review! Reviews are life blood for authors, and I appreciate every review I receive!

Want more from Michelle? Click below to receive *The Heartbreak of the Glen,* the free Glen Highland Romance short ebook, to read more about Gavin before starting this book! It also offers free ebooks, updates, and more in your inbox!

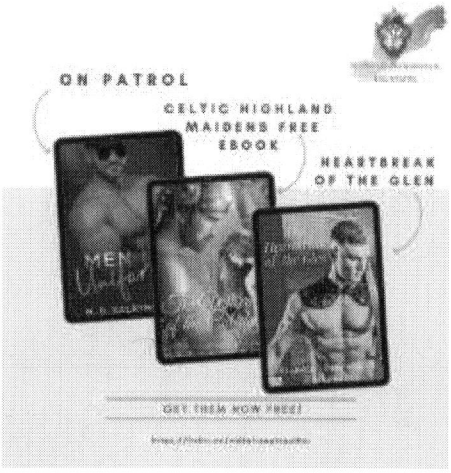

Find the newsletter link here: https://linktr.ee/mddalrympleauthor

The BlackGuard of the Glen

Table of Contents

The BlackGuard of the Glen _____ *1*

Chapter One: Considering Vengeance _____ *7*

Chapter Two: The Larder _____ *10*

Chapter Three: Meeting the King _____ *24*

Chapter Four: Secrets _____ *33*

Chapter Five: To Strike a Bargain _____ *41*

Chapter Six: Letters _____ *57*

Chapter Seven: All the King's Men _____ *68*

Chapter Eight: The Black Douglas _____ *80*

Chapter Nine: Life at Auchinleck _____ *93*

Chapter Ten: Private Conversations _____ *104*

Chapter Eleven: The Dreaded Wedding _____ *119*

Chapter Twelve: More Man than Monster ____ *132*

Chapter Thirteen: Well and Truly Wedded ____ *151*

Chapter Fourteen: A Shocking Lack of Training _____ *167*

Chapter Fifteen: Reclaiming Scotland _____ *184*

Chapter Sixteen: Are Ye Mine? _____ *193*

Chapter Seventeen: Private Trysts _____ *202*

Chapter Eighteen: An Unexpected Encounter ___ *214*

Chapter Nineteen: A Plan for Scotland _____ *228*

Chapter Twenty: Payback _____ *238*

Chapter Twenty-One: Sharing the News _____ *252*

Chapter Twenty-Two: A New Plan _____ *262*

Chapter Twenty-Three: Waiting _____ *270*

Chapter Twenty-Four: Shabib *289*

Chapter Twenty-Five: Heeding the Call to Arms *299*

Chapter Twenty-Six: The Future of Scotland *314*

An Excerpt From The Maiden of the Storm *327*

Historical Fevered Short Novella Series *330*

A Note on History – *333*

A Thank You– *335*

Also by the Author: *337*

Chapter One: Considering Vengeance

JAMES DUCKED BEHIND the yellow-budded gorse brush hidden in the eastern trees of the Douglas stronghold in Selkirk Wood. Douglas Castle. *His castle,* the one robbed from him by the vile King Edward Longshanks and granted to the loathsome Baron Robert Clifford, who rose to power by slaughtering fine Scots warriors, including the beloved Guardian of Scotland William Wallace. James's heart burned black at the mere thought of this man, nay, not a man, this devil that drew Scotland through hell.

Everything inside James was empty, a void carved out and burned to black ash by the English who had stolen everything from him — his mother and father, his lands, his castles. Even his very youth wasn't spent in his family lands, as his father sent him to France when their castle and the surrounding lands were seized. Hiding him from the King of England. *Hiding him!* The towering, powerful James Douglas?

Rather, the reckless James Douglas, if rumors held true. And he had to admit, those rumors held more truth than not.

Robert the Bruce, who had taken up the banner for Scotland after the death of Wallace, would assuredly welcome James with open arms. James hadn't been there at the failure of Methven, but he'd heard about it, and vowed to have his moment where he might swear his alliance, his sword, and his friendship to the bumbling lord-turned-King. When Robert escaped, with the Douglas clan's help, James realized 'twas time to leave his refuge and come home.

The first thing James had tried when he'd arrived in England was to petition for the return of his ancestral lands. He'd begun by requesting a meeting with King Edward Longshanks of England to see about taking his clan lands back. Lord Robert Clifford had been installed at Castle Douglas after the English had razed the Douglas lands. Since James had been absent for all of that, the king might not think him to have allegiance to the Scots. Clinging to that one, unlikely hope, James had traveled to England with his companions.

And Longshanks, hearing the mere mention of his name, rejected him, kicked him and his men out of the castle and out of England.

And the rock-hard, burning ball of fury in his gut only increased.

James would have his lands back.

Once he'd returned to Scotland, 'twas easy to hear of the Bruce's acceptance by the clans, and how he was building his army.

James informed his men they, too, would be joining the Bruce. But they had something that needed to be done first.

Chapter Two: The Larder

Douglasdale, Scotland Late March 1307

ONLY A HANDFUL of men were brave enough to join James on this senseless scheme. But if he played his strategy right, he would only need a handful.

James studied the stout tower, drab and gray against the cloudy sky. The seat of his clan, his birthright, stood as dark and subdued as he felt. As dismal as his life had been for the past several years hiding in France.

He wasn't focused on the stones of the tower that called him home like a siren called sailors to their doom. Instead, his aloof gray eyes, harder than the stone of the tower and as gray as the skies that hid the bright sun from those undeserving, studied the men surrounding the keep — those pathetic English soldiers who couldn't fight their way out of a burlap sack. Lazy, skinny, encased in overly large metal plates and mail that prevented them from running or fighting like true warriors.

Hell, half couldn't even raise a sword over their heads if needed.

Fools.

Two men (James couldn't bring himself to call them soldiers) stepped inside the gate, leaving it open, exposed.

Were these English so assured of their presence, of their prowess, that they left the open gate defenseless? He shook his raven-haired head.

Of course they were. James had watched them do it time and again over the past several days. The English were nothing if not predictable.

Two of James's own men joined him at the edge of the Selkirk forest brush line. They perched a few meters east of Douglasdale — his old friend and tenant farmer, Thomas Dickson with hair as black as his own, and his loyal confidant and paladin from France, the Moor Shabib, whose rich brown skin was reminiscent of the mountains in his homeland of Hispania.

"What are ye thinking, James?" Thomas asked in a whisper as he crouched behind his bush.

The man was devoutly loyal, having joined with James Douglas shortly after he watched helplessly as the English burned his crops, barn, and croft house to the ground. He'd fled with his wife and son to live with her Scott kin near Rutherford, then left to seek out the Douglas.

Shabib squatted on James's other side, his rich azure robes pooling on the ground as he peered through the bushes from under the edges of his turban-wrapped hood.

"You have mentioned that your people have a holiday soon. Is there a dictate that prevents you from military action on that date? If these English celebrate it, then their guard might be even more lax."

Ahh, James thought as he nodded. *Shabib is always one to see the larger picture.*

"Aye. The Lenten season ends with Easter and 'tis Palm Sunday in two days. Their commander, Clifford — the foul besom — is gone from the tower already for the season. Only a shell guard remains. Your idea has merit. They will no' expect an attack on one of the Lord's most holy days."

"James," Thomas's low voice dropped lower. "Ye canna do such a thing on the Lord's day. 'Tis sin upon sin. Some things must remain sacred even in times of war."

James's gray eyes hardened to slate, cutting Thomas in a murderous glare.

"Thomas, I love ye like a brother, but ye must understand. These English have stolen and desecrated my birthright, slaughtered my kin and clan, your kin and clan, and are using it as an English stronghold against the Scots. And when I forfeited my pride, shamed myself to crawl like a lowly dog and beg the English king to return my lands, he had me removed from his grounds and threatened my life if I ever dared return. I tell ye, Thomas, if I canna be personally responsible for Edward Longshanks's death, then by God himself, I will slaughter every last English soldier I can get my hands on. Including those whose horrendous English asses sit in my keep, sin or no'!"

Chastised, Thomas bowed his head. As a tenant farmer with distant kin, he'd never had a strong connection to the seat of the Douglas lands. He couldn't judge James for the actions he was compelled to take, but that didn't make an invasion on the day the Lord entered Jerusalem any more palatable. 'Twas an abuse of a sacrament, in Thomas's lowly opinion.

And in the opinion of most.

"Aye, James," Thomas whispered.

"Your friend has a solid argument, James. Nothing good is to be had when one offends his God."

James swiveled on his toes to face Shabib. Beads of dew had formed on his tightly curled hairline that escaped his hood and the shoulders of his robe, creating a shimmering aura on the man.

"These words may be sharp on your ears, Shabib, and I mean no offense to your relationship to your God, but my God, perchance He has abandoned the Douglases, and probably all of Scotland. There's no one left to offend. And even if He's still present, we have the saying that God helps those who help themselves."

James shifted his harsh gaze to Thomas, who had the good sense to hang his head at James's sound argument.

Shabib's face never shifted, not even a twitch of his cheek — 'twas one of the reasons James found the man so agreeable. He wore no emotion, keeping those useless feelings in check. Feelings, emotions, those were as useless as a one-winged bee in James's estimation, and Shabib never bothered James with such petty inconveniences.

Thomas, on the other hand . . .

"If you believe that, James, then we must accept it," Shabib intoned. "Even Allah permits fighting during sacred months in response to acts of aggression. And what these English have done, aggression is too light a word. So if you have no qualms about an invasion, then neither do I."

"Shabib," Thomas pleaded, "I would hope ye might talk some sense into this man. His compulsion knows no bounds."

"We all have a calling, Thomas. If this is James's, then I will assist him as he needs." Shabib shifted his doleful brown eyes to James. "That does not mean I won't pray for your soul, James. Allah knows, someone must."

James drew on the ground with a stick. The air was thick with mist, yet still dry. No rain, yet. James poked at two shapes in the damp dirt, then lifted his face to the skies. Those watching him might say his expression was prayerful, but Thomas and Shabib knew otherwise. What James was searching for was a hint as to the weather the next day. James sniffed, trying to sense if a storm was eminent.

The strategy would still go on as planned, regardless. 'Twould only be easier if the rain held back. James might have prayed if he were a godly man. As it were, he tasked Thomas and Shabib with any prayers.

"Tomorrow. Early. Most men will be at the kirk, for mass. We'll start here, at the gate, with two men." James drew lines in the dirt. "The rest will come from here, in a surprise Highland charge that 'twill overwhelm those few at the gate. Once we are inside, gather everything, everything, as I have told ye, here." He stuck the stick in the ground.

"What point is there to putting everyone in the cellar? What will ye do once ye move back into the tower?" the young Douglas warrior, Gabriel asked, his light hair bright against the gray skies.

James's stare cut that innocent brightness to shreds.

"We aren't moving back in, Gabe. No one is. I have alternate plans."

The difference in the skies between prime and sunrise brightened in a thin thread of sunlight that pierced the clouds. 'Twas more dark than light as James Douglas and his men crept to the stronghold. No guards kept watch, and they could have walked up in the noontime sun.

Thomas and Gabriel pressed forward to the gate. The rest of James's men tucked along the edge of the palisade, waiting for Thomas's high-pitched whistle, signaling the rest of the Highlanders to attack.

The thread of light widened, and with it, Thomas's whistle. With only the sounds of their feet in the muck, they moved as one being, blending into the stone and set with one singular focus. Destruction.

They slipped into the inner Bailey. No horses, no villeins, 'twas emptier than even James, in his most optimistic self, was surprised to see. Truly, the hubris of these English was boundless.

James tipped his head to his men, indicating it was time to take the church. A moue of guilt clenched James's chest at attacking a church on the Lord's day, but he flung it aside like a gnawed bone. Guilt would gain him nothing, certainly not his keep.

They reached the church, and James flung the sturdy oak doors open wide where they banged against the stone in announcement. Dim early-morning light filtered through the high window slits and illuminated the men who spun in their pews at the intrusion. James flicked his eyes to the priest-less altar. Figures.

"End them," he commanded, and his men melted between the pews with their broadswords drawn, striking down the defenseless men. A couple of Englishmen managed to unsheathe their swords, but not in enough time to save their lives.

Or their souls. They might be praying to God, and perchance God hadn't abandoned the English as He had the Douglases and the Scots, but these English demons were wasting their breaths. Heaven had no seat at its table for these unshriven souls.

One man wasn't exactly dead, and with a weak, bloodied arm, tried to drag his punctured body to the wall, as though he might escape his inevitable death. James didn't blink. He flipped his sword expertly in his hand and brought the blade across in a smooth arc, splitting the man's neck. The Englishman shuddered once and stopped, his neck's blood running in a river on the stones.

James wiped his blade on the man's tunic then rose to face his soldiers.

"Drag them out. Follow me."

Wrapping his hand in the dead man's tunic, James then dragged the man he'd finished off past the wide doors, down the steps, and into the dirt. His men followed his trail of blood to the main keep. James kicked in the door, searching for the knight that

Lord Robert Clifford had left in charge. The lazy fool wasn't in the church.

Probably couldn't be bothered to rise that early. They dragged the dead men to the stronghold's cellar, then spread out into the tower. Some of the men then found, they killed immediately. Others they bound. All were dragged to the cellars as well. James raced to the upper floors of the tower with Thomas and Shabib, until they found the second-in-command hiding in a plush, decorated chamber room.

My parent's chambers. James's head flashed red with blood and fury, and he raised his sword. Instead of using his blade that screamed for this man's death, James cracked the hilt of his sword against the man's head, and he dropped like a stone.

"Ye dinna want him dead?" Thomas asked.

James ripped a cord from a nearby tapestry, whipping it round his hand.

"He will be dead soon enough. I only lament that Clifford is not here. My vengeance will never be complete until that man is dead. These *sassenach* will have to do. They have their own culpability to account for."

James bound the man's hands behind his back until they turned purple, then dragged him down the steps to join his brethren in the cellar.

"Now, everything in the keep that is not tacked down, peat, hay, food, wine, tapestries, bedding, everything ye can find. Bring it here."

James started for the steps when Shabib grabbed his arm, his eyes blazing into James's soul. "James, friend. This is a dark path upon which you tread. 'Twill blacken your soul. Are you sure you wish to set onto this path? Otherwise, ye can leave, stand guard at the gate."

James's washed-out eyes searched his dear friend's face. His eyes were as empty as his chest, as empty as his soul.

"My soul is already blackened, my old friend. I've been walking this path too long for any other outcome."

Shabib placed a long-fingered hand on James's wide, weary shoulder. "'Tis never too late to step off the path. No matter how black your soul. If not today, perchance one day you will find the redemption you desire."

"I have no desire for anything, Shabib," James answered, opening his arms wide. "I welcome this blackness. I will no' begrudge ye if ye decide to sit out of these final events. But I must finish this. It must come to an end."

Shabib bobbed his head, then followed James to the main floor with his men. They spent hours throwing all they could lift into the cellars. One man had tipped a bottle of wine to his lips, and James smacked it away. The bottle fell to the stones and shattered in a burgundy mess.

"Dinna drink from this poisoned well," James commanded. His nostrils flared, and his brow was low, shadowing his eyes. His jaw was set and so sharp it might cut the very stone upon which they stood.

The man leaned to Gabe. "What fire burns in his mind? Why throw everything into the cellar? Like a nightmare larder. Are we going to waste it all?"

Gabriel shrugged as he rolled up another tapestry to toss into the cellar.

"I dinna know, but I'm sure the man has a reason for his madness," Gabe answered.

"Other than he is just mad?"

"Quit belly aching and help me with this."

Once the cellar was packed with food and furnishings, dead bodies and live prisoners, Douglas's men stood around the collection, their backs pressed against the dirty stone walls of the cellar. The pleading cries of the few who still lived sent chills down their spines.

Shabib brought kindling to James, who busied himself with it. He didn't raise his eyes to the men as he spoke.

"Thomas, ye and Shabib lead the men out of here. Get as far back from the keep as ye can. Back to the tree line."

The kindling James had been working caught and a slender orange flame lit his face and created a shadow around his head. A black halo.

"James, for the final time, are ye certain? This larder in your family's cellar may haunt ye all your life. Your castle will be forever destroyed and your soul will never recover," Thomas pleaded with him.

"I'd rather have a black soul and crumbling debris for a keep if it means the English can never use the lands against the Scots again. As for my soul, well, Thomas, ye well know this path I was on. My soul was already tainted. This will just complete it."

James nodded to Shabib, who ushered the men up the steps and out of the keep. Then he waited, listening to the sobbing. He didn't have to harden his heart against the sound, 'twas already hardened, as black as jet, and he'd accepted that lot. With a flip of his hand, he threw the inflamed kindling into the larder of food and furnishings, and moved closer to the steps, waiting and watching. He wanted assurances that the flames were well entrenched before he left. The wine and mead caught the flames, bringing the fire to life.

Smoke became dense, and James backed up several steps out of the growing, choking cloud. The sobbing in the cellar became screams when those captured smelled the sickeningly thick smoke. Those screams would haunt his nightmares if James let them.

He closed his ears to those dire sounds. The flames in the cellar erupted in bursts, here and there, and his eyes reflected those flames, as if the fire were inside his head, not in the cellar. When he was assured the fire was well established and wouldn't burn itself out, James ascended to the main floor and departed his childhood home, his birthright, his legacy, leaving it to burn to the ground.

Joining his men outside, he walked to the tree line and stared at the keep, steady with a keen patience only a man truly and unforgivably offended can maintain. The only sounds in the glen were of the popping flames and the low lamentations of those trapped in the cellar. His men drifted off, sat on the grass to eat, to rest, to wait for James to have his recompense. Shabib stood next to him the entire time.

Soon the flames licked out of the stones themselves, and the heavier rocks at the top of the tower slipped as the foundation crumbled to ash. Then the flames ate at those stones, charring them black, as black as James's soul.

By the time the late afternoon rain started to fall, most of the keep and even some of the surrounding inner bailey had been destroyed. The smoke in the air was thick, so thick even the rain didn't seem to be able to wash it away. Still, James watched with his arms crossed over his wide chest until the last flame's light licked out.

"'Tis done," Shabib told him. "You have destroyed your larder just as certain as the English had, and now they cannot use your castle against you. You must live with this the consequences of this foul deed. Do you feel any sense of remorse?" Shabib asked, his voice edged with a concern James had not heard in his friend's voice before.

James kept his gaze fixed on the ruined, steaming remains of Douglas Castle. He'd hoped the dark, bleak fury toward the English might have lightened with the destruction of his castle and the men contained therein, but that fury yet lingered. To James, this was a beginning, not an end.

"I feel nothing," James answered honestly.

Thomas, Gabe, and the other men had perked up at Shabib's voice, and they moved closer to James, hopeful to learn what they would do next. Especially since it meant spending the night in the rain now that the tower was destroyed.

"Well, then, my Black Douglas," Shabib asked, his eyebrows high on his forehead. "Did you have a contrivance for *after* this was accomplished?"

James uncrossed his arms, and with his hard-lined face, too hard for so young a man, he regarded each of those wretched souls who agreed to throw their lot in with him. 'Twas time think beyond himself.

"We've eliminated the English leeches here, but like the fat bloodsuckers, they still suck away at the life of Scotland. Our work is far from done. We will salt the wells, throw any remains in them, too, and pollute it. We shall make the land a black reminder of what the English have wrought on our land. Then we are to join the Bruce."

Chapter Three: Meeting the King

Dumfries, The Crown of Scotland, Early April 1307

THE CHAMBER ROBERT the Bruce occupied in Auchinleck Castle permitted every spring draft entrance as though they were invited. Though he wore his bear fur trimmed cape and stood directly in front of the fire, he shivered. Perchance 'twasn't the cold that embedded the chills into his bones.

Dark days loomed ahead of the Scots cause, with Robert himself at the helm.

John Sinclair's voice called to him. The Bruce shifted profile, and John's bright red head popped in, followed by his burly frame.

"King Robert, you have a strange visitor, one who requests your presence."

Strangely foreboding words from the normally light-hearted Sinclair man.

"Nay, an English emissary? My luck could never be so good," the king grumbled. John shook his head.

"Nay," James told him, his voice dropping low. "He claims to be James Douglas."

The Bruce froze, rooted to his spot on the woven rug. One eye narrowed at John, and his jaw clicked as he clenched it.

"Surely ye jest. That man has been long gone from the Scotland. His family lands fortified by the English."

"Rumors had spread that he tried to claim his lands from Edward, and Longshanks, upon hearing James's name, wouldn't even see the man and had him and his men sent away."

Robert didn't answer right away. He bit the inside of his cheek as he thought about the man standing outside his door.

"I would think Longshanks might have slaughtered the man and his soldiers right then."

John grunted. "Well, likely he regrets no' doing so now. Ye have heard of the Douglas larder?"

"I've heard that Douglas Castle was burned to the ground, and some have said 'twas James's own hand that committed that atrocious action," Robert answered in a terse tone.

He had indeed heard more, but much of it was so inconceivable, Robert didn't want to speak of it and give it any validity until he heard the truth for himself. He had doubted James had even returned to Scotland at all.

John's mouth worked, and he threw his shoulders back to face the king.

"Aye, well, 'twas a sight more than that. From what the rumors suggest, the man may no' be quite in his right mind."

"John," Robert said with a heavy breath, "Your words are too kind, if the rumors are true. Until we hear it from the man himself, however, we will no' sustain those tales."

"He's been called Black Douglas as of late, and while the man's hair is dark, I dinna believe they've given him this title for that reason."

The king nodded as his somber thoughts dug deeper. Robert well understood how black a man's heart, a man's soul, might become. William Wallace of yore was reputed to have one of the darkest souls in history, for all that he was a hero to the Scots. Heroism oft came at a dreadful price. He lifted a hand to John.

"Please tell Laird Douglas I would be honored to make his acquaintance."

"Laird James Douglas. The prodigal son has returned, and Scotland welcomes ye."

Robert's welcome sounded rehearsed, but the striking jolt to his chest at the sight of the reputed man made any words hollow.

James gave a slight bow to the brown-haired man who stood before him. The idea of a king was oft swollen and grandiose that a mere man himself couldn't compare. Robert was a bit of an exception. He wore no crown, only the unruly brown mane God graced him with. His heavy beard and lined face spoke of years of battle, yet his shoulders were still stiff, strong, proud, not curving under the weight of age or weariness. The broad man was of a fair height, almost as tall as James himself.

After seeing the thin, sickly-looking English nobles ruled by an old man who probably looked the same, encountering the powerfully hale Scots king, a man who lived up to his notoriety, sparked a light of hope in James's chest.

"I thank ye, King Robert. I've been long absent from my clan lands, and I am glad to have returned."

James straightened, and several seconds passed as the men regarded each other, James's iron-gray gaze meeting the Bruce's deep amber one directly.

"I've heard rumors, James, ones that speak volumes if they are true. Regarding Douglas Castle?"

James's stoic face hardened even more. "I believe ye mean the reputed Douglas larder."

The Bruce stiffened. The man didn't deny it.

"The rumors, James, they are true?"

James continued to stare at the Bruce, and his face shifted, a hint of a strange, dangerous smile tugging at his full lips.

"I believe ye mean to call me Black Douglas, my liege."

It took every ounce of Robert's will not to let his face change, not to react in any way. The man didn't deny it. A man who destroyed his own lands, adopted a scorched earth approach rather than permit the English to use that stronghold against the Scots people again — it spoke of a level of madness. Not that 'twas a bad thing. Many had said Wallace was as mad as they came. And the Bruce had followed that valiant man and taken up his very banner when Wallace died.

Douglas's madness grew from a separate root, one of obsession, of being robbed of one's birthright. And if that meant his military approach to the English was this dark, this furious, then by God, Robert wanted the Douglas laird in his army.

'Twould be easy enough to claim him, Robert knew. The man had nothing left but his name and his title.

"While I cannot necessarily condone what ye elected to do to your lands and those inhabiting them, I also know we are fighting senseless monsters. And when we fight monsters, we oft must take the most drastic measures humanly, or inhumanly possible."

Douglas remained silent, his flat, steely eyes studying the Bruce in such a way a lesser man might have squirmed under his glare. A way most men would not have used on their king.

"I need men in my army who can strategize, who are willing to make hard decisions against a ferocious enemy. Only then, will Scotland have her freedom. Ye, my dark laird, should have a seat at my table. Will ye accept this position?"

Again, silence. Then James gave the king another curt bow.

"I am honored to serve ye, my King."

Robert flipped the length of his cape behind his legs and stepped closer to Black Douglas. He flung his arms open wide.

"Then ye mad, black-hearted man, let me give ye a kinder welcome than the one ye received in Douglasdale."

James studied him for a space of several heartbeats, then stepped into the King's embrace. The Black Douglas was a weapon, a hard, ruthless weapon, but he was still a man who needed the camaraderie, the acceptance of his king. Bruce made it his mission to remember that fact, lest James lose the last trace of any humanity he had in his black heart.

The Bruce established James Douglas in a small set of chambers in the keep and his men in a pair of close set, decaying crofts not far from the stronghold. King Robert had requested Douglas's attendance at a meeting he was having with several advisers later in the day, much to James's surprise.

While news of his attack on his own castle spread more quickly than a wildfire throughout Scotland, he didn't believe that his loathsome attack could be the reason the king wanted him at his royal meeting.

Thomas scoffed when James mused this out loud. The lean, brown-haired man spread his plaid on a pile of hay for his makeshift bedding in the croft as he spoke to his laird.

"James, ye dinna know why the king might want ye at his meeting. But if lowly innkeepers have heard of your misdeeds against the English, I would wager my last coin that the king has heard of it as well. And someone with your, shall we say, *maligned* view of military strategy, may be just what the king needs to regain his kingdom against the English. The Good Lord knows the English have used similarly dire tactics against us Scots. Mayhap your reputation might precede ye, sending the fear of a gruesome death at your monstrous hands through the lot of them."

James flopped onto a hardback chair near the heart and grumbled under his breath. He had no response — Thomas was assuredly correct. His moniker of Black Douglas had become well entrenched in Scottish lowland lore, and nary a fortnight had passed since the dark event.

Shabib busied himself, looking about the croft to find the best place for his prayer rug. He was noticeably quiet.

James had an awareness that Shabib, while a devout and loyal friend, didn't fully approve of the dark path that James had embarked upon. But as a man grappling with his own demons, Shabib wasn't about to judge or comment. Instead he would get on his knees, bow to Mecca, and ask for forgiveness and absolution, and perchance peace for his tortured friend.

Shabib's lack of judgment was like a lone piece of floating wood in the sea, something James could hold onto so as not to drown in his own pit of despair.

James tried to push these thoughts away as he stared into the fire and let the heat warm his skin. How long had it been since he felt warm? Since he had a sense of home? Of family? The closest he came were Thomas, Gabe, and Shabib. And of those, only Shabib had been with him since France.

William Lamberton had been kind and tried to be a father figure for the lost lad when he'd arrived in France. After James's studies, the Bishop of St. Andrews had sent for him, making him a squire, and this move by Lamberton paved the way for James to become a hardened knight and even presented him at the British court to try to recoup his stronghold. The name Lamberton was the only reason Longshanks had considered meeting with James in the first place.

While he owed much to that great man, 'twasn't family. Dry biscuits and stringy beef by a lonely hearth, catechism studies, and squire duties did not a family make.

And here in Scotland now, he had his men, brethren he'd consider as close as brothers. But not a family in the way most understood. In the way Thomas or Shabib understood.

Mayhap 'tis what's made my soul as black as death, he pondered as he sat mesmerized by the dancing flames.

A banging at the door drew his attention from the fire, and he cast a quick glance at Shabib. The moor was wrapped in his richly colored robes and kneeling on his blanket — certainly not ready to accompany James on a meeting with King Robert the Bruce. Thomas and Gabe dropped their gazes. They too were unprepared to find themselves aligned with Black Douglas in the presence of the king.

James rubbed a bear-like hand through his riotous, shoulder-length black hair and marched to the door. A slender lad with a sword nearly longer than himself straightened when James swung the door open.

"The king requests your presence," the laddie squeaked.

James nodded, and grabbing his own broadsword sitting against the wall by the door, he ducked out the low door frame and followed the lad back to the king's temporary keep.

Humility didn't sit easily on James's shoulders, and he knew that if the king had Black Douglas on his side, the man was certain to reclaim his kingdom.

Chapter Four: Secrets

The Outskirts of Edinburgh, Late Spring 1307

"TOSIA, CAN YE bring me some eggs? We can boil them for dinner."

Flipping her chestnut hair over her shoulder, Tosia rushed to her mother's side. The woman had looked drawn as of late, tired, and her skin had a gray pallor that sent a lurch of fear over her spine whenever she thought on it.

Her mother's cough had been growing worse, sometimes making it difficult for her mother to even speak. And there was something more — something her mother wasn't telling her but made her mother cry herself to sleep at night when she thought Tosia wasn't listening.

Something dire was weighing on Maggie Fraser, and she wasn't telling her children.

"Aye, Mother. Can I get ye anything else?"

Maggie shook her head and began coughing, covering her mouth with a rough linen cloth. Tosia set her jaw and patted her mother's shoulder before heading outside into the drizzling rain in search of eggs.

Her brother, Tavish, was outside, his broadening shoulders and arms swinging an axe at a stack of split logs. The poor lad, well, not so much a lad anymore. Tavish had grown into a strapping young man, but with few prospects. Tosia sighed. Neither of them had prospects.

She hadn't been deaf to the rumor that she and her brother were bastards of some laird or other man of import. Her mother had never shared that information with them, keeping her scandalous history a secret. Tosia didn't know who her father might be, but being labeled as illegitimate meant no offers for her hand and few opportunities for Tavish. Since they also lived on the outskirts of Fraser land, they had little interaction with those in the village or in the clan at all.

Life for Tosia had been her mother and her brother. She had no idea how her mother supported them on the Fraser lands. They weren't tenant farmers — did her mother have to pay the

Fraser laird for usage of the land? Their rents? If so, where did that coin come from?

Most importantly, what would happen when her mother died?

Because that event was on the horizon. Tosia may not know much, but only a great fool could miss the signs. Tosia was many things, but she was no fool.

Tosia's mind whirled at these thoughts as she absently collected the small brown eggs scattered about the thatched chicken coop. Once her basket was full with all the eggs she could find nested in the grass and peat, she stepped outside into the drizzle.

Tavish met her at the door, his arms full of stacked wood. More scarce, it burned hotter than peat, and they needed all they could to chase away the chill, for their mother's sake.

"How is she?" Tavish asked before they entered. So many conversations about their mother began this way — questions about her health out of her earshot whilst they labored.

Tosia shook her damp head. "The cough is just as bad. I dinna know what to do for her anymore. Yet she will no' say what is going on."

Tavish shifted the lengths of firewood in his arms. "Mayhap 'tis time to confront her."

Though the idea had merit, Tosia dropped her gaze and dug at the mud with her toe.

"We canna force her to speak on it, and I will no' put her in that position. She will tell us when she is ready."

Maggie's cough grew more worrisome. Then one morning, blood clots accompanied the cough. That morning, instead of sending her children out for their chores, she asked them to join her at their narrow wooden table. She took Tosia's hand in her left and Tavish's in her right. Her gray skin hung on her frame, and Tosia's heart pounded erratically in her chest.

'Tis the moment. She's going to tell us she's dying, Tosia thought as her watery eyes gazed upon her beloved mother. What would Tosia do without her?

"Tosia," Maggie said with a glance at her daughter, then flicked her eyes to her son. "Tavish. I have a bit of news for ye, and I would ask that ye let me get through it afore ye ask questions. 'Tis much, to be sure."

Tosia tightened on her stool and the pounding in her chest stretched to her temples. But she did as she was bid and remained silent. A furtive look to her brother showed that he, too, was as still, as stiff, as she. Their shared panic filled the room more fully than the weak heat from the hearth.

"Ye've had questions about your father, and I've avoided many of them. I know it has angered ye. But I swore to the man I would no' mention his name to ye. To anyone. That I would keep the secret of ye to myself out of respect for him and his family."

Family. The word bit like a dog. Their father had a family somewhere? A family that didn't include them? Already Tosia disliked the man. Even if he was her father.

"Dinna judge the man too harshly. He was away from his family for a long time, and I was there. He gifted me the two best gifts a woman could ask for. And for the past twenty years, he's made certain our needs h ave been well met. This sturdy roof over our heads, food in our bellies, and a bit o'coin in our purse."

Twenty years? The man paid for their care for twenty years and Tosia had not known? How had her mother managed such a task of keeping that a secret?

"What has happened, mother? Is the man no longer paying because Tavish and I are older? Does he expect us to be on our own now?"

How could any man call himself a man and leave a woman in dire straights? The deep-seated anger at how this man left her mother inflamed Tosia's cheeks and burned in a hard ball in her stomach. She hated this man she'd never met.

Her mother must have seen a movement on Tosia's face, for she patted her lass's hand.

"Now, Tosia. Dinna judge harshly. I knew what would happen when I agreed to be with him for the short time I was. I loved him, and he loved me, and if all I had was those few years, then they were worth it. And he did as best he could for his children he couldn't claim. I never begrudged him that."

Tosia disagreed but didn't press the issue and let her gaze fall to the worn tabletop.

"He's no longer providing for your care, because he died last fall. As a high commander of the Bruce's army, he was captured by the English, hanged, drawn, and quartered, and his head now resided on a pike next to Wallace's."

Good riddance, Tosia thought spitefully, but the catch in her mother's voice when she spoke of her father's death gave her pause. Did her mother still love this man who'd left her? From the sadness in Maggie's voice, Tosia believed she must.

"I'm sorry for his death, Mother. But—"

"Let me finish Tosia. There is quite a bit more. Ye see, your father was an important man, and no' only to the Bruce. I know ye've heard rumors about who he might be. In truth, your father was Laird Simon Fraser. Ye are the illegitimate children of one of the most powerful men in Scotland, who was, until his death, a close confidant, ally, and warrior for King Robert the Bruce himself. Ye see why he couldn't claim ye? Why ye had to remain a secret?"

Tosia couldn't respond. Her mouth dried out, and with it her words. What could she possibly say to this shocking information?

She was part of the great Fraser legacy? And his family didn't know? And her mother lived alone all this time to protect the man's lineage and his standing?

Tosia raised one eye to her mother, almost afraid to look at her in this new light. Maggie had a strength Tosia hadn't known was possible.

Her mother had said quite a bit more. Surely there couldn't be more information? Was there? Tosia struggled with what she had learned thus far.

"I've a letter here in my pocket from King Robert the Bruce," Maggie continued, ignoring the shocked expressions of her children. She released their hands and withdrew the missive from a fold in her skirt.

Tosia and Tavish could both read. Maggie had been taught by this great man himself, and she'd made sure to teach both of her children. Men should be able to read, she'd claimed. For women, reading might serve in a dire time of need one day, Maggie had told her, so she'd taught Tosia basic letters and reading as well.

The letter Maggie withdrew had a broken seal, but enough of it was still intact for Tosia to make out the emblem. The brownish-red seal portrayed a mounted soldier bearing a sword. The seal of King Robert the Bruce.

The pounding in her head and chest grew insufferably worse. Why did her mother have a letter from the king? Tosia cut her mother a skeptical gaze — who was this woman she thought she knew?

Maggie took a moment to cough tiredly into a rag, and Tosia tried not to notice the heavy red streaks left behind. Then Maggie opened the letter and let her eyes peruse the words before she spoke again.

Chapter Five: To Strike a Bargain

Dumfries, Summer, 1307

THE AIR AT Dumfries was stifling, not from the weather and heat of the day, but from the smug feeling of victory.

Robert the Bruce inhaled deeply, taking in that aura of conceit, of victory, and breathing out the past ten years of heartache, oppression, and strife.

He wasn't done. He wasn't close to being done. Scotland was still hindered by the English yoke. He was still separated from his wife and daughter who were yet imprisoned by the king of England. Would Robert see them again in this lifetime? Only God knew the answer to that question. But for now, larger issues for Scotland loomed.

And smaller ones as well.

For the larger issues, the Scots military accomplishment had truly been unprecedented. After years of the English quashing the Scots attempts at independence, even under the staunch leadership of Sir William Wallace, the changes as of late had been unparalleled.

And Robert had Black Douglas to thank for it.

The man had a bleak and terrifying way of looking at the world, of seeing a harrowing strategy when none could be found, implementing those strategies in the most vicious way, leading to a successful outcome.

Robert's soul might be forever cursed in following Douglas's advice and recommendations against the English, but he'd smile the entire way to Hell. So far, having the fiend James Douglas as a commander and tactician in his army had been the best decision he'd made.

Black Douglas fought as though he had nothing to lose. And therein laid the problem.

He didn't.

The man's family was slain, his clan dispersed to the ends of Scotland, and he gutted, poisoned, and burned his own stronghold to the ground to prevent any further occupation of Douglasdale by the English.

If Robert didn't know any better, he'd think Black Douglas was well and truly mad.

Mayhap he was. His actions bore that out.

Regardless, the man had well earned the title of Black Douglas. And Robert had benefited.

A man like that, while so very, very valuable in war, could yet be a liability. Unlike James, other men, men such as Robert the Bruce, did have something left to lose.

As king, he needed to find a way to balance the horrific darkness of James with a sense of potential loss so the man didn't make a final, overreaching step from which he might not return. The Douglas was adrift, even with his clansman and his Moorish friend. They didn't anchor him, not in the same way having a family might.

Robert had been struggling with that issue — how to anchor Douglas, provide a counterbalance for his somber pain that drove him to the brink of lunacy. Otherwise, Robert might find his own soul past the point of no return.

And as God had been doing for the past several months, He dropped the solution to this Douglas problem right in his lap in the form of a slender, pleading missive.

Would Douglas accept it? Only if his king commanded it. And by God, Robert would command it. He had the solution mapped out.

All he required was for James to say aye.

A heavy rapping at the door of the study interrupted the Bruce's thoughts. He moved to his seat behind the desk and settled himself.

"Enter," he commanded.

The giant Douglas man entered on confident feet and in two long strides was before the Bruce. He bowed briefly then leaned his own gigantic frame on the armchair back that squealed in protest. Robert flicked his eyes to the offended seat, wondering if it would splinter under James's weight.

Robert the Bruce was a man of fair size. Some even claimed him to be large — quite appropriate for a Scots warrior. Other men, many from the Highlands like the red-headed Sinclair and his brothers, bordered on immense, making Robert feel small in comparison.

There were none that Robert had met who compared in size or demeanor to Black Douglas.

The man wasn't just tall — 'twas like setting an ancient pine next to a sapling and calling the pine tall. Even giant didn't fit, as it was too small a word. Was there a word that fit a man such as James? If so, Robert didn't know it.

And it wasn't only his height. Many men in the Scottish Highlands were tall, but the breadth of James — his shoulders, his chest, his back, his legs — the sole comparison Robert could muster was the Greek story of the half-bull monster that lived in the maze. James was a veritable Minotaur.

Black as a title fit him well, not for his disposition, but for his rich black mane that brushed his shoulders in a matted wave, his gray eyes lined in deep black lashes, and the grim expression the man wore without end. Even his voice was a grumbling, rolling voice that easily struck fear into most men.

Aye, Black Douglas was a fitting name.

A name Robert wanted to scale back, at least a hint, to save both his soul and James's.

James's gray eyes studied Robert in the way he imagined a wildcat might study a vole. With stark and unending patience, waiting for the perfect moment to strike. A chill coursed over Robert's back.

Douglas *must* accept this request.

Robert bided his time for several moments, shifting through the parchments on the desk before turning his gaze to James.

"I've a letter, James," Robert began, working to frame his words in the best light possible. James prided himself on his hard nature, his warrior status, his ability with a sword. Marriage, if not love, was not something James was searching for. If anything, Robert knew the man was running from those earthly trappings.

He'd heard the rumors, and many lasses found the Black Douglas exciting, mysterious, a man they might conquer. Beautiful lasses, ones any man would be pleased to find in his bed. Yet Douglas shunned them all. From what Robert's men had said, Douglas didn't take anyone to his bed since he'd arrived.

Guarding his heart? Guarding his body? Was the man so jaded he didn't feel safe or comfortable finding his release with maids at the keep? Even when they had been ensconced at Threave earlier in the spring, he hadn't allowed anyone close to him.

Only Thomas and his dark friend the Shabib the Moor were permitted close conference.

Well, they and Robert himself.

Robert shook his head. No, James wasn't going to receive this information well at all.

"What's in your letter? Something from one of your Highland clans?"

James's voice reflected the man. Deep and resonating.

"Ye may want to sit for this," Robert told James, sweeping his hand to the wood-backed chair presently threatening to buckle. If James were mad, as many suggested, as his own history suggested, then having that giant, black-haired man sitting instead of towering over him was a prudent idea.

James stared at Robert unmoving then lifted one bushy eyebrow and settled his girth into the chair that protested all the more. From the corner of his eye, Robert noted the Moor had followed Douglas to the study and now shifted to stand behind Black Douglas, his dark, long-fingered hands lost in the draping folds of his blue cape. Between the two of them, they commanded any room in which they stood, overpowering even the presence of a King, Robert begrudgingly acknowledged. Aye, a fine weapon indeed.

But a weapon that must be controlled.

Robert's hand grasped the letter that potentially held a measure of that control.

James dark green and brown kilt drooped between his legs, and he leaned his elbows on his knees. He was on alert, and not for the first time, Robert fidgeted under James's steely gaze.

"'Tis no' a letter from a clan laird or chieftain. 'Tis from a woman who was the mistress to Simon Fraser."

James started slightly, sat back, and folded his arms over his wall-like chest. His rogue eyebrow rose higher.

"I knew the man had a wandering eye, but he must have hid it well. I have no' heard of any mistress."

"Then prepare yourself for this news," Robert continued.

"What does this have to do with me?" The suspicion in James's voice dripped from his lips.

Robert cleared his throat and gripped the edge of his desk, preparing himself for James's reaction.

"Ye may have heard that Simon Fraser was put to death by the English late last year, his head on a pike right next to the great Wallace himself. His family's line will continue to flourish on the Fraser lands in a free Scotland, but Simon left something else behind that few knew about. I dinna believe he was aware that *I* knew about it."

Robert extracted a curled parchment from his stack and placed it on the opposite side of the desk for James to review.

"Maggie Fraser was a woman with whom Fraser spent much time. He was away from his wife and family for a long while as he worked with the other lairds and Wallace. Fraser spent so much time with this woman that he sired two children by her. A lad, now a young man, and a lass, a woman. For the past twenty years, he provided coin, paid their rents, provided food and other necessaries for the woman and her children."

James's eyes never left Robert's face. He didn't even try to read the parchment. Robert sighed. This conversation was about to become difficult.

"The money he'd secretly provided the woman has run out —"

"And now she seeks recourse from ye?" James interrupted.

Robert shook his head and inhaled again.

"Nay. No' quite that. She wants no handouts because she is not for long in this world. She has the coughing disease and would see her daughter and son set before she expires."

Robert dropped his gaze. That was half the truth.

"But there's something more."

"Your king has a command for ye, James. Ye may no' think 'tis important, and ye might think me a bit foolish, but 'tis for the good of ye, of myself, of the Douglas's, and of Scotland as a whole. I have most of the details worked out. All ye have to do to please your king is say aye."

James's already hard, silvery gaze narrowed. He waited several heartbeats before dipping his head at his king.

"What is your request, King Robert?"

His words were harder than the black stones of the mountains. Robert cleared this throat to continue.

"Ye are the finest warrior the Scots have. Your mind is brilliant when it comes to military success. However, most of your strategies, your applications, come with a sharp edge. One that is harrowing and burdens your soul. If your soul is burdened, then so is mine, so is that of your men. But I have a solution to help lighten that burden and resolve a commitment to one of my fine commanders who has fallen under the iron fist of the English."

James's expression never wavered.

"And?"

James's expression might have remained unmoved, but the man leaned forward, resting his well-muscled arms on his knees again. His eyes burned into Robert like a branding iron.

"She wants ye to have them established?"

"Especially in this dangerous time. Her son has seventeen years, so he can become a squire to any of the knights here, including ye if ye so choose. Truthfully, 'tis what I prefer."

James's jaw clenched, twitching under the force of the movement. Robert tried not to react — how could even a king stay calm and collected under James's stony glare?

"And what of the lass?"

Robert worked to frame his words in the best light possible. James prided himself on his severe nature, his warrior status, his ability with a sword. Marriage, or love, was not something James was searching for.

"What are your intentions with the lass?" James's voice was like the man. Deep and threatening.

He knew. Robert set his own jaw, struggling to find a way that James might accept his ploy. The alternative, striking the man's ire, was not what Robert wanted to encounter this day.

"The mother has asked that the daughter of Simon Fraser be wed to a man of higher stature, to a man who can provide for her, care for her, protect her in these uncertain times —"

James's chest rumbled in what appeared to be a low laugh, and he sat back in his chair with his thumb to his lips. One side of his mouth curled up, and that curled lip was almost more terrifying than his previously stern face. Robert swallowed hard. Now he would have to do some convincing.

"Surely ye jest. I am a man of war, no' a husband. I have no home to speak of, my strongholds gone, and if ye recall, I am a monster. The stuff of nightmares. The Black Douglas. No lass, no matter how desperate, should be saddled with me."

Robert leaned forward, bracing for James's ire. So far, Black Douglas had handled this request well. He'd rejected it . . . But at least he'd listened and hadn't tried to throw the king across the room. He flicked his eyes to the ever-stoic Shabib whose own face belied the fact he, too, was interested in such an arrangement for James, and felt confident enough to press on.

"I disagree, Douglas. Your name, your reputation, what better protection for the forlorn lass of Simon Fraser?"

James tipped his head to the side.

"And where, my good king, might she live? I have no home. Should she play the whore, following the army from camp to camp? Will ye keep her here, in what passes for court at Auchinleck?"

At this, Robert's mouth worked into his own smile. Here is where his plan would work. He'd anticipated James's arguments and was more than ready to respond to them.

"We left a small garrison at Threave. Most of my men have relocated here and will travel with me as we storm across Scotland and oust the English. As I am doing that, I need someone to keep the English out of the lowlands and rout them from our southern strongholds. I will gift ye Threave and control of the southern Scotland in exchange for the hand of Fraser's illegitimate daughter."

"Threave? We just left that pile of rocks! What manner of gift is that?"

James wasn't wrong in his estimation of that keep. However, the location was sound and granting it to Douglas meant he could build on it, or his progeny, in the future.

"Aye, 'tis little more than rocks and the moment, but we lived there quite well until we took over Dumfries. And ye can build your own stronghold there, however ye want, so your children and your children's children will have the legacy that was robbed from ye by Longshanks."

James half-rose from this seat, his irritation blazing off him like a raging fire burned under his skin.

"Ye must be mad to ask me such a thing. I am no' the type of man to take a wife. I dinna *want* a wife. I am a soldier with the singular goal of destroying all the English I can until they slay me in the process. What woman wants that in a husband? Nay. My answer is nay."

Robert raised his glowering eyes to James and set his shoulders back to appear as commanding as he needed to be. Robert's arguments had been sound, one even a fool of a man would consider. But James wasn't in the right frame of mind to appreciate the sound offer.

"I'm no' asking, James. I am commanding ye. This is an order from your commander, your king. And ye will do as your king demands."

James clenched his hands into tight fists. The unabiding desire to hit something, the wall, Shabib, the king, roiled through James with a fury. What in the name of Christ's blood was the king thinking?

"Why, Robert? I've overcome much to join ye, and I've done the work of the devil on the way. I'm a man with no land, no stronghold, no coin. I've my horse, my sword, and the friendship of the King, which I am doubting right now, and that does no' a husband make."

James's throat ached as he tried to choke back the words. They wanted to pour out in a furious scream, one that would bring the walls crumbling down, but this was still the King of Scotland before him, a man to whom he'd sworn fealty a few months before. A measure of control was prudent.

"James, please sit and listen to your king," Robert told him in a level voice. James sat stiffly and on edge, ready to leap up again. "I have several reasons for demanding this. I will numerate them for ye, and I hope one of them reaches your mind. First, I owe Simon much, and I can return his loyalty by ensuring his children are established. Second, ye won't be landless much longer. Ye shall have chambers here in Auchinleck whilst we are here. And ye still have the Douglas land — 'tis still yours though ye need a keep. To that end, as I promised, I am offering ye Threave as your new stronghold. Land, stronghold, coin." He counted them on his stout fingers.

James tried not to grimace at the prospect of a sinking pile of rocks in the middle of a loch as a reward. Robert continued speaking, trying to convince him that his idea had merit.

"As for ye as a husband, I can attest to what a mighty soldier and loyal sword ye are. As a strategist, ye are unmatched. Ye have many noble traits that make for a great man, and if ye apply those to a marriage, they can make ye a great husband as well. I know ye worry for your soul — ye are no' called Black Douglas without reason."

James tipped his head and tried to wipe the sly grin off his face. That reputation was dark and deplorable, but it had grown on James over the past month. He had come to embrace it. Robert's voice dropped low as his emotions took over.

"A woman, a good woman, a wife, can help us achieve a measure of forgiveness, of solace, that we might not otherwise find ourselves. Perchance ye might find peace in a domestic partnership."

Behind him, Shabib shifted. James knew Shabib had the same worries for James's soul, and he would readily agree with Robert on that point. James would never hear the end of *that* one. He fidgeted in the uncomfortable chair.

"Most importantly, James, when so much darkness haunts a man, I worry for ye. I'm no priest — your soul is no' my greatest concern. Your mind, however, that I need. Ye can think of schemes and strategies and tactics in a way I've never seen before. Ye have a familiarity with historical military strategy and can modify it to work for us. Ye think yourself a warrior, James, but ye are more an academic, a brilliant man. The problem is if the darkness grows too great, it can overwhelm the mind and drive ye mad. Yet, if we — ye, me, your adviser Shabib even — can help you deal with the darkness, ye might save your mind."

James hated every word that the King spoke, but he couldn't disagree with a single word of it — especially the final assessment of his mind.

During the burning of Douglas Castle, his actions with the now-renowned Douglas Larder, his mind burned like 'twas lit with vitriol — an unending burning he couldn't extinguish. Nothing had been able to cool that fervent pain in his head. Shabib had commented that the pain was his morality fighting with the violent actions that needed to be done, and James had begun to worry that if he didn't balance those two opposing forces, he would indeed go mad.

He had certainly felt mad when he was lighting his stronghold on fire.

Yet, the idea of a wife sucked the air from his lungs. He was not a husband. He didn't know how to be a husband. Any woman stuck with him would surely be cheerless and cursed for the rest of her days.

But the king believed James needed something to ground him. And if the king commanded that he marry, then what other choice did he have?

None.

James lifted his brooding eyes to his king. With a sour taste in the back of his throat, James grasped the king's hand and kissed his large signet ring.

"Your wish is my command," James said, rolling his eyes before spinning on his booted toe and departing.

Chapter Six: Letters

TOSIA'S MIND SPUN, as did the room. She placed her hand on her forehead and grabbed the rough edge of the table with the other.

Suddenly, everything she thought she knew about her mother, their life in this small croft, herself in this world, was called into question, and her view of her mother was clouded when she lifted her eyes.

"I had written a letter over a fortnight ago, and the Good King Robert the Bruce took time from his busy command and graced me with a response. I wrote him when the funds from your father began to run low. And he has offered a solution."

Tosia and Tavish stared at their mother with hanging mouths and stunned silence. Their mother had a relationship with the great Simon Fraser? She wrote to the king? Better yet, he wrote her back?

A spike of fear shot over Tosia's back at that thought. The King wrote *back*. By God, what solution could a man focused on war offer? She gulped the lump in her throat back down and focused on her mother's words.

"Tavish," their mother's gaze crested past Tosia to her brother. His wide-eyed face blanched to a pasty white. Tosia reached out a hand to help steady him as their mother continued. "The king has offered to take you into his household to be employed as a squire. This is a noble calling. One day, by the grace of God and our king, ye might be a formidable knight in the Bruce's army."

Tavish shuddered under Tosia's palm. If becoming a squire in the king's army was her brother's fate, what could hers be? The king's wife was held prisoner, did he have a court for ladies' maids? What other option did the king have for her? Or was she to remain here with her mother?

Her mother coughed into a rag and wiped her face which was nearly as pasty as Tavish. Nay, staying with her mother was not an option — even a great fool could see the woman was not for long in this world.

Tosia's lips quivered, and she bit her lip, willing herself not to cry.

"Tosia, the king has quite a different solution for ye. Please keep an open mind and know that neither your mother nor the good king, for whom your father was a staunch supporter, would steer ye wrong."

At her mother's words, Tosia couldn't stop the tears. Full, warm drops rimmed her eyelashes and dropped to her cheeks. Her fate was worse.

"Dinna weep, Tosia, for many a lass would give everything they have to be in your position. The king has decided that ye are to be wed to one of his closest advisers, one of his most powerful knights, the very man who is helping to turn the tide on the English."

Tosia heard none of that. The only word that permeated the fog of her mind was the word wed.

What? Marry one of the king's men?

She'd never been prepared for something like that, never been trained to be the wife of one of the king's men. She was a crofter's daughter! She had no dowry, no position, nothing.

Why would the king arrange a marriage for her? And to so important a man? Just how prominent was her father?

"Tosia, have ye heard me? Ye are to wed an important man!"

"Who?" Tavish finally spoke up. His eyes narrowed at their mother. "Ye refer to him as the king's man, an important man, yet ye dinna speak his name. What are ye hiding, Mother? Is the man verra old? What is so wrong that ye will no' speak his name?"

"Tavish!" she gasped with a sharp tone. "Dinna speak that way, especially of the king."

Tavish dropped his gaze but didn't pause his words that poured forth as Tosia sat and stared at him. "What's wrong with this man, Mother, that the king would be willing to marry him off to an unknown lass?"

Their mother took a wet breath and wiped at her mouth with the blood-stained rag.

"The man. 'Tis Sir James Douglas."

Several silent heartbeats passed before anyone spoke. No one needed to. The very name sent a shaft of fear into the chest of anyone who heard it. They might live on the outskirts of civilization, but everyone in Scotland knew that name.

Nay, Tosia thought. *Nay, nay, nay . . .*

"Black Douglas?" Tavish whispered. "The villainous blackguard of the King's commanders? That Black James Douglas?"

Tosia's tongue was as frozen as the rest of her. Everything inside her protested, screamed *nay* so loudly her brain cringed. But not a single word formed on her lips.

Douglas? The Black Douglas? The mountain-sized, black haired warrior? The man renowned for his loathsome and bloody attacks against the English?

Her mother must have misread the missive. Surely, she must be wrong.

Tosia's shaking began low in her wame and spread to the rest of her body. Tavish placed a hand on her shoulder, offering his silent support, giving her the one connection to the world she needed, lest she faint away.

"Mother, ye must be wrong," her voice was less than a whisper. "That man can marry anyone. A powerful lass of a laird. Even as a favor to his king, why pick me?"

Her mother reached across the table to pat Tosia's shaky hand.

"Ye may think ye aren't powerful, but ye are the daughter of Simon Fraser, illegitimate or no'. That name alone carries weight with the king, who feels he owes much for the man who at present occupies a spot on a pike next to Sir William Wallace."

Tosia paled and cleared her throat. "Surely there are other young women, though. He doesn't know me. Know us."

"Douglas needs a wife. He doesn't seem interested in anyone who's been close to the king's court, so much as 'tis right now. Perchance a woman from outside might warm the Douglas's heart."

"His icy heart," Tavish said in a snide tone as he crossed his arms over his chest.

"Mother, this does no' make sense!" Tosia wailed.

"Quiet!" Her mother's voice rose before breaking into another fit of bloody coughing. She bent over, spitting into the rag.

"Mother!" Tosia cried. Tavish knocked over his stool as he raced to her side, cradling Maggie in his sinewy arms.

What little color that had remained in their mother's pallor was gone. She choked and spat.

"Mother —" Tosia began, but her mother waved her hand.

"Ye are to wed this man. Your brother will be a squire in his house. I will write a letter of introduction to the king. Dinna tally. He is already expecting ye, so dinna think to remain here. Please, dinna arouse the king's ire. He's doing me, us, a great favor. Please, promise me this, that ye will go right to the king."

Tosia's tears fell freely at her mother's pleas, wetting her cheeks and her mother's kirtle. She held her hand as Tavish lifted her frail form in his steady arms.

"Bring me my ink and quill to the bed, with a tray," her mother commanded weakly. "I have a letter to write."

Tosia waited until her mother busied herself at the bedtable with her quill before bolting from their simple home and racing for the heather-filled field beyond the house. In her rush to leave, to catch her breath from the harrowing news, she'd left her arasaid hanging on its peg beside the hearth.

But she didn't need it. The air held warm notes, but they didn't compare to the heat boiling under Tosia's skin.

She ran until her breath was lost in the wind, whipping her hair in a wild swirl around her head. She ran until her chest was ready to burst and the soles of her feet were sore from the stones that bit through the thin leather of her shoes. The chill in the air went unnoticed until she'd thrown herself into the damp grass, and the roots of a rowan tree caught her when she collapsed against the trunk. The cool dew seeped through her kirtle.

Why? Why had her mother agreed to such an arrangement?

The Black Douglas? The vile man who had decimated his own lands? Who fed men into a Scottish killing field? Who slaughtered without thought or conscience? Where did his violent nature end? A man, nay a demon such as that, would kill her for sure.

The Black Douglas's reputation had spread from the lowlands to the Highlands, of how he put a whole castle of English to death with only his small band of men. Of how he decapitated his enemies and burned everything — everything! — in his own keep, his own birthright, his very home, and the men inside it, to the ground rather than let the English live there. Who did such a thing? How did anyone conceive such a contemptible idea? He wasn't a man. He was a monster.

Tosia rested her arms across her knees and dropped her head to her forearms, trying to close out the world. The sooner the world fell away, the sooner she could pretend that her mother was mistaken, that she wasn't cursed to marry a monster.

How was *this* the best solution for her? For her brother? Her tears whetted her dirty skirts as she wept away this horrid news.

"Tosia, please. 'Tis no' that bad," Tavish's voice carried over the hill to her space under the comforting rowan leaves. His voice deepened as he walked closer. "He canna be all bad if he is a friend to the king."

"How do ye know?" Tosia countered, her voice muffled by her sleeves. "He is the king's vicious dog, and ye dinna know the king. If he permits his beast to ravage the glen, then how can the king be a good man?"

Tavish sat heavily next to her, bumping his shoulder against hers. "The king is fighting for us, for the Scots, after years of tyranny by the English. That stands for something."

Wiping her damp face on her sleeve, Tosia raised her eyes to Tavish's matching hazel gaze, one that must have been a gift from their absent father, as their mother had eyes as green as the hills in the morn. Tavish's eyes were soft, his concern for her painted on his face. Not that his fate was any better, but at least he didn't have to dread the prospect of marrying the Black Douglas.

Or share a wedding bed with him.

Tosia shuddered.

She didn't answer her brother — instead she stared into the distance, wondering how far she might make it if she started running and didn't stop. Tavish nudged her again.

"The King would find ye. There is no place ye can hide, so put that foolish notion from your mind," Tavish advised.

Tosia pursed her lips. Tavish always seemed to know what she was thinking — they were close enough in age to be oft mistaken as twins, and Tavish acted the role of an older brother often enough. The idea of running had crossed her mind.

"How did ye know what I was thinking?"

Tavish groaned as he stretched his long legs in front of him. "Ye canna hide anything on your face. It speaks louder than your mouth."

Her lips squeezed harder.

"What am I going to do, Tavish? I canna wed the man. His vile reputation aside, I dinna even know him!"

"Aye, I can see your problem with that. But, this is a union sanctioned by the king to a mighty Laird. Ye will be a lady. And what if the man is a beast with a heart of gold? Stranger things have happened. And he, too, is fighting for his land. And rumor has a way of gaining traction where it shouldn't. Maybe he's no' the demon rumor makes him out to be."

The wind gusted up and blew locks of her honey-bronze hair across her face. She brushed them aside as she glared at her brother. She hated to admit his words might have merit. This time, she nudged him.

His shoulder was hard, solid muscle. Tosia sighed. When had he grown from a boy to a man?

"Ugh. I hate it when ye make sense. I have no argument against what ye say."

Tavish got to his feet and reached a dirt-encrusted hand to her. "Come. The sunlight fades and mother will be wanting dinner." He helped her stand, then whirled her to face him when she bent to brush dirt crumbs from her skirts. "And, my dear sister, I shall be there with ye, and I vow I will no' let the men lay a wayward hand upon ye."

Tosia clasped her slender fingers atop his. "Tavish, ye shall be little more than a squire, beholden to your laird. If ye tells ye to step away, your loyalties will have to be with him. Dinna misconstrue this, brother, ye are just as stuck in this new union as I."

She placed a tender hand on the patchy scruff of his cheek, then stepped away, heading home in the gray gloaming of the night.

Toward home for one of the last times.

They buried their mother on a Sunday, with only the priest in attendance at the church yard. Her lonely grave was set into the far reaches of the cemetery, near the stone wall.

So far from everything, Tosia thought as she studied the loose brown earth on her mother's grave. *So far from me.*

Her mother had left instructions, that the king's men were to arrive on the morrow and retrieve them, to pack lightly, and to keep her in their minds and hearts. That last command was a silly one — Tosia would never forget her mother. Even if she had set up this farce of a marriage.

Tavish remained close to her the rest of the day, which was as gray as they both felt. They spoke little, but what did they have to say? Nothing, nothing that wouldn't bring sobs and painful reminders of their mother.

Packing what few belongings they was easy. Her nicer flaxen yellow gown, her combs, and she also took her mother's clean shift, the one she hadn't been buried in. Tosia thought she might wear it when she felt lonely, and thus expected to wear it often. She hadn't known how severe her ache for her mother would be until she was gone, and it was an immediate knife in her heart, twisting into that unending pain.

She paused in her packing. Tavish stood next to her, placing his own items in his pack, and she took his hand. They stood there, side by side, holding hands as they stared into the air. It was just the two of them, and Tosia wanted to hold onto him, the last bastion of her home, for as long as she could.

Chapter Seven: All the King's Men

TOSIA ROSE EARLY the next morn, but Tavish had beaten her awake. Muffled speech floated past the door, but she didn't have to listen to know what was being said. A neighboring crofter, MacIntyre, agreed to take the animals for a fair price, and Tavish was probably helping him load the smaller animals into a cart.

She wondered how long before the king's men might arrive when Tavish rushed in, his hair and breacan flapping.

"Tosia, ready yourself. Riders on the western horizon!"

"So soon? Did they ride all night?"

Tavish shrugged and raced to the bucket to wash his hands as Tosia scrambled to dress behind the curtain that separated her bedding from the rest of the croft. Her worn brown kirtle from yesterday still hung on its peg, and she threw it over her shift, lacing up the front as she searched for her kerchief. Her rich waves of hair had to forgo the taming of a comb, and she needed something to makes herself presentable. She didn't know who the king was sending to bring them to Dumfries, but she wanted to make the best impression she could, and as a poor crofter, she had few options.

There 'tis! She found the kerchief on the low stool near her bed and managed to tie it under her hair as the drumming sound of horses rode up to their quaint cottage. This far from Edinburgh, the sounds of horses were rare, and the vibration made her chest quake under her shift. The time had come to leave the only home she'd ever known, travel across Scotland, and be wed to a man she'd never met.

Tosia had one final consideration to run away until Tavish flung open the door to welcome their escorts.

Hard men with rough hands and even harder eyes assembled outside the doorway.

"Tavish Fraser?" A deep, rumbling voice asked. Tosia appeared around the curtain with her pack and stood next to her brother in a pathetic display of solidarity.

"Aye," Tavish responded in a strong voice. He didn't fool Tosia, though, who felt him quaking under his breacan. "And my sister, Tosia."

The rugged man flicked his stony gray eyes to Tosia and back to Tavish. "Do ye have your belongings? We are from the king, to bring ye to Auchinleck. The ride should take a full day, and we should arrive on the morrow. Dinna tarry."

That final phrase was a command, one that neither Tosia nor Tavish would disobey. Tavish gathered his bag and joined Tosia as they walked out to the horses.

"Can ye ride, man?" A stocky, blonde man asked Tavish. He nodded, and the man led Tavish from Tosia to a saddled horse at the rear.

"Ye ride with me, lass," a voice spoke behind her. Tosia's heart leapt into her throat as she spun around.

The rough man who'd first spoke to them stood behind her, looming impossibly large, his gruff face hinting that perchance he didn't care for this duty. His cold, sharp eyes impaled her. Tosia swallowed, and unable to dislodge the ever-burgeoning lump in her throat, nodded instead of speaking.

With a surprisingly light touch, the dark-haired man took her elbow in one hand and led her to his destrier, a rich brown monster of a beast. His strong hands wrapped around her waist and lifted her as though she was naught more than a kitten and settled her side-seated on the front of the saddle. Then, in a nimble move for such a giant man, he swept himself into the saddle, his arms on either side of her as he gathered the reins.

No names, no introductions, nothing more than the transferring of property. Tosia longed to ask their names, learn who these men were, find some point of familiarity, but their terse visages robbed her voice from her throat. These were not men who participated in idle banter.

These were men of war on a mission, and they would not be deterred.

The silence between the troupe lingered, hanging heavy in the air like the very mist itself. If the men weren't talking, then Tosia wasn't going to disturb that. God knew, her voice probably wouldn't make sound, as dazed and frightened as she was.

She tilted her head to gaze northward at the snow-tipped, purple mountains peeking out from the morning mists. The mountains stood as sentinels for the Highlands, powerful warrior landscapes defending Scotland from invasion with their mere presence. Her eyes flicked to the men riding with her, sitting tall in their saddles resembling the mountains, mighty warriors ready to defend the land.

How could she, a woman who'd never been more than a few hours walk from her home, live among men such as these?

She might as well take her chances in the mountains. At least she'd seen them before.

They rode for hours, chasing the sun as it coursed across the sky. 'Twas late in the day when the charred remains of a lone, crumbling outbuilding appeared in the distance. Tosia focused on that to help her forget the agonizing soreness in her backside.

It might have been a croft or a barn at one time, and it stood forlorn in the distant. Why had it burned? Had the family made it out? The enigmatic, blackened remains wore at Tosia's mind. Finally she couldn't contain her curiosity, and her words burst from her mouth.

"What is that?" Tosia risked asking as she pointed her finger at the building.

The giant behind her grunted.

"That building? The burned one?" she tried again.

He shifted and grunted again. "A ruthless memory of the English, lass."

His response only elicited more questions.

"What do you mean?" Tosia squinted, trying to see if the building bore a mark or the like, indicating its English attachments.

"The English oft preyed on the better nature of the Scots, encouraging men to find common ground by agreeing to a meeting. When the Scots arrived, gathering in anticipation of civilized discourse with the English dogs, the bastards barred the door and set the building aflame."

Tosia gasped and grabbed her plaid cape tighter around her neck. "Nay! Surely such a thing is only lore, a story. Such atrocities, they dinna really happen?"

The man stiffened and his arms clenched against her.

"Ye think I lie?"

Tosia tore her gaze from the building and forced her eyes straight ahead. "Nay, I —"

"They happen, lass," the austere man continued. "Wallace learned to turn the English's tricks against them. Yet the English dogs commit this manner of crime to this day, only we Scots have become wise to the ploy. That building is one of the last times the English tried that guise against us."

Tosia fell silent again, contemplating the man's words. How sheltered she'd been with her mother and brother. Until the death of her father, little of conflict with the English touched her. So much death and destruction, so much pain and hatred. How did men, women, and families emerge from this with their wits about them? And here she was, riding right into the thick of this conflict, to live near the king and wed his top man. Another shudder chilled her to her bones.

"Are ye cold, lass?" the man asked.

She barely found her voice. "Nay. I'm well."

As if he didn't quite believe her, the man's arm fell away, and he wiggled behind her and brought the edge of his plaid breacan around her shoulders. The wool was still warm from his body and rather than smelling of horse, which she'd expected, scents of leather and male surrounded her. A sense of security came with the plaid, false though she knew it to be, yet she welcomed its comfort.

They camped late, with Tavish close to her for assurance and warmth, and the rose in the misty light before the sun fully graced the earth. Another day of silent travel, and shortly after midday, a stone monolith rose in the brightening rays of sunlight.

Auchinleck Castle.

Present home of the king.

And of the Black Douglas.

They entered through a stone-framed gate into the inner yard of the stronghold. Tosia wasn't sure what she expected, but the mildly domestic scene of women carrying baskets and washing laundry, chickens and small goats ambling among the patchy grass, and rough, bearded men in dull tunics assembling weapons was not it.

Were families here? Was Dumfries *not* the center of a war? Not that Tosia was even certain of what war was supposed to look like. As her eyes jumped from one side of the yard to the other, she once again realized how sheltered she'd been for her entire life.

The horse approached the main doors of the castle, and a man in a black tunic and braies and subtle streaks of gray in his chestnut hair stood at the top of the steps. He leaned onto the low, stone balustrade, watching their entry. The men halted their horses, dismounted, and threw the reins to lanky lads who scrambled to house the horses to their stables.

The brawny man behind her dismounted, and before Tosia was able to gather her wits, his hands grasped her waist again and hauled her down. He held her aloft until her feet steadied under her, for which she was grateful. She didn't want to fall into the dirt and make her first introduction to the king and her future husband in stained skirts. As soon as she was steady, he released her and stepped to the bottom of the step, his arms crossed over his chest.

Riding in front of the man had shaken Tosia to her bones and relief flooded her once she was released from that awkwardly intimate position. Yet her heart pounded in her chest. Where was Tavish? Why were they standing here in the yard? Was someone going to direct her where to go?

Then a warm hand pressed against hers, and Tavish stood next to her, his presence providing her a measure of encouragement in this unfamiliar place. The man at the top of the steps spoke, commanding Tosia's attention.

"Tosia Fraser. Tavish Fraser." The man bowed his head slightly, Tosia, uncertain of what to do, curtsied in return.

"Welcome to Auchinleck. I hope your travels weren't too arduous. I am Robert the Bruce."

Tosia's heart threatened to stop in her chest, and her mind swam in her head. Tavish pressed his arm against her to steady her, lest she faint away. This was the king? This casual man in humble clothing? What of robes? A crown?

And then a second, sinking sensation clenched her stomach. Did that mean she was to meet the Black Douglas now? Here in the yard? Without the chance to prepare?

The king nodded toward the giant man who'd ridden behind Tosia to the keep. Her eyes started at his feet, mud-covered leather boots, and rose slowly over his loose braies, the plaid draping from his hip to shoulder, and his stony green-gray eyes, sharp nose, and mass of black hair. This time, she thought she *would* faint.

Nay . . . it couldn't be. . . She had ridden with that man, that blackguard plague of the Highlands?

"And if ye haven't formally met him yet, may I introduce your husband-to-be, Sir James Douglas."

Then everything went black.

When she opened her eyes, Tavish's concerned face hovered above her. His eyes, the only part she could see of him, really, wide and a hue of cinnamon and spice, searched her face.

"Tosia! Are ye well?"

She lifted her shoulders and rested on her elbows. Several other men surrounded her, including the earnest-looking king, and the beast of Scotland himself, Douglas. She rubbed her face with her hand, more embarrassed than injured.

"Aye, Tavish. Dinna fret. 'Tis been a long series of days, methinks."

The king squatted next to her, taking her hand in his. Indeed, her life had shifted in an inconceivable way. Was the King of Scotland truly offering her succor?

"Then we must get ye to your chambers. I'll have a maid bring ye water. Your brother will escort ye, then find his place."

Then he rose and helped Tosia to her feet. She teetered slightly, and the king put a reassuring arm across her back. The Black Douglas, fortunately stayed away. She wasn't sure she could have kept her feet if he'd been the one to assist her.

Tavish took her arm and led her inside where a young woman who introduced herself as Brigid held a pitcher of water and led them to the stairs. Tosia focused on the maid to distract herself from the complicating largess of her present life. Brigid was a petite young woman, buxom, with dark blonde hair pulled back under a linen kerchief. A perpetual smile seemed embedded on the lass's pretty face, and Tosia's heart clenched at Brigid's welcoming visage.

Would I ever smile again?

"'Tis no' the end of the world, Tosia," Tavish whispered to her. "Douglas is an important man, the king's right-hand man. There are worse things."

Tosia gripped her brother's arm. "Really, Tavish? Ye say such things to me? I am to be shackled to a monster —"

Tavish stopped walking and flashed his gaze at the maid to make sure she hadn't overheard, then turned his hard eyes on Tosia. She'd never seen so fierce an expression on her brother before, and she trembled under that fiery glare.

"I dinna see a monster, Tosia. The man was kind, considerate even, on our ride here. Aye, there are rumors about him, but will ye judge a man based on rumor? Or rather on what he shows ye in his actions to ye? The king has given ye a gift, Tosia, us a gift, one we most likely dinna deserve, and to spit on it is dangerous. He's given us position and permitted us to stay together. Give his man a chance."

Tavish tugged on her arm, yanking her up the stairs as he resumed walking. They caught up with Brigid who waited at the door at the end of the dim hallway.

Tosia's chest was hollow, an empty pit, at her brother's words. He spoke the truth, aye, but it didn't lessen the dismay that threatened to bring Tosia to her knees.

Brigid gestured them into the narrow room with a smart flip of her hand. Tavish led Tosia to a straw-filled bed and sat her down gently.

"I have to go, my dear sister. I will check in on ye as much as I can, but please, *please*, find peace here. I canna do my duties knowing the strife ye feel."

Tosia lifted her face to her brother and cupped his still-smooth cheek with her cool palm. *So young, yet so wise for his age.* What had she done to deserve this love from her brother?

"Go. Thank ye for your sage counsel, brother. I shall be fine."

Tavish stood tall, tugging on his tunic. She was proud at his attempt at courage, even if he only put on that courageous air to appease her.

"I'll see ye soon, I hope. Dinna despair, Tosia, and know that your brother loves ye, always."

He bowed slightly and turned, leaving her alone in the chambers with the maid.

Chapter Eight: The Black Douglas

ONCE TAVISH EXITED the chambers, Brigid prattled away, including mentioning that Douglas would soon move to his own keep at Threave, recently gifted from the king himself. She didn't seem frightened of the villain, rather she spoke in tones of awe, which perplexed Tosia. How did anyone not live in fear of the man's shadow?

The news of moving to Threave sent another shot of cold panic through her. Would Tavish come too? What if he was not attached to Douglas but with the king? How would she survive without her brother with her?

Brigid offered to draw Tosia a bath, but even the call of warm, calming waters wasn't enough to draw her from her despairing thoughts. She sent Brigid off with a limp wave of her hand and sat on the edge of the bedding, which emitted a crinkling sound of packed hay. At least that sound was familiar.

The chambers were cramped — unimportant guest bedding at best. Still, it was a sight better than anything she'd had at home. Here she had a door that closed, mayhap even bolted, and she might sleep in peace under the soft wool coverlet knowing that the monster who was her husband-to-be couldn't enter.

Until they were wed. That was a whole other problem, and Tosia's head swam enough as it was even before considering what it would be like to marry the blackguard.

A tiny hearth was built into the wall next to the window slit, and Tosia was grateful springtime was well entrenched. That hearth wouldn't warm a croft, let alone this stone chamber. The kindling was gray and cold as it was.

The window slit emitted a narrow patch of sunlight, the lone shard of brightness in this otherwise dim chamber, this dim life, Tosia found herself in.

Her wallowing in self-pity increased as she stared at that patch of light, and before she managed to lift a hand and wipe them away, hot tears squeezed from her eyes and streamed down her face. Then she lost all control, collapsing into the wool and sobbing with abandon. Her brother's words waned in her misery.

Everything — the death of her mother, being ripped from her home, the loss of her brother's immediate companionship, and her betrothal to the Black Douglas — it was too much. Her heart shattered in her chest. How could she survive? Her sobbing wracked her body.

She must have fallen asleep in her tears, for the sweeping of her chamber door against the stones as it opened drew her from her fitful slumber.

"I still dinna need anything," Tosia called to the maid, keeping her face squashed in the damp plaid blanket.

"I'm no' the maid," a deep voice rumbled, and if she'd had the energy to cower, she would have. As it was, the crying had taken much out of her, and Tosia slowly lifted herself on her elbow.

Black Douglas dwarfed the room — how did one man take up so much space? He must have bathed, or leastwise cleaned up, for his beard was trimmed to little more than a shadow on his jaw, and his hair had been tamed, clipped at the sides with tiny queues braided at the back. He had changed his tunic, this one clean and the color of white summer heather on the glen. His black and gray plaid was clasped at his neck with a brooch etched with a fiery salamander. He looked the part of the esteemed second in command to the king.

But he was yet the Black Douglas in Tosia's eyes. No amount of washing cleansed that cursed name from him.

She wiped her face with the draping sleeve of her kirtle — she was flushed from sleep and at being discovered crying.

James remained by the door, keeping his distance. He said nothing, waiting for her collect herself. Tosia sat up fully on the bed and patted at her hair. She must be such a sight!

"Lass," he said, his voice surprisingly tender, "I canna imagine the distress ye feel right now."

Her lips quivered, but she held her tongue as she slowly shook her head. Nay, he could not imagine.

"But I am not unfamiliar with loss," he continued in that same lulling tone.

Tosia tipped her head, intrigued by his words. Nay, he wasn't unfamiliar. If anything, he was as intimately acquainted with it as she.

"The king has granted ye a sennight to settle in at Auchinleck 'afore we are wed. We will then stay here until the king decides our next movements, then I will relocate ye to my temporary keep at Threave. Your brother will remain by my side as my squire, and thus be near to ye until our battles take us elsewhere with the king."

His kindness at detailing what her future held touched something deep in her heart. She'd feared she'd be wed to the man the same day they arrived. Knowing she had a bit of time to grow accustomed to her new surroundings, mayhap get to know her future husband, and have her brother nearby for the meantime, lifted a weight from her shoulders.

And the tone of his voice . . . She'd not considered the beast to have a tender side at all.

His words regarding his own loss were raw. Perchance she'd judged the man too harshly.

Then he moved suddenly, and she stiffened as he knelt on one knee in front of her. He was so close! Why did her body feel like a fire blazed at the hearth with his nearness?

He clasped her shaking hands in his calloused ones and gazed at her with eyes as more green than gray, reminding her of a loch in spring.

"The king has commanded we join our lives, and I would have ye know that despite the horrors ye may have heard about me, I would never bring you harm." Then he bowed that black head and his hands tightened, his grip impossible to break. "I vow to ye, Tosia Fraser, the protection of my body, the security of my sword, and would lay down my life for ye if necessary. No matter what ye've heard, I vow to keep ye safe from all manner of violence, even mine."

Tosia couldn't move, yet her insides quivered from his nearness and the power of his words. Her heart pounded against her chest, and she struggled to take in a breath. This was nothing of what she had expected. The monster of Scotland on his knees, swearing an oath to her? Had the world turned upside down? How had she been put on this strange road to the king of the Scots and his men?

James didn't move. He remained on his knee, his head bowed, his hands clasping hers.

Is he waiting for something? She cleared the lump from her throat.

"Why?" she whispered in a wobbly voice.

His head lifted, and his shimmering moss-green eyes, so different than the hard gray flint from earlier, searched her face.

"I swore fealty to the king. What the king commands, I do, and he's no' led me astray yet. His latest venture is to bind me to you. And I protect what is mine."

Mine.

The word held such weight, and a shiver coursed over her back.

His in every sense of the word.

But he had vowed not to harm her. Perchance 'twas a start.

"And I am yours," he continued. "Your needs, your desires, I will fulfill them as best I can."

Hers.

She hadn't considered her part of the marriage in that way. Or that he would think of her like that.

Aye, she'd have to reconsider her presumptions of the man.

Tosia withdrew her hand from his and lifted it, unsure of what she was doing in that movement. At first she thought to rest it on his freshly washed head, to touch that sinfully black hair.

But her nerves got the best of her, and she instead dropped it where it rested on his forearm.

His eyes flicked down at her hand, as if assessing her touch. He'd assuredly had women before — he was a man after all — but a soft touch in such a hard life? By a woman to whom he had a claim?

Perchance not.

James shifted his own hand and with one long finger traced the thin veins under her skin in the most gentle caress. Too gentle for the Black Douglas.

Then his finger was gone, moving as quickly as the man moved to rise. He strode to the door before speaking again.

"The king will expect you for the eventide meal. I must sit by his side, but I will see to ye before and after the meal. Is there anything ye need before then?"

Tosia shook her head. "Nay. But gratitude for your consideration."

James studied her for a long moment, then nodded and stepped beyond the door.

Only then did Tosia breathe fully.

※

James marched down the hall, a small spark of hope in his chest that he'd managed to quell at least some of the lass's anxieties. As it was, his time was at a premium, and now the Bruce had shackled him with an unwanted wife, whom he would assuredly neglect in his attendance to the king.

What at the Bruce been thinking?

But the Bruce's whims were not the fault of the young lady, and as forlorn as she appeared to be, she didn't deserve a stern husband on top of her present discomfort. She had seemed receptive to James's private oath, even reaching out to him. He'd taken the chance to caress her hand, expecting her to cower away from, but she hadn't.

That, James believed, was a strong start.

James was not a sentimental man by any means, yet something in his chest had contracted when he'd first set eyes on her. Everything about the lass was *uisge-beatha* at sunset — brown and golden and amber, with wide eyes and a dazed expression that sent a surge of protectiveness through him, an emotion he'd only experienced in defending his men against the English.

Never had that sensation extended to a woman. And he'd been between the thighs of many.

Something about this lass — her skittishness, or the fact she was his — he wanted to keep her safe. And mayhap, just mayhap, make her happy.

James had seen the way her brother hovered around her, protective in his own youthful way, and how her eyes had watched him as he walked away when they had arrived.

Obviously they had a close relationship. With how isolated her croft had been, he wasn't surprised. But that meant keeping her brother safe if he were to keep Tosia content.

Being a soldier in the Bruce army was not conducive to safety, that James had seen all too readily with his own eyes. Christ's blood, 'twas why he had become so hard and jaded in his life!

He reached the top of the stair, empty and surprisingly quiet. Leaning against the stone wall, he pressed his fingers into his eyes until he saw stars.

Och, but did this lass and her brother complicate his life. Shabib would chuckle softly, saying it was Allah's way to temper James's fiery brain.

What had the king been thinking?

A clamor echoed up the stairwell, familiar enough to James. Robert had arrived in the hall for his midday meal, and he would want to meet with his men after. Taking Auchinleck had been a monumental accomplishment for the Scots army, a blow to the English and one desperately needed.

James's mind switched like a fork in the road, and his concerns for the woman in the small guest chambers were pushed to the back of his mind as he assessed what the Bruce would need to do next in his movements against the English.

James searched his mind for strategy as he shoved off the wall and descended the stairs, ready to do the King's bidding.

The midday meal with the king, a simple fare of leek soup and rough oat bread, passed quickly, as the Bruce commanded his men to returned to his solar, which he used as a disorganized war room. Before he left the main hall, James spoke to a kitchen maid who carried a large bronze pitcher and requested a simple meal to be brought to Tosia. The last thing he needed was for her to wither away. While she might not eat, James would ensure she'd have nourishment at her disposal.

The men packed the room, which stank of musk and mud. The bright red Sinclair reclined at the foot of Bruce's table, while several other men — the Adonis-like MacCollough and his man, Torin, included — clustered at the sides. The powerful figure of Robert the Bruce stood at the head of the table with his brother Edward, recently arrived from Ireland on his left, and a chair on the other side of him, waiting for James. Closing the door behind him, James approached the chair. The Bruce pointed to the tattered map on the table as James approached.

"Douglas, the groom-to-be! We are fortunate ye decided to join us!"

The Bruce's rich baritone vibrated throughout the chamber, and the men at the table roared in laughter. James waved a hand at the men, dismissing their mockery.

"I'd though ye'd have abandoned us to spend time getting to know your betrothed. Ye look the part of the handsome bridegroom, for certain." Robert raised one dark brown eyebrow.

"Your match-making knows no bounds," James retorted. "Dinna laugh, men. Ye might find yourself betrothed under the king's command. Look what happened to Sinclair's brother!"

The men laughed again, and even James's lips twitched into a suggestion of a smile. Robert pounded his back.

"At least my captain has no' lost his sense of humor," the king said in a sardonic tone. "But let us focus now on our next movements. Come, James. What do ye see?"

Black X's marked places where the Bruce's army had defeated the English. James didn't miss the X scrawled atop his own now-decimated keep in Douglasdale. The X's scarred the map, and a finer piece of art James couldn't imagine.

Circles, however, yet littered too much of the map — those places where the English were still well entrenched.

"With the defeat of Valence, and the taking of Auchinleck, Longshanks will be none too pleased. I expect he's on his way north as we speak." Asper Sinclair spoke up from his end of the table.

"I've yet heard his health is precarious. Will he try for Scotland if he's ill?" Thomas inquired.

The Bruce scratched at his beard. "Nay, he'd have his men carry him on his deathbed for the north. I believe we must anticipate he will at least try to invade. But when that will happen, 'tis anyone's guess."

James kept his eyes riveted on the map. "What are your intentions, my king?"

"We need your strategy again, but this time for a more personal intention." The Bruce paused and scanned the grizzled men. James shifted where he stood. *A personal intention?* "I would have my vengeance on the MacDoualls for their part in the deaths of my brothers Thomas and Alexander. Garthland Castle here, in Galloway, off the North Channel, is where we will find those fiends."

With his finger, James circled the larger area of Dumfries and the Scottish lowlands. "I know ye want to take the Highlands as soon as ye might, but if ye desire to wreak vengeance on the MacDoualls, we could use that to our advantage."

"In what way?" the Bruce asked.

"Why not establish our presence more securely in the lowlands before moving to the Highlands? 'Tis June in a few days. We dinna know when Longshanks will arrive. What better than to have more of the lowlands under our control to halt his onslaught before it even begins? Once we feel the lowlands are secure, ye assign a Sheriff to maintain control and then we start for the Highlands. The men there are more ready to be on our side. Taking back those lands might be a sight easier as a result."

Robert's face split into a wide smile, his entire face brightening. For a man in the throes of war, every line on his face relaxed at the prospect of military success. He pounded James heartily on his back.

"Och, Black Douglas. Has there ever been a strategist such as ye? What say ye men? Should we rout the *sassenachs* here ahead of pressing north?"

The men pounded the table in agreement, and Robert smacked James's back again.

"Well, good for ye, lad. Ye won't be too far from your bride this summer, which should please her."

James kept his mouth shut and cut a sidelong look to his King. He wasn't sure his bride-to-be agreed.

Chapter Nine: Life at Auchinleck

NEVER HAD SHE seen such a spectacle in all her days. Brigid had led Tosia down the steps and jerked back when Tosia froze where she stood.

So many people. She'd known the king had moved his men and those attached to him from a keep farther south to Auchinleck when he'd defeated de Valence in the spring, but that knowledge didn't prepare her for this sheer number of people in the hall. And from the open doors at the front, many more people gathered outside.

Tables were crammed into every nook and cranny, and the king sat at a raised table at the front of the hall. James sat to his right, ever at the king's right hand. Above the table hung a saffron banner emblazoned with the snarling red dragon — the banner of the Bruce and Scotland. So many colors, so many people, so much noise!

When she'd lived with her mother and brother, meals were merely the three of them. Simple fare in their narrow croft. She'd encountered larger groups of people on market days, yet nothing like this.

The reverberating sound alone made her ears ache, and she had to force herself not to clamp her hands over her ears. How did one hear oneself speak in this noise?

Brigid threw a reassuring smile over her shoulder and dragged Tosia to a table not far from the kitchen entryway.

"Dinna fret, lass," Brigid said loudly, helping her sit. "Ye will get used to it soon enough."

She would? Tosia gave Brigid a tight smile in return. She couldn't imagine ever growing accustomed to this noise, this many people.

Brigid pointed to her left. "The Bruce sits aloft, and your man, James, sits on his right, always. Yet James wanted to know ye are here, so I will tell him afore I return to the kitchens. Dinna be surprised if he searches ye out or sends someone to sit with ye."

"Sends someone?" Tosia asked, her hand clenched in her skirts. "What—"

But Brigid was gone, threading her way expertly through the mass of rough men and several of their women toward the raised table at the front of the hall. Brigid leaned in toward the Black Douglas, who cut a fine figure in a burgundy-brown tunic that fit his powerful chest and strapping shoulders as though 'twas crafted just for him. His eyes, a deep forest gray-green in the heated light of the hall, found her, and the steeled, brooding lines of his face relaxed. He bowed his head at her, and Tosia, her blood burning from her head to her wame, nodded back.

A rustling next to her drew her attention from the darkly hard man at the front of the room. A blonde woman, so beautiful it pained the eyes to look on her too long, settled gracefully on the bench next to Tosia. Her mouth popped open, meaning to ask who she was, then snapped shut — her surprise robbing her of any words that might form.

The stunning woman gave Tosia a slip of a smile, one that might have readily calmed her if she wasn't in such a state as it was. Tosia's lips parted again, in an effort to greet the beauty, when another woman sat across from her, speaking loudly enough to be heard over the rugged din of men's voices.

"Ye must be Tosia, the lass who's to wed James Douglas?" she inquired without pause. Her forthright manner stole Tosia's words, leaving her speechless again.

This woman held her own beauty, a refined, almost regal loveliness, with rich chestnut hair that fell in a river around her shoulders and silver eyes that focused on Tosia as forcefully as knives. Tosia choked on her own breath as she tried to nod.

Who are these women?

The refined woman's face split into a wide-mouthed smile. "Och, then. We're in the right place. Welcome to Auchinleck, lass. I'm almost certain ye did no' receive a proper welcome when ye arrived. The king's hall is a raucous place, to be sure."

Tosia blinked at the woman. They were welcoming her?

"I am Lady Elayne MacNally MacCollough, lass. Wife of Laird Declan MacCollough, there." She pointed a long, slender finger toward the well-muscled blonde man sitting at a table near the king. "And the giant bear of a man sitting next to him? He's Declan's second, Torin."

Lady Elayne's finger flicked to the blonde woman. "Her husband. This stunning woman is Caitrin. Declan is her brother."

Tosia's gaze snapped from one woman to the other. Was she expected to remember all this?

"Several other wives of lairds and the king's men are here as well. Ye will meet them soon enough. But Caitrin and I well know how rough and tumble men can be, now they don't stand on etiquette, so we wanted to make sure ye were welcomed properly."

The woman finally paused. Tosia cleared her throat, trying to find her voice.

"Thank ye," she said, uncertain if the woman heard her over the deep chatter of the men.

Both women smiled at her, and the blonde Caitrin rested a light hand on Tosia's arm.

"Dinna fret. I well know how daunting it can be here." The woman's voice was gentle, a perfect match to her features. "But keep in mind, ye are no' alone. Call on us if ye need anything, even if 'tis the company of women among these loud men."

Tosia gave the woman a tight smile, words still absent from her lips. Why had these women sought her out? Why were they being so kind? She was nothing more than a beleaguered orphan in the king's home. Their kind words, though, did their job, soothing Tosia, and she appreciated them.

A roar of laughter from the front of the hall drew their attention, and they turned their heads. James's glinting eyes caught Tosia's, and she dropped her face to her hands in her lap.

She suddenly knew why they were offering their welcome and company. Not for her, but for the man she was to wed, for the darkly handsome and imposing second in command to the king.

The evening meal passed quickly, for which Tosia was grateful. Declining assistance and a bath from the effervescent Brigid, she unlaced her kirtle and hung it on a peg near her narrow bed, then lay on the crinkling straw mattress clad only in her shift. The sound of hay as she shifted was a calming one, the same as her own bedding she'd had in her mother's house.

Her entire body ached to her very bones, and her eyes burned behind her lids. She was beyond exhausted from the events of the day and was certain sleep would claim her quickly. Though her eyes were tired, her mind was not, and continued to flip through everything she'd encountered over the day.

At the evening meal, she'd only picked at her food. The Lady and Caitrin were in demand, and once they finished their meals, they'd bid farewell to Tosia. Lady Elayne had reminded Tosia to search her out for any need, then departed with Caitrin to attend other concerns.

Once they'd left, Tosia wasn't certain what to do with herself. Her gaze flicked back to the head table and James, whose hooded gaze remained on her as though she might flee the hall. In truth, she'd considered it. She wanted to escape the hall, find Tavish at the stables, run as far as she could with him.

But to what end? Where would they go? Instead, she'd risen, and James watched her, giving her a small nod in acknowledgment. Tosia had returned the gesture and found Brigid at her side, ready to escort her to her meager chambers.

She hadn't seen Tavish for the rest of the day — he'd spent his time at the stables or wherever squires were required. She didn't know when she'd see him again. Hot tears burned behind her eyelids as she longed for her old life, for her mother snatched to soon from her earthly veil, for her brother always at her side, for her simple life filled with love and laughter.

As sleep swept her into its warm embrace, she wondered if she'd ever have that again, that measure of laughter? Of simplicity? Of love?

The week passed quickly as Tosia busied herself in the kitchens. Feeding an army of men was no small task, and the kitchen maids welcomed her presence with open arms. The chatelaine set her to preparing and cutting vegetables in the corner of the kitchen near the hearth — early summer peas and vibrant carrots, kale and purple cabbages. Tosia found the work fulfilling. In her work, she was able to lose herself and not think on this strange change in her life or her dreaded upcoming nuptials.

She lifted the last cabbage from the basket and set it to the side. It was filthy, requiring a wash, yet more was needed for the stew. Vegetables thickened a stew well when meat was at a premium, but one cabbage head wasn't enough. Tosia nodded to the chatelaine as she stepped into the gardens at the side of the keep, looking for more ripe cabbage she might add to the stew.

A shadow fell over her as she searched for any cabbage heads, and she whirled around, expecting Tavish, or worse, James.

Instead, James's brown-skinned companion stood behind her, his long blue robes wrapped around his lean form.

"My apologies," his penetrating voice intoned. "I did not mean to startle you."

"Nay, I'm well. Merely preoccupied." Tosia gestured to her basket, her hand trembling. What did James's man want with her?

The Moor flicked his gaze behind her. "Preoccupied by cabbages?" The corners of his black eyes crinkled, and a hint of white teeth escaped under his lips. Tosia found herself almost smiling back.

"Aye, well, that."

"Again, my apologies for the interruption. I had wanted to find you, introduce myself since you are to marry James." He bowed slightly, his robes flapping as he moved. "I am Shabib al Massouri."

Tosia lifted the edge of her skirt in a short curtsy. "Tosia Fraser."

"The pleasure is mine. I have to admit, I was surprised to hear the king desired James to marry. Yet, it pleases me, as he is a man with a dark side that must be tempered. A fine wife is just the thing to provide a balm to a man's demons. And ye appear to be quite the fine person."

The reminder of her upcoming nuptials caused her to stiffen, and Shabib must have noticed. He tilted his head at her.

"Please know, I have been James's close companion for several years. He has a reputation, yes, but he is one of the most forthright men I've met. He will guard you with his very life, give you a safe haven. He will treat you as fine as any wife deserves."

The memory of James's vow at her feet on her first day here echoed, where he promised to never bring her harm. She prayed the Moor's words were truth. On the tail end of that memory, curiosity sparked. The phrasing of his words intrigued her.

"Is that why ye are here? Your own demons?" she inquired, suddenly more interested in the stranger.

His lips tightened, either in memory or to halt a smile, and Tosia wondered if she'd overstepped in her question.

"I was in France for a long while. I had left the Spanish peninsula after several harrowing events at the hands of my own people and my enemies. I vowed to never go back unless it was to slay everything and everyone in my path. Like James, I was grappling with my own demons."

"And ye met James there?"

At her question, his tight lips shifted and became more of a smile. The expression softened the hard lines of his lean face, and Tosia grew more fond of the man by the minute.

"I can't say *met*. More like fell in with. I was at a tavern in northern France. The innkeeper wouldn't rent me a room, as you can imagine, but he offered me space in the stables, which I readily accepted. I was bedding down for the night when a loud drunkard crashed through the doors, looking for a place to piss. He was shocked to find me, to say the least, and grew angry when he learned my coin wasn't good enough for the tavern owner. He joined me in the stables that night and offered his companionship for the rest of his stay in France. He was the first man to treat me like a man, not like an oddity since I'd left Spain. When he told me his story and of his quest to regain his lands in Scotland, I could think of nothing better than to accompany him as his right-hand man."

Tosia enjoyed the cadence of his speech and the tone of his story. He, too, was a broken man searching for his place in the world. He wasn't so different than she.

"And now ye are sitting in the presence of the King of Scotland. What a strange path life has led you on, Shabib."

His smiled tugged at his cheek, forming a slight dimple, and he eyed her intently.

"Much the same as yourself?"

Tosia stilled, a chill dancing over her skin even in the sunlight. She had believed herself so alone, and here was a man in much the same position as herself.

"Ye speak the truth. Being with James, being here, in service to the king, has it helped ye manage your demons?"

Shabib's eyes dropped to the folded sleeves of his robe. "As much as I could hope. 'Tis why I am eager for your wedding to James. It pains me to see him battle his own tormented side, and the rumors have only made that battle more difficult for him. It is my hope that your wedding will be a bright spot that he needs in his life."

Shabib bowed again and turned to leave the gardens. Tosia grabbed at his flapping robe, stopping him before he went too far.

"I hope the same for ye, Shabib, to quell the pain of your own demons."

He tipped his head slightly, then pulled his robes from her fingertips and left.

Chapter Ten: Private Conversations

TOO SOON, HER wedding was a mere day away. Tosia's jitters, her nerves, her disquiet grew with every passing hour, passing minute . . . King Robert's household, James's men, even her own brother tried to assuage her apprehension, and she tried to take their counsel to heart, she did. But whenever James's intense, black-lashed gaze landed on her, or his gruff voice spoke to her, trepidation surged through her, pounding in her head and making her hands shake. The rumors of his dark nature, his reputation as the beast of Scotland, outweighed any other words about the man.

The night before she was to wed, she came late to the evening meal in the main hall, having spent most of night in the kitchens preparing oats and onions for the blood pudding. Her fingers stank of the arid tang of onion, and her eyes had watered the entire time. She lost herself in her task, true, but she knew in her heart she was also trying to avoid those in the main hall. She couldn't bring herself to lay eyes on the Douglas man who tomorrow would be her husband.

Only when Brigid kicked her out of the kitchen to find her meal did Tosia enter the hall, hesitant and subdued , and she sat at the first bench where a platter of venison and peeled turnips sat undisturbed. She picked at the food. A hot ball of unease filled her stomach, making it impossible to eat.

"Och lass. I was afeard ye would've missed the evening meal."

The thundering voice behind her made her jump. The enormous hulk of James stood behind her, his companions Shabib and Thomas next to him. The Moor gave her a slight nod, one to calm her jumpiness no doubt, but to no avail. The king himself was walking through the tables toward them.

As if her heightened nerves needed further vexation. She lowered the knife on the table and the hot ball in her belly burned more.

"I've no' been hungry, milord," she said in a slight voice as she dropped her gaze to her lap.

"'Tis understandable, lass. Much has happened over the past sennight, and with tomorrow —" He kept his voice level, trying to sooth her anxiety, but with these three men crowding her, Tosia was lost.

"Pardon me, please, milord." Rising awkwardly, she gave the men a quick curtsy and raced for the darkened stairwell as fast as her legs could carry her.

Once she was hidden in her room, Tosia exhaled. Her stomach roiled as she breathed, and she dove for the chamber pot, thinking she'd lose what little she had eaten that day. But there was nothing left, and she only dry heaved until she was weak.

Sitting on the floor, she shifted to lean against her bedding. Tears formed in the corners of her eyes, and she wiped them away with the stained sleeve of her kirtle. Her head fell back against the bed and she gazed at the ceiling beams, wishing she were back in her cramped croft with her mother and brother, wishing she were anywhere but here.

***

"Ye frightened the poor lass well enough," Robert commented as he closed the door to his cramped study. "Ye'll have to talk to her, James. She canna wed ye if she fears ye. What manner of wife would that be? If she is to be your calming balm, ye must show her that ye do have a caring side."

James raised an eyebrow. He had long thought the king's sense to be skewed, prone to folly, and here he was, the victim of it. The lass was attractive, he could not deny that, her hair as rich and earthy as his former Douglas holdings and eyes as ruddy as the Scots *uisge-beatha*. But he barely saw those eyes for all she kept her gaze lowered. She was also well-built, not one of the sickly, small women who'd struggle to lift a bucket.

He had hoped that his vow to her the day she'd arrived assuaged at least a few of her concerns, but from how she'd reacted to him, that didn't seem to be the case. Wedding a woman who feared him more than the devil didn't interest him in the least. He wasn't the type to welcome an unwilling woman to his bed. What was he to do?

"What makes ye think I have a caring side?"

"Ye agreed to the union. And your friend Shabib seems to think ye have some redeeming qualities, other than your talent for war. I'll admit, I have yet to see them, but Shabib assures me they are there, albeit buried deep."

Shabib needs to keep his mouth shut, James thought.

James rubbed his face with his calloused hands, then faced his king.

"I'll try. But those qualities may be buried too far to be resurrected."

"Well, if our Lord can do it after being dead for three days, I'm inclined to believe the Black Douglas can do it whilst still alive. I'll have the lass sent to your chambers at my behest. Speak to her, show her 'tis more to the beast than his hard exterior. Best she care for ye before ye wed. I'd not have the lass live in fear of ye as her husband."

Neither would I.

James averted his eyes and bowed slightly and then retired to his chambers to await his petrified bride to be.

For more times that she could count, Tosia wanted to run for the Highlands. Instead, she found herself at the chamber door to the Black Douglas. She raised her fist to knock on his door, but her hand hesitated, hanging in the air. She couldn't bring herself to do it. Enter the lion's den? *Nay.*

As she swirled away to run back down the hall, the door flung open, and the man stood at the threshold, his unblinking gaze assessing her.

"Thank ye for joining me. Please enter."

His voice was low, softer than she'd expected, and the hard lines of his cheekbones and nose weren't as razor sharp as she'd recalled from days past. Yet his tall, brawny form was as formidable as ever. She swallowed hard, gathered her courage as she gathered her skirts, and stepped inside.

James moved to the hearth, keeping a suitable distance between them. He moved easily, relaxed in the security of his private chambers. They were not much larger than hers with nothing to indicate he was a man of note, a laird, the right hand of the king.

Tosia hesitated near the door, ready for a quick escape if necessary, and clenched her hands open and closed as she waited for James to speak of why the King had commanded her here.

James reclined against the stones of the hearth. "Ye fear me because of what ye've heard, aye?"

The question caught her off guard. James's deep voice rumbled in the sparse area of his chambers in the King's temporary keep. The room resembled the character of James himself — barren, empty, devoid of any personal touch. And this was the man who was to be her husband?

Tosia wanted to lie to him, feign any knowledge of his escapades on behalf of the Scot's cause, but that would be a foolish thing to do. He'd know she was lying — everyone in Scotland knew of his reputation as a demon on earth. Lying didn't become her.

She nodded at his question. "Aye, I've heard of ye. Of the Glen Trool victory. Of the Douglas Larder." Her voice drifted to nothing on that last word. Such a simple word that, because of the black-furred man standing in front of her, had a new and terrible meaning. One only had to speak the word "larder" and the skin prickled in horrified fright. He was a man larger than life, larger than the King in many ways. and if she were honest with herself, she feared this blackguard more than she feared The Bruce.

And here she was, in his chambers, soon to be his bride. Tosia shuddered.

James's hard face didn't change or shift at the mention of his vile acts. Rather, he tipped his head slightly, his piercing eyes studying her as she stood by the foot of the bed. He possessed the look of a wild cat preparing to pounce on its prey, and she fidgeted under that gaze.

"Ye think me a villain? That I am no better than the English dogs?"

A hot lump formed in Tosia's throat. How was she to answer such a question? What woman called her soon-to-be husband a villain or an English dog?

Tosia was many things, but not a fool. Her mother, God rest her soul, had raised her better than that.

She shook her head. "I dinna believe I am in the place to call anyone such a thing. I dinna know ye well enough," she told him with as much confident honesty as she could muster.

James licked his lips, a slight touch of pink against his black facial hair. The gesture was odd to Tosia, a human touch to an inhuman being.

"Fair enough," he growled. James shifted against the hearthstones, leaning toward her. "Why don't ye ask about me?

Instead of relying on the grim rumors that surely abound in the Highlands?"

Ask him? What could she possibly ask that wouldn't sound like an accusation? Like doubt? And how would he take that?

Tosia bit at her dry lip and played with her skirts as she considered. He waited patiently, his arms crossed over his chest (*his impossibly broad chest! How did the King manage to find every Scottish giant for his army?*) as his gaze rested on her.

"There are rumors that ye are the King's tactician. Is that true?" That sounded like a valid question, more like she was questioning the rumors, not him.

He nodded, his swath of black waves brushing against his collar. "Aye, myself and several other men — MacCollough and his man Torin Dunnuck, John and Asper Sinclair, Edward — we serve as advisers."

His answer was direct, to the point, and in the same tone as when she'd first entered the room. He didn't appear upset or angered that she'd asked.

The chambers suddenly seemed overly-warm, and droplets of perspiration rolled down her back under her chemise. She wanted to lift her hair from her sweaty neck, but her fingers were frozen in the fold of her skirt. Yet his patient nature emboldened her.

"Glen Trool, 'twas your strategy?"

James inclined his head. "Aye. The funnel strategy. 'Twas successful and the Bruce had his first true victory over the English. We repeated it again here to overtake this keep. But 'tis no' my idea. I could only wish to be so clever."

Tosia stiffened and tilted her head. It wasn't his idea? But he said the rumors had been accurate! Why did he speak with such mystery?

"I dinna understand. Ye said ye are the king's tactician. Was it another adviser's idea then? How did ye get credit?"

At this, James's check twitched, and if Tosia didn't know any better, she might think he was hiding a smile. But this was Black Douglas. This man didn't smile — he had no softness in him.

"No' quite. I was the one to speak the idea to the Bruce, but the idea itself wasn't mine. I was educated in France and studied there most of my life. I wasn't always a wild demon, aye?"

He raised a sardonic eyebrow, and Tosia's hand flew to her mouth. He admitted to being such a creature?

"The idea belongs to a Spartan king in Ancient Greece. King Leonidas, have ye heard of him?" Tosia shook her head. Her own education was limited to a few pieces of literature, basic sums, and sewing. She had heard of Ancient Greece but had learned little about such an enigmatic place.

"He was a king in a tight place, much like our own Bruce. A better organized and more powerful enemy, the Persian empire, was knocking at their gates, and King Leonidas was not going to bend his knee, no matter what the Persian king demanded. They forced the Persian army to thread in a thin line through the Pass of Thermopylae and managed to keep the Persian army at bay until reinforcements arrived. I was taking a lesson from a much smarter man — so smart a man, our own beloved William Wallace did the same thing at Stirling Bridge. I only took a brilliant historical strategy and shared it with our king so he might put it into effect."

Tosia's whole body stilled as she tried to understand what James was saying. He wasn't architect of monstrous military strategy? That these tactics were used in wars before now?

He again relaxed against the stones, so casual, as though they were discussing the harvest and not the history of death and destruction. So she asked another question.

"The larder?" She could barely speak the word — it came out as a breath. At this James stood straight, and her heart stopped in her chest. Was that it? Had she crossed a line?

"Aye, the larder." He grumbled, yet his eyes, those hard stormy eyes, were not as hard as she remembered.

He took a step toward her, and Tosia backed up until the post of his bed struck her back. The air left her lungs as she struggled to take in any breath. Had she angered him? Was he going to take his fury out on her?

"The larder," he repeated. He had halted a few feet from her, close enough that she could reach out and touch that fearsome, broad chest, if she so desired. How could anyone dare to desire?

"It seems so dreadful, aye? Such a dark and dire act, to condemn so many men to a vicious death and burn it all to the ground. To poison the water. To make the land uninhabitable. To curse that piece of land for eternity? To seemingly curse my own soul? Even Shabib had a bit of a qualm with it, but even he too, came around. If 'tis possible he may hate the English more than I."

He admitted it! Was he cursed? Tosia's hand crept to her neck as her eyes remained riveted on his face.

"Do ye think I acted without thought? Too aggressively? That 'twas too much evil for one man?"

Tosia's mind swirled, and she was certain she was going to faint. She was alone in the chambers of an admitted demon! The words stuck to her tongue.

"The larder," he said in an almost nostalgic tone as he rubbed his beard. "Aye, seems dramatic, but 'twasn't my idea either."

Was he telling himself that to make it easier? "Another ancient tactic?" she ventured.

That twitching cheek again. "The Romans. After they destroyed Carthage in battle, having attacked homes one by one in a horrific slaughter, they then took apart the city stone by stone, and then burned the rest of it to the ground, so that Carthage might never rise against Rome again. Razing the enemy's land is another historic military tactic, and one I believed sent a message to the English."

Dinna ask! Tosia commanded to her lips, but they disobeyed.

"What message is that?" she asked, her voice wavering under the looming shadow James cast in the firelight — a devil from the very flames of hell.

"That we Scots are willing to watch the world burn to secure our freedom, no matter who we kill."

"No matter who?" Tosia choked out. Was her own life at stake?

In a flash, James was nearly touching her, his hellish heat enveloping her, and his wide palm cupping her cheek. She had nowhere to go to avoid his touch, her back was compressed so hard into the bedstead, she was sure it left marks.

"Of the English, lass. What we do, what I do, is for my people, my country, and I would do anything, anything, to have their freedom from these violent oppressors. And for ye, my bride, though we may no' have sought this arrangement for ourselves, that vow extends to you. I'd burn the world to ash for ye, to protect ye."

He moved in closer, so his muscled chest brushed against her breasts, and with his hand, lifted her face to his. His breath was warm on her skin, scented with mead and bread.

"With my wedding to ye, I give ye no' only my name, but the protection of my body, until my last breath is yanked from it against my will. As long as ye are mine, I will guard ye against every evil thing in this world."

He moved his head so his lips were perched right over hers.

"Every evil thing, but me," he said then caressed her lips with his in a movement that was so gentle, she couldn't believe the kiss came from the man known as a monster.

His touch was light, as his knuckles caressed her jaw. He held her with such delicate arms, he seemed to be a completely different man, not a demon. Her lips responded in kind, meeting his and parting slightly when coaxed by his tongue. Her hand clutched at her skirts in heady desperation and her sense whirled. Who was this man who was at once a devil and a lover? Who was both hard and gentle? What was she to make of him?

The more she tried to grasp her thoughts, the more they twisted from her mind, until his lips left hers. He raised his head and dropped his fingers from her face, and all that remained of the man and his kiss was her red skin roughened by his beard.

"Ye should go. Ye are no' yet my wife, and I would no' have your reputation sullied. That is, if ye have no further questions?"

One thick, raven eyebrow slanted high on his brow and he moved to the door, opening it. Tosia's words failed her again, only this time not from fear, but from something deeper and unfamiliar. As her hands still twined in her skirts, she curtsied quickly and escaped through the door into the dimly lit hallway.

Only then did her breathing resume.

※

James stood firm and straight as the lass rushed from his chambers, as though all the demons of Galloway chased after her.

And didn't they? James scratched his thick beard with one hand and reached to his groin to adjust his ballocks with the other. The lass, in all her fearful beauty, created a yearning deep inside — something he hadn't felt in years. Decades. If ever. As a man accustomed to finding his release between the willing thighs of a tavern maid or a whore, the prospect of a wife, forced though it might have been, intrigued him.

And she might fear him for their entire marriage, as long as it lasted — James could easily find himself at the wrong end of an English sword or Edward's beastly trebuchet — but at least the lass would have the protection of his name for the rest of *her* life.

He vowed to protect her with everything he had, and he would, even if it was only his name from beyond the grave.

Protecting her with his body? James glanced at his torso and arms. His chest and arms, hidden presently by a fine tunic gifted to him by the Bruce, bore witness to scars, a patchwork of near-deaths and agonizing pain and fear of pus. The lass wasn't getting a milquetoast gentleman. He hoped she was prepared to meet the monster under his clothing.

Yet, when he kissed her, he didn't feel much like the monster he was accused of being. Rather, he felt like a man, a skin and hair man with a rising cock and throbbing heart, and a desire to hold this lass and love her as a man loved his wife.

James shook his head and departed his chambers to join the Bruce for an evening of drinking, one which promised an abundance of mead and fine *uisge-beatha* to celebrate James's upcoming nuptials. The king mayhap had a sound idea in bringing the lass to Auchinleck castle to wed him.

He'd certainly felt the monstrous side of him temper the longer he was in the room with her. And when his lips brushed hers, no monster at all.

Only a man, through and through.

Chapter Eleven: The Dreaded Wedding

TOSIA'S WEDDING KIRTLE was a gown fit for a queen, at least in Tosia's estimation. Accustomed to rough woolen dresses and misshapen leather shoes, the pale sky-blue gown with draping sleeves and thistles embroidered in green and lavender, fit like something from a dream. Tosia felt much like a fae creature from one of her mother's stories.

The thought of her mother tugged at her heart, and tears filled her eyes. She touched a fingertip to the corner of her eyes, trying to stop the weeping she feared would ensue. A daughter should have her mother by her side at her wedding, and here she was, alone.

Well, not exactly alone. Brigid had helped her dress, and once the gown was laced up the back and sleek brown slippers adorned her feet, Brigid sat Tosia on a stool to brush out her hair and tie it back. Her lush sunset locks were knotted, and Brigid had to work her fingers through her hair to pull them out.

Once she was satisfied with the narrow queues that she'd braided back from Tosia's temples, Brigid then tied them off with ribbons and threads that matched her gown. When Tosia thought she was done, Brigid laid a strong hand on her shoulder, keeping her seated.

"Your groom has sent ye a wee, sentimental gift. Here."

Brigid thrust a floral crown before Tosia's eyes, and Tosia gasped.

"I've already received far too many gifts. I dinna know where the King found such a fine gown, but he gifted me with it for this day. And these slippers." Tosia lifted the soft woolen skirt to expose a dainty toe. "I canna accept anything more."

Brigid clicked her tongue. "From your groom-to-be, ye can. Let's put in your hair. It matches your gown like 'twas made for it."

She spoke the truth. The crown bore slender young fern leaves, sprigs of summer heather, and round heads of purple thistle. Tosia imagined she was fae when Brigid tucked it into her hair.

"There!" Brigid exclaimed. "Now dry your eyes and let's see if the king is ready to walk ye to the stairs of the kirk."

So she hadn't missed the tears Tosia tried to hide. The maid was too sharp by half.

"The king will walk me?" Tosia asked, realizing what the maid had said.

Brigid took Tosia's hands to help her rise and smiled widely.

"Och, ye are without a guardian and are to wed the king's second in command. Ye think ye are worthy of anything less?"

Tosia's stomach fell to her feet. The idea of the king at her wedding made her head swirl. But to have him walk her to meet her groom? She feared she's faint again.

And the prospect of standing in front of the priest with the Black Douglas himself? If she managed to keep her feet, it would be a miracle.

Though the beastly man had done a fine job of trying to reach out to her, assuage her fears and let her know he was a man, not a demon in disguise, it was a different matter altogether to be marrying the man with the dark reputation.

And then to find her bed with him? Tosia swooned and gripped Brigid's arm. Better to not faint on her wedding day. The Black Douglas didn't want a feeble-hearted lass at his side. He needed a strong wife.

Tavish had assured her she could be just that. He'd reminded her of that the day before when he found her in the gardens. She'd believed that her brother would be the one to give her to James, but he wasn't of an age, only a squire to the great man himself.

"Are ye ready, lass?" Brigid asked, excitement making her voice rise to a glass-shattering pitch.

"Aye," Tosia squeaked out, lying.

No matter what vows he made or what his men said about him, she would never be ready to wed the monster. She only prayed that she might grow accustomed to him, and that he'd forget about her soon enough.

Tavish waited below in the hall with King Robert, scrubbed clean for the event. They stood amid the light that dappled through the unshuttered windows, on woven rushes that had been freshly replaced. He smiled up at her as she descended the steps.

When was the last time she had seen Tavish so clean? From his tunic to his tartan to his shoes, he looked more a man than a boy, and Tosia's heart hammered in her chest at the sight. Though he was growing into a man far too quickly for her, he'd always be her younger brother. Her heart trembled at the man he was becoming, and the joy that she'd be able to experience that growth with him.

She patted his cheek, and he dipped his head with a dimpled smile. *There's the lad I know,* she thought as a touch brushed her elbow. She turned to find the king held out his arm to her.

The king himself was a remarkable sight. Clad in black from shoulder to toe, he commanded any space in which he stood. His burnished-brown hair, still damp and glistening in the pale sunlight, was brushed back from his face, framing his cheeks and jaw before touching the collar of his black tunic. He often wore black — unlike other royalty she'd heard rumored to wear bright colors – light blues and purples. The Bruce was a king of his people, and in Tosia's opinion, he certainly dressed the part.

Had she ever believed to meet the great man? Nay, not in this lifetime. Yet here she was, her arm threaded through his as he led her to his second in command so that she might wed him. Could the world work any more strangely? God's plans surely were more than her mind could begin to comprehend.

The two men walked on either side of her, ushering her to the formidable stone chapel on the far side of the outer bailey, where the Black Douglas, her future husband, awaited her on the gray steps.

When she reached the pathway to the chapel, she forced herself to lift her eyes and gazed upon the man who would be tied to her for the rest of her life.

More shocking than the soft cheeks of her brother or the refined figure of Robert the Bruce was the bushy, wild-looking Black Douglas, or rather, the lack of him.

He didn't look like the Black Douglas she'd seen over the past sennight. Gone was the roughly clipped beard and sweeping black waves that reached his neck. Someone had taken a razor to his cheeks, all the way up his scalp on the sides. What remained of his hair was slicked back, a shining black helm in the patchy sunlight. With his face and head shaved, his body seemed larger, more immense under his freshly laundered dark blue and green Douglas plaid. He looked as regal as the king himself.

But it was his face that caught her attention. With his jaw shaved, she could see him, the *real* James Douglas, not the infamous Black Douglas. 'Twas like she was marrying someone different, not the beast of the Scots. His jaw was as formidable as the rest of his, angular, with a cleft in his chin.

As she gathered herself to recall she was standing with this man on the steps of the chapel, she wondered if he had dimples when he smiled.

Then he spoke to her, and she blinked several times, trying to focus on the event at hand.

"Pardon?" she whispered. Was she missing her own wedding?

His lips curled suggestively to one side. "Are ye ready?" he asked.

She couldn't stop herself. Tosia lifted her hand to stroke the smooth planes of his jaw that distracted her completely. The curl in his lips twitched, and Tosia snatched her hand back, shocked at her bold move.

James raised a jet eyebrow at her and grasped her hands, and Tosia dropped her gaze.

"Aye. I'm ready," she answered.

He leaned in close as the priest lifted his hands to begin the ceremony. "Calm, lassie. I dinna bite."

She started and pulled back, but he held tight to her hands, keeping her close.

"No' unless ye ask me to," he finished.

Tosia's frantic eyes gawked at him, and that curled smile returned.

The rest of the day was a blur to James, as his eyes remained riveted on the woman at his side who glowed brighter than the sunset — amber and gold and bronze, the richest treasure. He ignored the king's gloating, matchmaker smile, instead savoring the vision of the woman he now called wife.

Tosia was nervous, 'twas obvious to anyone who cast their eyes upon her. Unlike James, she kept her gaze lowered at the meal in the main hall and her hands twined in her skirts. But

James was enchanted, his gaze following a luxuriant coppery lock of hair that spilled from her queue at her crown, over her milky shoulder to settle on the delicate curve of her breast.

She had touched him earlier. Why was she so uneasy now? Was it the excitement of their wedding, or did she fret about entering his bedchamber? As he let the rest of the hall fall away to concentrate only on this lovely creature, he presumed it was both.

Wasn't she in the same predicament as he? Forced into a marriage at the behest of the king? The difference between them was James had experience in the bed, could send her away at will, and bend her to his dictates. She had no recourse. She wasn't only at the mercy of the king; she was at the mercy of James as well.

That thought caused the hard wall he'd built around his heart to start to crumble. Even when the English had commandeered his castle, he at least had the option to burn it to the ground. This poor, downcast lassie had no such recourse. That wall in his chest crumbled more.

He had vowed to protect her, and he'd meant it. But how could she know that? In the past fortnight, she'd only known loss and upheaval and rumors of the monster she'd just wed.

No wonder she sat bowed, seeming to fold in on herself.

In that moment, he made another vow that she'd only know peace with him. That he would bring her as much joy as his twisted existence could muster. That he wouldn't send her away, rather than ensure the bright light he saw in her glowed as brilliantly as possible. He had to convince her he wasn't the monster from the tales she'd heard if they were to be a married couple.

James reached for her hand, and she flinched away.

Och, poor lass.

"Tosia," he asked in the most tender voice his throat could form, "I dinna mean ye harm. Please have a measure of faith in me."

While the rest of the hall found their amusements in their drink and feast, James and Tosia's mutton and apple compote grew cold, and their mead cups remained untouched. For the two of them, nothing else in the hall existed. Tosia's eyes shifted to his like a frightened doe. James leaned closer to her and plucked her hand from its hiding place in her skirts.

"Dinna fret. I'd like to hold your hand, if 'tis acceptable?"

Her lips were sealed, but she didn't fight against him. Repeating her movement from earlier, he placed her hand against his smoothly shaven cheek. It was cool to his touch, and he held her palm against his skin, sharing his warmth with her.

He expected her to yank her hand back as though she'd been burned, but she didn't.

Did her curiosity outweigh her apprehension? James preferred to think so.

She lifted her furtive hazel eyes to his deep gray-green ones, holding his gaze as she held his face. Their shared look intoxicated him, putting the whiskey in their cups to shame. A flare of hunger inflamed in his chest as their gaze drew out.

"I dinna want ye to fear me," he said in a ragged tone, then slipped her hand over his lips to kiss the soft skin of her palm. She stiffened, yet kept her face turned to his. "I made ye a vow, and 'Tis one I intend to keep. I am nothing if no' a man of my word."

She nodded, more smooth locks sliding over the swells of her burgeoning breasts that peeked above her rounded neckline and panted as she breathed. He had to force his eyes to her piqued face. Undressing her with his lustful gaze wouldn't alleviate her fears at all.

"I know that of ye. Your men, the king, my own brother, have vouched for your fidelity."

That lock of hair was too much, and he entwined it around his finger that brushed against the fair skin of her chest. Her breathing heightened; she was still nervous, yet she didn't move, and her tenacity under his touch inflamed him even more.

"Then why do ye yet fear me?"

She blinked at his question. "I yet fear the unknown."

James nodded at her answer. "Aye, I can imagine our marriage bed might be a fretful prospect, but I —"

Tosia shook her head, tearing the lock of hair from his fingertip.

"No' just the bed. I mean, aye, I have the concerns that any maid would, but ye, milord, ye are the unknown."

She dropped her gaze, her bravado exhausted in that one statement. She tried to withdraw her hand, but James didn't let her. This connection, at once powerful and tenuous, he didn't want broken.

"Then I would have ye know me. We've spoken little, but that does no' do much against the tales ye've heard that have crisscrossed Scotland. Most are accurate as I've told ye, but what do ye want to know of me that aren't of those tales? What of me, directly?"

A bit of a gambit — what if she asked a question that only frightened her more?

She swallowed and flicked her face to him, then back to her lap.

"Ye were in France?" she asked in a hesitant voice. He nodded. "How long?"

"Several years."

"And ye speak French?"

"*Oui, un petit peux*," he answered.

"Ye are truly well-educated. 'Tis a difficult language to learn?"

James shook his head. "It can be learned easily enough." He leaned into her. "Would ye like me to teach ye some words?"

Her shoulders relaxed, and she peeked her eyes up at him. "Aye. 'Twould be nice."

"Anything else?"

"Do ye miss your family?" she asked.

The depth of the question caught him by surprise. He sucked on his lower lip as an old familiar pain, tender as an ancient bruise, ached deep in his chest. She'd lost family, as he had. A shared loss, another connection to her.

"Aye," he choked out. "I was young when I left for France and wasn't here when they died. 'Tis a lonely thing for a son no' to bury his parents."

"I buried my mam," she responded, then lifted her clear face to regard him fully. "It does no' lessen the weight."

"Ye speak a harsh truth," he said, then moved so his lips were nearly brushing her cheek. "I would help ye bear that weight. For your loss and in all things."

She turned her head slightly, so their lips were a breath from each other. "Why? Ye likely know less of me than I do of ye."

His shuddering breath blew wisps of her hair. "Again, ye speak the truth. But ye are now my wife, and I owe ye a duty. When I vowed my body, my life, I meant it in all things. 'Tis something else ye now know about me."

Her shaky breath was warm on his skin, and her cheek brushed against his. He yet held her hand and again slipped her fingertips to his mouth, kissing each fingertip as her breathing grew more rapid.

"I would have ye know more of me," he told her in a husky voice, his lips caressing hers but not quite kissing her. More like brushing her in a gentle touch, a promise of something more. Then he stood suddenly and turned to the Bruce.

"My apologies, my king, but I can wait no longer. I would retire with my new bride?" He bowed slightly and the Bruce smiled with drink-induced crazed joy.

"I'll no' suffer ye to wait any longer. Take a platter when ye leave. I doubt we will see ye again this eve, and ye will need nourishment for this night."

Then the Bruce, the Sinclair who sat next to him, and several other men roared at the king's bawdy suggestion. James glared at the men, then took Tosia's arm in his and lifted the closest wooden platter with the other.

He led Tosia from the hall and up the stairs toward his chambers.

Chapter Twelve: More Man than Monster

JAMES SLAMMED THE door shut with a kick of his booted foot as he swept Tosia into the room. Perspiration droplets rolled down her back under the tight bodice of her gown, and her insides shuddered against his touch.

So soon? Now? She was supposed to expose herself, give her body to this man she'd only met a sennight ago and whom she'd spoken to but thrice in that time?

What madness was this?

Truthfully, she didn't know what to expect. Her mother had explained in a general sense what happens between a man and a woman, though Tosia hadn't fully believed it. She'd heard gossip and rumors and jokes from the kitchen and scullery maids concerning the virility of men and the things they did under the covers.

Bathed in a heated blush, Tosia had quickly found other duties far from those giggling, wagging tongues.

But here, now? Perchance she should have listened more to those wagging tongues.

Instead of rushing her to the bed, James set her steadily on her feet and moved around the room, snuffing out a few of the candles and unwrapping his plaid from his shoulders to hang it on a peg near the hearth.

In the dim light, Tosia noted that her meager belongings had been brought to here from her tiny chamber and set on his trunk, ready to become part of the Black Douglas's chambers. Tosia shivered again.

Once the room was set the way James desired, he turned to her. Tosia's quivering stomach dropped, and a hot flush overwhelmed her. If it hadn't been for the narrow oak table at her backside, she would have swooned to the floor.

His lustful eyes, icy, reminding her of pine treetops in midwinter, studied her, and Tosia felt a bit like a mouse under the predatory gaze of a lynx. She played with her fingers behind her back, wondering if there was something she was supposed to do or say. Or just let him look?

James tipped his head and rubbed his knuckles against his shaven chin. He did have a dimple there! A cleft normally hidden by his whiskers, its appearance only made his jaw seem more sharp, his face more lethal.

"We are wed, lass. But I find there to be an issue."

She was suddenly dizzy, and her knees went weak. An issue with her? Did he regret wedding her? Was he now going to set her aside? The moisture in her mouth dried up, and she had no words in response. What could she possibly say?

"We've spoken together all of three times. Each of those times, I tried to convey that I will no' bring ye harm, that ye are mine and I guard that which is mine. I've lost too much, aye?"

His eyes squinted at her. Tosia still had no voice, but she nodded slightly. Where was he going with this? 'Twas not how she expected her wedding night to start.

Not that she had any presumptions about *that* to begin with.

"But we've only had those three conversations. Not exactly what I'd call wooing. Do ye agree?"

Here she could readily nod. She'd had the same clarity from the moment she woke that morn.

"And as a new wife, I assume a virgin wife, I might also presume ye have many fears and questions about what will transpire this night."

"My mother —" her voice trailed off. He shifted his head toward her.

"Pardon?"

"My mother explained to me what transpires. And the maids gossip." Her voice barely broke the air as she spoke.

"Mmmm," James mumbled, his lips thinning in a suggestion of a grin.

"But being told how to ride a horse and actually riding one are two completely different things, aye?"

Tosia's hand flew to her neck as her eyes blazed wide. "Surely ye canna compare to a horse?"

She'd seen the members of many a horse. Try as she might, Tosia couldn't stop her eyes from flicking to the waistband of his kilt.

"Nay! No' like that, I mean."

Tosia straightened and had to fight against the surprising smile that tugged at her cheek. For the first time in their conversations, she had knocked away his stiff and unyielding demeanor. Maybe it was his small taunt about biting at their wedding, maybe it was that she was starting to feel a sense of ease from the man, their wedding night notwithstanding, but giving him a sense of discomfiture made him appear more human, less monster, in her eyes.

She crossed her arms over her breasts, waiting for him to continue.

"What I mean," he put a hard, gruff emphasis on his words, "is that hearing of it is far different from completing the action. I can make that easier for ye, if I may."

Seeing the change in James piqued her curiosity.

"In what way?" she asked.

"Weel, again, like with horses. Do ye ken how to have a new horse become familiar to ye?"

Tosia bit at her lips before answering. "I fear I'm no' overly familiar with horses."

James nodded, his face softening as he gazed at her. "Ye dinna just rush in, aye? A horse is skittish, and the two must become acquainted. Ye do that by first sharing your presence with the horse, moving gently around him until he is comfortable with your nearness. Only then might ye touch. The horse may no' move, and your touches must be slow, easy, until the horse adjusts to ye. Only then might ye begin to really pat the horse, or try to ride him. It may take a while, but once that happens, the horse and rider can move as one."

Tosia didn't answer right away. She blinked slowly, trying to take in all he'd told her. This was *not* the conversation she'd anticipated on her wedding night, but then, what was?

"What are ye trying to say? What's your suggestion?"

James inhaled, inflating the breadth of his chest as his eyes glittered in the candlelight.

"Ye must get to know me, more than our brief encounters have permitted. I shall be as the horse, unmoving. Ye can study me, undress me, touch me to your liking, and I will no' move an inch."

Tosia cocked her head as her rosebud lips pressed together.

Was he crazy? What man could just stand there under the attentions of a woman? Not move at all? His offer seemed implausible at best.

"Not move at all?" she questioned.

"No' until ye are ready. But." Here his eyes narrowed slightly. "Once ye bid me move, though I will do the best I can to be gentle for ye on your wedding night, 'twill be rather like ye've released the wild animal side of the beast. And ye must be prepared. Only grant me move if ye are certain ye are ready for me."

One amber eyebrow rose on her forehead. "Ye vow no' to move, no' touch me, until I give ye leave?"

James took a deep breath. "Aye. This I vow."

'Twas an impossible offer. There was no way he could remain still and not move until she permitted. He was a hot-tempered man who acted rashly and oft without thought of consequence. Could he now control himself enough to hold still that long?

Tosia signed silently. In truth, she had no option but for the one he offered. She was his wife. He could take her as he might. If he were giving her the opportunity to familiarize herself with him, extending her a courtesy that he didn't have to, then what else could she do?

James stood stock-still in the center of his own chambers, his booted feet firmly affixed to the freshly woven mat that covered the stone floor. The candlelight danced off his skin and cast shadows on his tunic and kilt. She left the relative safety of the table's edge and moved to stand before him. He spread his feet shoulder width apart and clasped his hands behind his back, patiently awaiting her investigations.

Tosia started by eying him in a sidelong look, as if she feared looking at him straight on. Even when his hands were bound by his own promise, she hesitated. Her eyes dropped to his legs, so she decided to start there.

His well-formed legs were on the lean side, covered in long muscle and a bit of rough black hair that made his skin appear darker than it was. His kilt brushed right above his knees, and she could barely make out the firm line of his thigh before it disappeared under the plaid.

His waist was tight, not paunchy like some men she'd seen who enjoyed too much mead or whiskey and meat. His body was a warrior's body, rigid and carved, as if from stone. From his waist, his chest flared out, and matching his arms under the short, loose sleeves of his tunic, packed with muscle — further testament to his days spent wielding a sword.

She shifted then, made to walk around him, but her eyes flashed the question to him first. Was she allowed to move around in her rather unorthodox *introduction*? His chin dipped almost imperceptibly. Thus encouraged, she lifted her skirt and circled him, noting the broad expanse of his backside and how his black waves of hair, so short on the sides, yet curled to the neck of his tunic. So he hadn't clipped it entirely.

Tosia continued her trek to face him again. His eyes didn't drop to hers, but remained forward, as if he were on guard and couldn't lose his focus.

Under her scrutiny, perchance, that was how he felt. If he lost his focus, he'd break his vow. The strong lines of his cheek, now visible like the cleft in his chin, were as sharp as cut stone and as hard as the rest of him. His intense eyes, that shifted from engaging to soft to flinty in a matter of moments, stared over her head to the wall.

Only a few days past, he had touched her lips with his, drawing her into a dizzying world of emotions she struggled to understand.

His lips were the first part of him she touched, returning the favor. He exhaled a wavering breath that tickled across her fingers. All that power surging under his skin, barely checked and controlled.

That same wry smile she'd experienced earlier returned to her face. So, she wasn't the only one unnerved by this interaction.

Her fingertip traced the fullness of his lips before trailing a line down his warm neck to the edge of his tunic. The rough fabric covered him from neck to waist and most of his upper arm. Was she supposed to remove his clothing? From his suggestion before he fell silent, it seemed she should.

She dropped her hand to the hem of his tunic and tugged. He moved with her, lifting it over his head. He clasped his hands behind him again, dropping the tunic at his heels.

His chest rose and fell in front of her eyes as he tried to control his breathing. Her eyes roved over his bare skin, and something in her own chest, something strange and compelling, flooded her and made her head swim. The chiseled muscles of his chest rose and fell. She felt that she should feel awkward, shamed even, for staring at him as openly as she did, but he gave no indication that she should stop. In fact, from his steely presence, he seemed to encourage her to continue.

Other than Tavish, had she seen a half-naked man this close before? Nay, certainly not. And definitely not one she could reach out and touch at will. That knowledge made her even more dizzy.

A smattering of black hair, as dark as the hair on his head, covered the expanse of his chest and narrowed to a fine arrow at the waist of James's plaid. With a tentative hand, Tosia reached it and let her fingertips stroke the beast's fur. For that's what it truly was. Then she let her fingers sink beyond the thatch of hair to the skin of his panting chest.

It was like touching a large, powerful animal, warm, with a steady rise and fall that seemed somehow larger than the man himself. The Black Douglas may have told her he was just a man, but his furred chest, his heavy breathing, the flare of his nose as he forced himself to remain still under her ministrations, told her that he was, indeed, more beast than man.

His skin was marked, covered in scars, a life of hardship and battle written upon his skin.

She walked around him again, her fingers sliding across his side, over the ruched muscles of his back, which were also covered in scars and marks.

What hadn't he done to his body? she wondered. Were all warriors thusly marked?

In a sudden bold move, her hand dipped lower, over the plaid, pressing against the hard rounded globes of his lower backside. He twitched at her touch, surprised by her more intimate gesture. She'd seen the tight, rounded backside of him when he wore his braies, and it was as firm as it appeared. Her heart raced her in chest as her side smile returned.

There was something to be said for having this much power under her control.

Would it always be like this? He'd made a vow to her, said that he was hers. Did that mean his barely controlled power was hers to command?

The thought sent another shiver that bloomed hotly between her thighs.

Her fingers rose up on his hip to his belly as Tosia finished circling him. She glanced at his legs, still clad in his boots. She pointed at his feet.

"Your boots?"

Without hesitation, his feet went to work, the toe of each boot taking turns to loosen the heel before lifting one leg at a time and pulling the limbs free. James tossed the boots behind him without looking. His eyes remained fixed on the wall.

Tosia was impressed at his commitment to his vow not to move unless she gave him permission.

Now the only thing that stood between her and her new husband's naked form was a swath of dark plaid and the belt that held it on his hips.

Was she courageous enough, bold enough, to bring her hand there?

She started at his waist, using her finger to follow the thick edge of his brown leather belt. At his hip, she patted her hand over his plaid, like she'd pat a goat, then brought her hand back up to his belt. Her fingertips hovered over his groin, barely touching his copper belt buckle.

His belly quivered and danced under her fingers, and his breathing grew more ragged in the quiet of the room, sending a rush of his breath against her hair. She flicked her gaze up to see that his head had dropped a bit, his eyes angled downward as he focused those blazing green eyes at her.

No longer stoic or perfectly still. He was losing his control, yet fought with his own inner beast to keep his vow not to move.

Emboldened by his faltering control, her hand shifted, pressing against the hard member of his arousal that bulged against her palm. James gasped sharply. Tosia wanted to snatch her hand away — he *was* like a horse! — but forced herself to keep her hand pressed against the rigid shaft under his plaid.

She was certain that now he'd move, now he'd tell her this game he made of promising not to move was at an end, but he didn't. The only movement he made was a narrowing of his eyes and the pulsing of his manhood.

While her own chest quivered, that blossoming heat between her legs grew, becoming hotter and spreading lower on her thighs and up to her chest.

With both hands, she slipped the belt from the buckle, and his skin shook as she withdrew the belt. The plaid caught on his hips, precariously balanced, and after a heartbeat of hesitation, Tosia tucked a finger into the waistband, forcing the wool to drop to his feet.

She was at once shocked and mesmerized at the sight of his straining manhood, hard as a sword yet smooth and pulsing toward her as if it already knew the way home.

Her hand reached out and she stroked the hot, silky length, caressing her fingers over the purplish, rounded top of his staff. The ragged, shivering breath he took told her James was at his breaking point.

Then she enveloped his cock in her hand, and his arm shot out from behind him and grabbed her wrist with such a grip she thought he'd crush the bones of her hand.

Instead of cowering away, she kept her own grip on his manhood and turned her eyes to his. If his eyes had teeth, he would have devoured her whole, but she still met his gaze straight on.

"Ye vowed ye wouldn't move until I released ye," she whispered.

"Didn't ye though?" he rejoined, his voice gruff and ragged.

"Nay. No' quite." She turned her head slightly, peering at him from under her heavy lashes. Her lips relaxed into that half-smile again. "Do ye wish me to release ye? To give ye leave to move?"

His hand clenched her wrist as his gaze burned into hers, challenging her that he might remain in control when they both knew he was nearing the point of no return.

As was she.

"Answer me, James," she demanded, again shocked at her impertinence. When had she become so brazen? "Do ye desire that I give ye leave?"

His whole body shuddered.

"Aye."

What power she wielded — what power he had bestowed upon her.

She squeezed his throbbing shaft again, and his groan was so loud and raw that it shook her to her core. She leaned into him so her lips were near his chin. Taking a deep breath to prepare herself for what was to come, she spoke the words.

"Then I release ye."

With a low snarl like the beast he was, James moved with such speed that she barely finished the words when she was on her back in the bed.

He lay atop her, though she was fully dressed, and his eyes searched her face, her heaving bosom, and lower to her waist. Then he cupped her face in his hands and spoke plainly.

"I will do all that I can to ease this transition for ye. If I can make ye feel half the excitement and passion for me that I feel for ye right now, then ye might find your own heights. If ye dinna, I vow that every night after this one, ye will know naught but the greatest ecstasy."

The promise was an odd one — how could he make such a vow? And were such sensations possible on one's wedding night? She had not heard any rumors of the like.

Tosia didn't have time to ponder it, as one of his hands cupped her backside, pressing her hips against his as the other worked at the laces at the back of her gown, freeing them with ease.

Once her gown was loose, he wasted no time in sliding it down her body, followed by her thin chemise that didn't hide anything as it was, until her body was free, and she was as naked as he. She expected him to move then, to take her as quickly as his ragged desire suggested he would, but he didn't. Rather he paused, feasting upon her with his heated gaze.

James's own passion rose inside him, and as much as he wanted to plow her pink furrow with wild abandon, he couldn't. She wasn't a hussy to be used and tossed aside. Tosia was *his* woman. He belonged to her, and while she might feel the pain of first love this might, he swore to himself he'd do everything in his power to make sure he worshiped her body as it deserved to be worshiped.

It was the least he could do for this gift that lay before him.

Her legs dangled off the bed, smooth as poured milk. The apex of her legs that hid her treasure shimmered like dark heather honey in the candlelight, rich with amber and rose and malt, and would surely taste just as sweet. His cock pulsed at the view she presented.

His eyes continued their upward movement as she breathed heavily under his gaze, panting as much as he was, making her plump breasts jiggle under the exertion. Her nipples, dusky pink in the dim light, peaked, and offered themselves as a succulent meal. Her hood eyes never left his face, watching him with the same intensity as she had when he stood naked in the center of the room.

Her lips formed a perfect bow, and he leaned over her, his hot shaft pressing against her hip, and she quivered at the sensation. She'd called him a horse, and while that was a wild comparison at best, he'd been flattered and didn't want to frighten her more than she already was.

When he caught her lips with, caressing them with a gentle kiss that demanded every measure of restraint from him, her lips received him and returned the kiss with slow, smoldering movements. Her lips tasted as honeyed as he'd believed they would be. She squeaked when the tip of his tongue pressed forward, invading the warmth of her mouth, giving her a taste of what was to come.

One of his hands lingered on her shoulder, brushing her arm before reaching her full breast that he stroked with his fingertip. The luscious offering of her breasts was too much, and his kisses grazed her neck and chest before reaching her breast. His tongue traced a line of heat over the sweetness of her skin, sweet and salty as the finest mead, and if he could he'd drink on her all night. Her nipple tightened against his palm and he stroked it before replacing his palm with his mouth.

Under his intense licking and sucking, Tosia mewled and squirmed beneath him, as if she were fighting to leave and to get closer to him at the same time. As his tongue lapped at her tremulous skin, his hand slipped between them to explore the uncharted skin between her legs.

She gasped in his ear when his fingers found the cleft between her intimate petals, touching their warm velvet softness, skimming across her quivering thighs. When he moved his finger to rub between her womanly folds at her bud of desire, she arched off the bed. Her fingernails dug into his back, adding to his scars, and his hand became wet under his attentions to her unchartered treasure.

Shifting so his lips found hers, he breathed into her mouth.

"Ye are ready, lass. I am more than ready. I've been ready since I've met ye. I will be as gentle as I might, and the pain should last but a moment. Your heights will soon follow, this I vow."

Then he pressed forward in a gentle movement, the pulsing, purplish head of his cock parting her in a slow, nearly-aching thrust. Her sheath accepted him more quickly than he anticipated, and her gasping became a bit-off cry once he embedded himself fully within her.

They were joined, and the quivering motions of her sheath on his iron-hard flesh sucked everything from him. He lost himself in her, kissing her lips and thrusting his hips as deeply into her as he could.

The first few thrusts drew more gasping cries from her, ones he tried to chase away with long kisses and tender licks of his tongue on hers. Soon, her gasps of surprise and ache ebbed, and her breathing changed into puffs and pants against his mouth. They found a steady tempo that bound their bodies together, and soon her hips rose and fell with his, welcoming him into her body.

She murmured his name into his lips until his need for her grew to a crushing crescendo. James closed his eyes as his penetrating desire roiled in his groin and spread to his entire body, a fire catching on kindling and spreading to ignite every part of him. His manhood pulsed and his ballocks clenched against him, and at his moment, he threw his head back, pressing his cock as far into her as he could, spilling his seed and roaring his climax from the deep within his chest.

He remained rooted to his place between her legs, a sensation of belonging and possession as he filled her thighs. His panting slowed, and when he finally opened his eyes, her burning hazel gaze caught him like a snare. Savoring the feeling of spent satisfaction for a moment longer, James dipped his head, kissed her with a light tease of her lips, then withdrew his dripping member to lie next to her on the bed.

His hand yet lingered on her breast, unwilling to fully separate from her. All the angst and rage he'd held inside had spilled with his seed, and for the first time in years, he had a sense of contentment he'd lacked with this woman who was now his.

Tosia's head turned to the side and her gaze studied him. His fingers played absently with her breast.

"I did no' hurt ye too badly?" he asked. She shook her head.

"No' too badly. It ached, to be sure, a shocking and sudden pain, but it faded. 'Twas replaced with something else. A peculiar sense of fulfillment."

"I have an odd sense of fulfillment, too, but one borne of contentment," he told her. "Nary a person has brought that to me in years, mayhap longer. Ye, Tosia, are the calm in my storm that I have so desperately needed."

She ran her fingers through his shortened, damp hair. "Then perchance we are well met, milord."

A lazy grin slipped over James's lips.

"Och, lass. Well met indeed."

Chapter Thirteen: Well and Truly Wedded

TOSIA DOZED NEXT to him, her hair entwined in his arm as she slept the sleep of the innocent. James's cheek twitched at that thought. No longer so innocent.

Rolling to his side, he disentangled her hair from his skin, and he moved with stealth off the bed to his discarded clothing from the day before. He folded the rich black tunic into a neat pile, ready to return it to their proper owner, and opened his trunk. The aged wood squeaked in the silent gray light, and he froze, his gaze darting to the woman in his bed. She didn't move.

James placed his kilt inside and withdrew his own worn tunic and braies from the trunk, then closed it with clenched shoulders. When it didn't squeak again, he exhaled and placed his borrowed wedding finery atop the trunk where Brigid or another maid might find it.

Once dressed, James lifted his tartan cloak where he'd hung it on its peg the day before and held his breath when he opened the door, waiting for another irritating squeak. Thank Christ it was silent, and he stepped into the hall and closed it quietly.

James hated himself for sneaking out, but his mind was in turmoil from his wedding night. He hadn't wanted to wed the lass yet did as commanded by his king. Upon meeting the nervous creature, his heart went out to the shy-eyed young woman who'd recently lost her mother, her home, and was forced into the union with a man of his terrible, deserved reputation. If anything, he marveled at her restraint. Unlike him, she didn't have the resources or skill to lay waste to those who put her in that situation. Despite his better judgment, James worked earnestly to calm her fears. He protected her as they rode to Auchinleck, answered her questions with full honesty, and spoke to her in the sweetest of tones he could muster.

Then, he'd expected to send her off to Threave and refocus his energies on the king and Scotland's independence.

But yesterday, last night . . .

He had no understanding of what had transpired. But he had a better grasp of what Robert the Bruce endured every day that his own wife was imprisoned by the English. If anyone tried to remove Tosia from his side, he'd make the reputed Douglas Larder look like a springtime walk in the moors.

What ached his head was he had no reason for those emotions. Firstly, King Robert had been correct in his belief that a fine wife could calm the beast that was Black Douglas. That knowledge vexed him to no end. And other than the undeniable fact that Tosia Fraser Douglas was now his, in the eyes of both God and the law, he couldn't wait to find himself between her legs again. Only next time, he'd make sure she experienced the same consuming heights as he had.

Since he wasn't prepared to speak to his new wife, the notion of exposing his conflicting emotions to her a knife in his chest, 'twas better to sneak out before she woke.

The torches in the hall had burned to blackened stumps and fell into shadows where the bleak sunrise didn't reach. So Shabib's sudden appearance at the top of the stair made him clutch one fist to his chest and lash out with the other. He stopped his flying fist just before it made contact with Shabib's full lips.

"How do ye do that? Ye materialize from the shadows like a specter! I could have stuck ye senseless!"

Shabib didn't recoil — instead, the white gleam of his teeth crested into a half moon, mocking James.

"Oh, sirrah. Was your attention focused elsewhere? Perchance on the fair lass you snuck away from?"

James pursed his lips and crossed his arms over his broad chest. For so lean a man, Shabib had no fear or mocking those who might land a punch. Or at least mocking James. And James had no doubt Shabib wouldn't even flinch from the strike and would hit back just as hard. He'd seen Shabib do it more than once.

"I wasn't sneaking."

"Oh. Well, I know you have an abundance of practice at it with other women. I had assumed that, since this lass was now your wife, you'd be more inclined to tarry by her side for a bit longer."

James stiffened and narrowed his eyes but said nothing. The white gleam of Shabib's teeth widened in the dim hall.

"So, you wanted to stay. Could it be the iron-hard beast of Scotland has found his heart softened and now doesn't know what to do with it?"

How did Shabib read him so well? James prided himself on his stoic face and tried to maintain that under the Moor's taunts.

"Ye know no' of what ye speak."

Shabib's smile faltered. "Don't I though? A man might burn his land to ash for king and country, but he'd scorch the entire world for a woman."

Aye, Shabib well knew. He had done the same for those who'd had a hand in his wife and daughter's death in northern Spain, Moors and Christians alike. Their violent deaths crushed Shabib's heart so fully that he had indeed laid waste, fire and sword, against everyone who had executed his family so indiscriminately, as if they were nothing more than garbage to throw out with offal. Shabib's sword and torch had killed and burned as indiscriminately, and he hated all those who lived south of the Holy Roman Empire. He especially despised his own people whom he'd expected to help protect his wife and daughter and instead left them to die.

It was one of the reasons he'd stood beside James when he'd destroyed his own keep.

Aye, Shabib truly understood what a man would do for the woman who held his heart.

"It is not without irony that love makes us better men at the same time."

"I dinna love her."

He said the words without thinking, but he didn't believe them himself. Why was he so conflicted otherwise?

"Oh, but you are well on your way. I've seen the change in you when she is near. You won't realize it until it hits you hard, like a stone striking your head. And then you will do anything and everything for that person. You'd move the world for a look, a smile, a kiss."

James rolled his eyes skyward. Shabib meant well, but the man was shockingly emotional for a hardened warrior.

"Don't dismiss it. Don't you think that if I could destroy the world to have my heart back, I'd do it without thought?"

James did know, that much was certain. Shabib's religion forbade drink, and for the most part, the man was devout. Except for one night in France when Shabib's depression was palatable, a sickly sad taste that he could only drown with sour red wine, James found him deep in his cups. The typically stoic Shabib, his tongue loosened by drink, confessed every grisly detail of his wife and daughter's murder by the Spaniards after being accused of improper behavior and shut out of their village. Trampled by Spanish horses, unaided by any of his people, and left for dead in the hot sun. For nothing more than an untrue rumor of illicit behavior that Shabib couldn't return in time to rectify.

Shabib had seen red. He had grabbed a torch off the wall and set fire to the houses in his town before taking his sword to any Spaniard he met on the road. After a particularly violent fight that left the skin of his cheek ragged and dripping and the rest of him barely alive in a ditch, Shabib had found a surgeon to stitch up his face and left his cursed home, and those he now despised, in his past.

His hood often covered the scar, but it couldn't cover the scars of his heart. Only rarely did he bring up his wife, as he did now, and James allowed his brain to absorb Shabib's counsel.

The lanky Moor smacked James's back and gestured toward the stairs.

"Since you are not yet ready to declare your love for the lass, let us break your fast. You can show your adoration for her later. Though you will have to come up with a better fabrication for the king, who might think you are rejecting the bountiful gift he's granted to you."

James gave Shabib a knowing, side-long look as they descended the stairs and elbowed him in the ribs.

His companion spoke an undeniable truth. Tosia was a bountiful gift indeed.

Tosia had just finished lacing up her worn, everyday kirtle when the door to James's chambers (*nay, our chambers, nay mine*) creaked open.

"Good day, dear sister," Tavish greeted as he stepped inside. His brows were high on his forehead, his eyes bright. "How do ye fare this day?"

Tosia's cheeks inflamed, and she averted her eyes. She knew the real question he was asking.

Had James adhered to his vow to not hurt her?

Had he been gentle?

Tosia swallowed her embarrassment and gave her brother a tight smile. What point did it serve to be coy? Everyone in the keep knew what had transpired between her and James the night before. And if he hadn't been gentle? What recourse did they have if her new husband was as violent with his wife as he was with his enemies? None.

But James hadn't been violent. Her mind still whirled in confusion over her wedding night. Other than the brief pain of taking her maidenhood, James was the most gentle man she could imagine. He had made sure her body was quaking and as ready for him as it could be, and when he did enter her, he was slow, easing into her gently, and his words of love and passion were a steady chant in her ears. She had been his religion, his church, and he had worshiped her body and praised her, lavished adoration upon her as though she were more holy than the Madonna herself.

How could a man burdened with a reputation as a violent beast, one with no care for agency, treat her like fine glass, almost as if she could command the man himself — if she were so bold to do so.

"He was verra gentle," she said noncommittally as she averted her gaze and gripped her skirts. This was a *most* unpleasant conversation with her brother.

Tavish cleared his throat. "Weel, that is an auspicious beginning then. Are ye growing to know him as ye wanted to? Ye believe the king as done well by ye?"

He sounded like a hopefully young lad, doe-eyed and eager to serve his laird and his king. Tosia's eyes misted over at the sight of this laddie in a man's body. She moved close to him and ruffled his auburn waves. Time spent outside in the intermittent summer sun had added golden locks to his hair, and he seemed almost brighter for having come to Auchinleck.

At least one of us is, she thought with irrational bitterness. Why was she so inflexible against the prospect of finding a measure of joy in this new path of her life?

"Aye," she told him, unsure of the truth of her words. She gave Tavish another tight smile. "We will make the best of it."

If Tavish doubted her, he didn't show it. His cherubic grin tugged at her heart, and in that moment, she made a decision.

She vowed to give her marriage to the Black Douglas, and their service to the king, an honest chance. Not necessarily for herself, but for her hopeful and excited brother.

"Go now," she waved him toward the door. "I must finish dressing, and I'm certain that Sir James has a list of chores for ye this more. He rose with the sun."

Tavish dipped his head and swirled toward the door. Before he disappeared, he looked back over his shoulder at her.

"I am happy for ye, Tosia. I had only hoped for the best for ye."

Then he was gone in an amber flash of his tunic, and she was again alone the James's chambers.

She regarded the quarters in which she sat, noting several of the amenities she had missed the night before. Though relatively austere, the room did hold a few comforts. Larger than her cramped, pre-wedding chamber, with a navy and cream-colored tapestry of horses hanging on the wall by the door, the room was tidy. A smaller matching tapestry hanging over the narrow window, and tucked into the corner between the window and the hearth sat a table which held a wooden bowl of water for washing. Not what she expected from a brutal warrior.

Any clothing he had was put away, for no evidence of it, not even a tartan cape or extra tunic, hung in sight. Someone had brought her belongings in the night before, and they sat in a neat pile next to his trunk under the tapestry. Aye, not the chambers of a rough man, but of a disciplined one.

"Our chambers," she said aloud to herself, letting the sound of it roll off her tongue. Could she grow accustomed to that phrase? And as she learned more about him, the real James, could she grow accustomed to the man?

Recalling the sensations he drew from her the night before, a new realization flashed in her mind like lightening.

Perchance she could.

The day passed quickly, full of smiles and cheer at her new position as James Douglas's wife. Too soon, however, night claimed the land, and she found herself in their chambers, on his bed, completely nude under his voracious gaze. He'd vowed to have her find her ecstasy this night, and now he was following through.

"Lean back, lass," James whispered above her.

He shifted to sit on the bed, and Tosia did as he bid, so her nubile body was stretched in front of him. His eyes flashed at her offering, the fire in them burning to match the fire at the hearth.

"Touch yourself," he commanded.

Tosia froze, her hand on her thigh. *Touch myself? What does he mean? I'm touching my leg!*

When she didn't respond, James chuckled, a deeply resounding vibration in his chest that made the air around Tosia thick. She could taste his need, salt and leather and male. He reached for her hand.

"Like this," he told her as he took her finger and placed it between her quivering woman's lips.

He stole her breath from her when he handled her, and she quivered all the more, only not from passion. What was he doing? Why did he want her to touch herself there?

"Ye have a place there, aye?" James's voice was as thick as the air in the room. "Special to a woman that brings her pleasure. I know ye didn't fell the fullness of passion on our first few nights together, and I swear that ye will know that passion every night we spend together for the rest of your life. Now, brush your finger across, right, there."

His finger pressed hers into her own flesh, and as he guided her, she swiped across a small round bud between her legs that made the deep quivering in her belly when they were alone together blossom into a tempest. Every part of her body wanted to launch off the bed, and when he guided her finger over it again, she had to bite back a scream.

What has this intimate spot on her body that had been hidden this whole time?

"Aye, lass," James's breathy voice rumbled into her core, matching the vibrating deep in body. "I would have ye find your pleasure as ye will. It is my joy to bring ye to it, but if I ever can no', I'll no' have ye left unsated."

Her finger moved across her nub between her legs, and her quivering and shaking bloomed more, igniting like a fire until it had a mind of her own. Then a shock went through her, a hot wave washing over her from head to toe, and she arched her back as she lost herself in the all-consuming sensations. There was nothing else in the world but that shock of ecstasy that robbed her of breath and thought.

Her hand fell away from her woman's mound, and before her mind could regain control, James thrust his shoulders under her thighs. She squeaked in surprise.

"'Tis your honey pot, flavored just for me, and I long to taste your pleasure. Bring ye to your rise again," he told her, his voice ragged.

Any words of surprise or protest were lost on her lips — her body wasn't her own, and he dragged his tongue over her inner lips, teasing her sensitive bud again. His tongue was slippery as it dipped low again before cresting her bud again. Tosia shuddered as she inhaled. What was all this? How did her body give her this sense of perfect, uncontrollable delight?

She gripped his black hair, holding onto it in fear she might fall off the world. Then his head popped up, his sage green eyes dancing with mirth and his face shining with the wetness of her own juices.

His lips fell to her belly, kissing his way to her jaw. Her hands held his head as he moved his lips to hers, kissing her deeply, savoring the taste of her own salt and sour.

"Did you find your pleasure?" he asked against her mouth.

She moaned lightly. "Aye, now 'Tis time to find yours."

She surprised herself with her bold words, and James reacted immediately. He lifted his lips from hers and grinned wickedly. 'Twas like he embodied the demons that haunted him — he was her own personal demon in her bed and between her legs.

His hips moved in response to her demand and tickled her already ripe pleasure bud as he entered her. Her desire for him overrode everything else and her hips lifted to his. James groaned deep in his chest. He placed his hand under her backside, clamping her hips to his in an iron grip, grinding into her over and over. His eyes remained fixed on hers, that slightly wicked grin plastered on his face as his hips worked, his manhood grinding into her again, deeper.

She closed her eyes and lost herself in her arched body that he used for his own needs just as her body reached a crescendo. He penetrated her, reaching to the very core of her, and as peaked again in thunderous waves, James worked into a frenzy, roaring his climax into her, raw and animalistic.

His body clenched against her, and when she opened her eyes, he was panting above her, his damp head hanging against her breasts. His broad shoulders blocked everything else from her view, and in this moment as their frenzied passion calmed, only the two of them existed, joined as one against the harshness of the world.

Tosia skimmed her hands over his sweaty back, pulling him down so they touched skin to skin, and James accepted her comforting embrace. She held him as though this hardened warrior were a fragile glass, as though here in bed was the one place she might keep him safe and drive away any lingering demons.

If she could forget the world in the passion he stoked in her, then she might do the same for him.

When he finally rolled away, the cool air raised pimples on her skin. James flipped a fur over them, chasing away the chill. Then he turned to his side and placed an arm over her, drawing her close, and pressed a kiss on her shoulder.

In these chambers, in his arms, Tosia felt a new sense of security, one she hadn't experienced before. Oh, she hadn't thought such a feeling possible with the Black Douglas! Yet he was her own beast, one that circled her protectively, guarded her, and brought her immeasurable joy.

Like the joy he'd shown her this night. She shivered at the lasting memory of it. James tugged the fur higher on her shoulder.

"Are ye chilled, lass?" he asked, wiping her hair to the side to kiss the back of her neck. She shivered again.

"Nay. 'Tis the sensations ye give me."

He chuckled behind her, his breath warm against her neck. "Ye found your pleasure then?"

She warmed as a blush flared over her skin, turning her of a shade of pale rose. "Aye," she admitted in an embarrassed voice. "I did."

His hand caressed her shoulder and down to her waist, encircling her. "I would have ye find your pleasure with me every time. I want ye to know all the joy that ye might have in this world."

She moved her hand and found his hand. His fingers moved to clasp hers, as if he needed every part of their skin, even their fingers, to touch.

"'Tis a hard thing, to find joy in this world. I hope that ye find joy in it as well." She held her breath after she spoke. Had she overstepped in her words? Reminded him of his own hard life? His lips found the back of her neck again.

"I find joy in ye," he whispered against her skin, "and 'tis enough to bring me joy in this world."

Tosia smiled to herself as their breathing shifting, steadying as sleep embraced them. Any fears she'd had for her husband had evaporated, disappeared completely, and an undeniable realization washed over her. She was growing to love this man and would do everything in her meager power to keep him close to her.

And considering James's ability to rage and destroy if provoked, Tosia pitied anyone that might try to separate them.

Chapter Fourteen: A Shocking Lack of Training

JAMES WAS NOTHING if not the Bruce's man, and only a few days after their wedding, he fully resumed his role as captain, directing the king's armies among the lowlands and searching for rogue English and their treacherous Scottish allies.

Which meant James oft came to their chambers late, shed his harsh, military exterior as he shed his sword and tunic, and came to their bed to find his release with Tosia.

A man of few words, James put his stock in his actions, his behavior, keeping Tosia close whenever they were together.

And as the Bruce's man, he didn't share any military strategy with her. Whether it was due to his reticent nature or his desire to shelter her ears from his repugnant but necessary deeds, Tosia couldn't guess. Perchance a mix of both. What she did know was that any rough or beastly tendencies he might have, he kept out of their chambers. Instead he plied her with kisses, laving her skin with his bold tongue, and delicate touches — far too delicate for a man whose hands commanded death and destruction.

Well, *mostly* delicate.

His tease on their wedding day had sat in her mind, and one night as James's eyes flashed like green lightning and his hands found her most intimate folds, she had asked him about it.

"Why would I want ye to bite me?" she'd asked.

James had stilled, and a slight wolfish grin spread across his dark face.

"Is it because ye are oft called a beast? Or do couples sometimes bite?" she continued.

He had shifted atop her and gazed at the curve of her neck.

"Both," his raspy voice drawled before lowering his face and taking the thin skin under her jaw between his teeth.

Alternating between sucking and nibbling, James's mouth had sent shivers curling through her. His delicate biting had blazed a trail to the quivering bounty of her breasts, taking one pinking hub and holding it with his teeth as his tongue worked her into a frenzy.

Her fingertips had clawed into his back, and she had sucked in a fierce breath.

"Aye," she agreed into the darkness as she lost herself with him. "Both."

Too often, memories of their marital interludes caught her during the day when her mind should have been on other tasks, and a burning blush warmed her cheeks as her loins roiled.

For a man who had frightened her to her core less than a month before, he had shown her the many faceted sides of even the most devilish man. In truth, Tosia had come to feel safer in his arms than anywhere else.

"Och, I know that look. Has that Black Douglas found his way into your heart with as much pleasure as he's found in his bed?"

Tosia, who was supposed to be beating out the tapestry that hung from the line, whirled around to find the stately Lady Elayne standing behind her, a grin playing at one side of her refined face and a wee babe swaddled on her chest. Even with a bairn in hand, she held herself like a queen, and Tosia had to suppress the instinct to bow.

That impression wasn't far off. With the king's own beloved imprisoned by the English and few enough other women in the king's entourage at Auchinleck, Lady Elayne ran the keep with a firm hand and the household, transient though 'twas, ran with an efficiency that rivaled any royal court.

Tosia bowed her head slightly as she tucked an escaped lock of hair back into her kerchief. The tall woman's silvery gray gaze, usually hard and surveying, crinkled at the corners as she clicked her tongue at Tosia.

"Dinna fret on it, lass. Many a woman has been caught up in the attentions of an eager, new husband, no matter how the marriage came to be."

Lady Elayne's tone held a light note, and Tosia found courage in the woman's presence.

"Even if 'twas assigned by the king to a man who's known as an evil beast?"

Though she no longer saw James through that veil, she wasn't deaf to the gossip of what new, vile strategy James envisioned for the king's war for freedom, necessary though those strategies might be.

Elayne threw her head back and barked out a rich laugh. The swaddled babe squealed at the sound, its shock of blonde hair sticking past the plaid fabric. Elayne cast a soft gaze at her babe, then back at her.

"Och, Tosia. I forget ye are no' from the Highlands. How do ye think I found my husband, Laird MacCollough? Or Caitrin found hers? Do ye no' know who the MacColloughs are?"

Tosia shook her head, her eyes focused on the woman who possessed a fascinating tale, to be sure. Elayne's eyes sparkled as she spoke, her hand patting the babe's backside without thought.

"Declan MacCollough is laird of what was known for a long time as the beast clan. Wild men with nary a civilized soul among them. When Declan became laird, he'd recently served the Bruce and wanted to lead a clan that was worthy of that position. He'd made an offer for my hand to my father, as I had my own reputation as the willful, loudmouthed harpy. He wanted a strong wife to assist him in humanizing his clan. I didn't know the man when I arrived at his stronghold, only the disheartening rumor."

Elayne winked at Tosia. "There's more to a man, to anyone, than the rumors, than their history, than their kin. If ye take the full measure of a man, 'twill show ye his true nature."

Tosia nodded as she released a long breath. Thinking something on her own was one thing, to hear someone confirm it, someone in a similar situation, was quite another — and a relief.

"And now ye have a babe?" Tosia asked, smiling at the fair child. Elayne's face beamed at the babe again.

"Aye, a strapping son we call Gabriel."

"Och, like the angel!" Tosia cried. Elayne nodded.

"So, has he?" Elayne asked, one of her rich chestnut eyebrows rising high on her forehead.

Tosia's head flinched slightly. Was she asking if James had gotten her with babe? Such the invasive question! "Has he what?"

"Found his way into your heart? If the king entrusts the man with his life, I can assume ye could do no less. And there is something to be said of a man who would guard ye, champion ye, with his life."

Do my eyes sparkle like that when I speak of James? Tosia wondered wildly. If they did, then mayhap Lady Elayne's words were accurate.

James had done nothing to perpetuate any vile thoughts toward him and instead done all he could to make her feel welcome, safe, valued.

Elayne patted her shoulder. "If no' yet, perchance soon enough. I will leave ye to daydream at the tapestries."

Tosia's warm blush became a hot flush of embarrassment at her lolly-gagging, and she dropped her gaze to her feet. Elayne's boisterous laughter carried through the courtyard as she swept back to the keep, leaving Tosia to contemplate Elayne's words.

Try as she might, her mind still couldn't focus, and after repeatedly failing to beat the dust from the woven canvases, Tosia dropped her shoulders and returned the paddle back to its place by the kitchens. Mayhap Brigid had a chore in the kitchens that might engage her mind, so she didn't waste it on girlish fantasies regarding her husband.

Upon entering the kitchens, she was greeted not with smiles but with frantic rushing. Had something happened whilst she daydreamed away the day? Why the chaos? She closed the door behind her and grabbed the sleeve of a chambermaid whose arms held cloths as she shoved past the other kitchen maids.

"Is something amiss?" she asked the curly-haired lass who went by Alana.

"Aye. The king's men were attacked by the cowardly MacDoualls, caught by surprise. One's been injured." Then she ripped away and ran for the doorway to the main hall.

James! Tosia thought crazily. Who else would be a target than the man who'd wreaked havoc on the English and their allies over and over?

Lifting her skirts, Tosia broke into a run, following the woman to the main hall.

But it wasn't James who was carried in by the Bruce's men.

The men rushed into the hall in a storm, not with joyous celebration but in cautious tones.

"Call the midwife!" Asper called out as Tosia followed Brigid out of the kitchens.

The giant red man shoved a young clansman out the main doors, and the lad scrambled to do his bidding.

It wasn't the man hidden in the circle of men that drew Tosia's attention; it was the pale expression on James's face — a foreign look on a man intimate with death and blood. What caused him to look so wan?

Only one thing — if the injury were to her, something out of James's control. But she was fine, covered with a fine layer of oat flour, maybe. Which could only mean . . .

"Tavish!" she screamed, dropping the cloth she held as she ran to the men.

James caught her around the waist and swung her to his side.

"First, 'tis no' as bad as it looks," he whispered raggedly in her ear. "Second, ye must temper yourself so as no' to frighten him."

Tosia stared into James's ashen eyes, which were nearly as washed out as the rest of his face. She nodded slowly, and only then did James step to the side and permit Tosia to go to her brother.

The gash on Tavish's side appeared grievous, with blood seeping enough to taint his tunic a frighteningly maroon red. Tosia's heart raced in her chest, her own fear at her brother's seemingly dire state gnawing at her like a rat on grain. She reached out her hand and clasped his pale fingers.

"Och, Tosia. I regret ye find me in so pitiful a state. I'm not the warrior I thought myself to be."

"Posh, dinna say it. Many a great warrior has his battle scars as testament to his greatness. 'Tis only your sour fortune that your first one is larger than ye expected."

"Aye," James's normally harsh voice was tempered behind Tosia. "Ye've seen my back, a collection of scars that would set many men running. Ye are no' a true warrior until ye have the scars to prove it."

James's attempt to build Tavish back up slowed Tosia's erratic heart. She'd learned he wasn't quite the monster he'd been painted, and hearing him support her brother only softened her to him all the more.

"Move, move, let me pass," an authoritative, high-pitched voice announced, and they turned toward the invasive sound.

A stout woman with her entire head wrapped in a pale blue kerchief brushed by the men circling Tavish. The woman's crinkled brown eyes flicked at Tavish, and she clicked her tongue as she lifted his tunic, then turned her gaze to Tosia.

"Ye are his woman?"

Tosia smiled weakly. "His sister."

The stout woman nodded approvingly. "Well, ye can stay. Can someone get the rest of the mongrels from here?"

James and Robert immediately jumped to work, corralling the rest of the men out of the main hall.

"I'm called Morna. I'm a healer and midwife. From the looks of this wound, ye dinna need to fret overmuch. Stitching will be the worst, and then ye will have a fine scar to show off to the lassies." Morna chuckled to herself as she patted Tavish's shoulder.

Tavish shot a worried glance to Tosia, mirroring her own clenching worries, then looked back at the midwife.

"Aye? I'll recover?"

Morna dug in her satchel with one hand and flapped at Tavish with the other. "Ye did no' think that this was a fatal wound, did ye? Och, laddie, ye have much to learn about swordplay. I think yon king and his mannie will make sure ye learn all ye must, aye?"

She lifted a slender brown eyebrow but kept her gaze on the injured soul in front of her. James and Robert nodded and grunted in agreement.

"Fine. Here, bite down on this. 'Twill be sore for a bit, but in a fortnight or so, ye will be back serving your master, sword in hand."

Before Tavish could respond, Morna shoved a well-gnawed stick between his teeth. Then she cast a quick look over her shoulder.

"If ye would?" she asked, gesturing to Tavish. Robert and James scuttled to Tavish's side to hold him immobile as she worked. "If ye feel faint, lass, please take your leave. One injury is enough for me today."

Tosia bit her lip and nodded, vowing to herself to keep her wits about her. She barely had time to marvel at how easily this short woman commanded the King of Scotland as if he were nothing more than a lowly crofter, before her needle was threading through Tavish's skin, pulling it as the thread dragged through his ravaged skin.

He hissed and tried to arch his back, but the King and James were true to their word, holding Tavish down so Morna's fingers could work as quickly as possible. Soon, the sheared skin was rejoined in a jagged line of stitching, and only a few thin trickles of blood remained where once a bloody ragged gash had been.

Morna wiped the rest of the blood away with a rag, then wiped her own hands before wrapping a strip of cloth around Tavish's waist. "There. Keep it clean. Lass, ye can clip the threads out for the lad in two or three weeks. Watch for pus, and if it forms, call for me right away."

She patted Tavish's tunic again as she stood.

The air in the hall suddenly seemed thinner, cooler, and Tosia took a deep breath, trying to clear the clenching in her chest and the pounding in her head. Robert and James each stepped back from Tavish and inhaled deeply as well, searching for their own cooler breaths.

The king walked the healer to the main doors, slipping a coin into her skillful hands. James went to Tavish and ducked under his arm to help him rise from the stained bench. Tosia still clutched her brother's hand, and supported his other side as best she might.

"Ye get a cot in the chambers off the kitchens, oft reserved for servants of guests," James explained as they hobbled toward the archway. "That way the maids can see to ye as ye need. Ye will remain there until the stitching comes out, then ye are back with the other squires. However, this has shown me that I've been lax in your training. I should no' have brought ye with us until I was certain of your ability. Prepare yourself. Once those stitches are gone, your body will wish they were back. I shall work ye until ye drop. Your next scar will be one of no consequence, this I vow."

But he wasn't looking at Tavish as he spoke. James's gaze peered around Tavish's heaving chest at Tosia.

He was making the vow to her.

Once Tavish was settled in his cot, the kitchen maids were tasked with bringing him spiced mead and dried venison to help him regain some of the blood he lost. Tosia patted his hand and kissed his forehead before leaving. His brow was cool, and color was returning to his cheeks. The deathly pallor of his face was gone.

James placed his arm around Tosia's waist as they exited through the kitchens toward the stairwell.

"A moment, if ye please," James asked before they mounted the steps.

Tosia turned to him, a flicker of apprehension surging through her. James grasped both of her hands in his, and his glittering eyes searched her face.

"The blame for today resides in me. I asked him to accompany us as I would have any other squire, not bothering to see if the lad was ready to fight if called upon. I apologize if his injury caused ye any pain."

Not for the first time, strange emotions battled inside her. Here stood the mighty beast, the Black Douglas himself, renown for causing pain and destruction, and he was apologizing for causing her any pain. Would she ever resolve those two contrary aspects to the man?

Tosia released one of his hands and placed her palm on his scruffy jaw. His black beard and the sides of his hair that he had shaved to cleanly had started to grow back, returning his rough appearance to him. The hairs prickled against her skin as she rubbed them, and his face tipped to her hand, nuzzling it.

"'Tis our lot, James, to fight against the English. Tavish knew this once the king sent his missive, and he was the one convincing me that this was our new path in life. I canna fault ye for the actions of the English. I'd rather have ye at his side, at his back than any other. Ye of all people would bring hell upon earth before seeing him, or any of your men, harmed."

"Or ye." His voice cracked as he spoke, and her heart leapt into her throat. "I'd lay waste to everything on Earth and in hell to keep ye safe."

Her heart fluttered at his words. How did a man so hardened make her insides soften to the point her legs threatened to buckle? How had the Blackguard of Scotland managed to steal her heart?

"As I would ye. Dinna forget, James. Just as ye made a vow to me, I made one to ye as well."

Then his full, sensuous lips latched onto hers, his tongue caressing hers as if to seal their shared vow with their kiss.

The evening meal in the hall was a subdued affair. At Bruce's table, Robert's head bowed close to those of James and Asper Sinclair as they conferenced on serious events of the past several days.

June had ended in a bloody wake. Tavish had been the start of a series of violent escapades that the King's army had tracked back to the MacDoualls, and the king's frustrations seeped from his skin, marking his face with severe lines. His plan to quell the English and their lowland sympathizing clans had to be put on hold to deal with this more pressing issue.

"We can wait no longer. I've wanted my vengeance on the bloody MacDoualls, and now I might have it. Most of their attacks have occurred as evening claimed the day, as 'twas when they murdered my brother. I'm sure they expect us to attack in a similar measure, if they expect us to attack at all."

His statement hung in the air as a question, and he flicked his steady brown gaze to James, who dipped his head in a slight nod. James's set jaw and icy verdant gaze left no doubt as to where his mind was — assessing the best way to inflict the most damage to the MacDoualls, for both his king, and his wife.

Under hooded eyes, James glanced around the hall, but Tosia was nowhere to be found. She had taken her meals with her brother for the past several evenings, and he had missed her clear, bright face in the hall. As much as it chafed him, the lass, her modest strength, and acceptance of a man such as he for husband had endeared her to his heart.

What chafed him even more was that Shabib and Robert had been correct — Tosia *had* been good for him. A balm for his soul, for his heart. He hadn't lost that organ, no matter what the gossips claimed.

And if he lost it now, it was because the forest fae lass was stealing it from his chest.

The king had continued, and James rubbed his hand across the stubble of his sprouting beard to focus on the matters at hand.

"We'll take our lead from Douglas, and his renowned larder. Daybreak, after a night of drink. They may well be sleepy and sore from a night of imbibing, but we will give them full opportunity to raise sword against us. We will surprise them as light touches day, instead of attack in the dark like the cowards they are."

The Bruce's voice rumbled roughly on the word *cowards*, and James ginned at the king. The man had grown into his crown well, a warrior king, and Scotland deserved no less.

"James." The king shifted to face James directly. "Your man, the Moor, ye've said he has a talent of working well in the shadows?"

James tilted his head and glanced at his blue-robed friend. "Aye. And he's been waiting for ye to find him of use."

Robert nodded. "The tomorrow night, we will ride out. Stay to the woods but send your man to the Dumfries keep. Have him spy on the men, and if they are drunk enough, he can tell us. Then we will prepare our raid."

James nodded. "And if he overhears anything of note, the words will fall eagerly from his lips."

Robert slammed his fist on the table. "Then we are in accord. Gather the men on the morn, prepare for an attack. James, I trust ye will concoct a ploy for success?"

A slight shiver coursed over James's back, but he cleared his throat and leveled his gaze at his king.

"I am ever yours to command."

Chapter Fifteen: Reclaiming Scotland

TOSIA MIGHT HAVE had a measure of pity for her brother, if several of the kitchen and house maids hadn't made it their intent to ply Tavish with adoring attention. If it wasn't Chrissy with buttery treats from the ovens, then 'twas Grace sewing up Tavish's tunic and braies to fit Tavish's burgeoning form to perfection.

She leaned against the side of the stairway, watching as the lassies scrambled for a hint of consideration from Tavish. Tosia was pleased that her brother was coming into his own, finding his place with James and the king's men. Yet at the same time, the sight made her stomach tighten in a hard knot. He didn't need her anymore, and she'd miss the adoring brother he'd been.

A form came up behind her, pressing his hard body against her back. She leaned into the comfort of James's chest as he bent to whisper into her ear.

"The king will wait no longer to settle his vengeance against the MacDoualls. I will explain to your brother why he's not attending me. He shall be disheartened but understanding. Please know that while our charge on the MacDoualls is in retribution for the king's brothers, my sword will also lay waste in retribution for the injury to your brother."

She shouldn't have found comfort in his violent words, but she did. Knowing that James would slay the men who'd harmed her brother sent a wave of warmth through her, tinged with a new, icy concern. Tosia spun into his arm, her face upturned.

"And ye. I have confidence that ye will do as ye say, but I dinna desire to see *ye* harmed. I would have ye return to my arms."

That reluctant tug of a smile sparked on his face. Without answering, he lowered his head and nipped his teeth on her lip before claiming her in a lusty kiss.

Then he released her, gave a courteous bow, and entered the small servant chambers off the kitchens where Tavish reclined on a low pile of furs and tartans. The doting maids rushed from the room as if the hounds of hell themselves had entered.

"Milord," Tavish's lighthearted face grew serious at James's approach. He lifted up on his arms as if to rise from the bed. James waved him back.

"Stay. Ye are no' well enough to rise yet. And as such, ye will take this news with grace. The king has decided we can wait no longer to quash the MacDoualls. We ride tonight to learn what we can and prepare our attack."

"But I must go wi' ye! I'm your squire!" he squeaked out, and Tosia giggled behind her hand from the kitchen where she eavesdropped.

"Nay. A knight does no' permit one who is injured to come to more harm, which is what would happen if ye came with. Ye can barely stand. Know that we will have our retribution, both for the king's brothers and for ye, and when we next ride against the English and their allies, ye will be more than prepared to ride with us."

Tavish's mouth pulled into an irritated frown, but he nodded at James, acknowledging the command of his lord.

James turned and left the cramped quarters. When he passed Tosia in the kitchen, she gave him a grateful smile. He didn't stop but reached out and caressed her hand with his finger as he strode past.

A violent demon on the outside, but an adoring husband where none might see.

None but her.

Shabib emerged from the darkness like a spirit, a dark ghost in an even darker night. His deep blue robes were black in the shadows, and James started when he approached. The back of his head smacked against the tree trunk, and he sucked in his breath and rubbed the sore spot.

"It saves me from smacking you to pay attention, James," Shabib intoned as the other men surrounded him.

"Och, ye fiend. What did ye learn? Anything of use?"

Shabib bowed, whether it was in assent or mockery, James couldn't guess. The Moor was nothing if not mysterious. And he had an astute ear of overhearing conversation, which was why James tasked him with observing the MacDoualls from the shadows.

"The MacDoualls are within. They depart on the morn to meet with Richard MacCann from clan MacCann, and from their tone, it involves the English. And there is more, something you might find very interesting."

James straightened and stared down Shabib, waiting for the man to speak. Why did he always speak in such riddles?

"Shabib?" James asked with an edge to the word. James thought he saw a glint on Shabib's teeth when the man smiled.

"Your king had wondered if the Hammer of the Scots English liege was in stout enough health to try to invade Scotland once again?" James nodded, his teeth on edge. What had Shabib learned of Longshanks? "The king is dead. His health finally expired, and now his son has very recently been crowned King Edward the Second."

James stilled, his breathing shallow as his mind tried to process Shabib's news. The Hammer was dead? The old king had finally died? He didn't yet know what type of king the son would be, but James, as well as most of Robert's inner circle, knew the son to be a weakish fop.

"Let us find Robert. He will want to strike at the MacDouall's on the morrow, after they are well away from the keep."

"And news of the old king?"

James did something he rarely did ever. He smiled.

"We will save that best news for last."

In the moonlight, the king's face shone bright enough for all the men to see by.

"Truly? Ye heard them say that the Hammer is dead? That his son now reigns?"

Shabib bowed his head. "Yes, milord. The milquetoast son is now King Edward the Second."

Bruce's dark eyes caught James's, and he threw back his head, a burst of laughter exploding up from his chest.

"Och, the Lord is good. This is a sign for Scotland, 'Tis surely. God must bless our endeavor for a free Scotland, for why else did he send Longshanks to his death?"

"The weak king, he will still wager a war if for nothing else than to try to claim greatness on his father's back," James reminded him.

The Bruce flapped a dismissive hand. "True. And we are weary of war. But the lad is no' the commander his father was, and he will need time to regroup. We will take advantage of the change in power, decimate these MacDoualls, and then reclaim the lowlands before heading north. We yet have a war ahead of us, only now 'tis one I have no doubt we can win."

"Och, ye had doubts before?" Declan MacCollough asked.

The Bruce nodded his head — honesty was one of his more esteemed character traits. "Aye. I have confidence we shall cut a swath through these English, yet I'm a man just as ye. I've had many doubts over the past winter. Now, with ye men leading my army and the Hammer of the Scots dead and cold, most of those doubts have fled."

The king's positive attitude was infectious, spreading amongst the men as readily as a summer breeze.

"Now, I believe Douglas had his plan for us. What has your black heart designed for the attack on the morn?"

With that, the elated attitudes of the men dissipated, replaced by extreme focus on James as he drew in the dirt with a stick under the flickering light of a low torch.

By daybreak, the Bruce, James, and their men gathered at the edge of the wood, waiting for their moment. The mood was familiar to James, but now that summer was high upon them, instead of a misty, damp gloom emerging with the sun, brilliant yellows burst forth onto the land. The shadows of the trees lay long on the grass, like gray carpets leading the men to their undertaking.

James lifted his left hand and waved. Two groups of men behind him, Shabib and Thomas included, broke off and crept to the north and south to surround the stronghold and ride in when the MacDoualls focused on what they believed to be a single eastern attack.

The strategy worked a brilliantly as they had hoped, and many men fell to their swords. James's own sword drank the blood of the MacDoualls as a parched land drank water, and his ears were deaf to the dying cries of his enemies. He grimaced as another spurt of blood crossed his stained tunic, another testament to the Scots reclaiming their freedom.

But as they worked their way through the inner bailey, James's spirits dropped. Not enough men were present, and Laird Dungal MacDouall was nowhere to be found. An old man they'd spared shared what he knew under threat of a slit throat by Thomas, whose hand held the man's neck at his mercy.

"Nay, Laird Dungal departed two days past! For the MacCanns!" The old man gasped, the blade at his neck drawing a thin line of blood.

The Bruce cursed in a low voice and turned in a rush. He thrashed at the hay cart by the gate as he stormed out, roaring his curses replacing his hushed tone.

Shabib's eyes cut to James, who shrugged. Then his stony glare returned to the man who held no compunctions of sharing his clan's secrets. James gave a quick nod of his head, and with an easy swipe of his arm, Thomas ended the old man's treasonous misery.

James directed Thomas and the rest of the men to secure the keep before he and Shabib rejoined the king. His helm-covered head was bowed as he pinched the bridge of his nose.

"Ye spied on the keep and no' a one said that Dungal was no' here?"

Shabib shook his head, his own gaze focused on his folded arm. "Nay, milord," his deep voice intoned. "Perchance it explains why the men imbibed as heavily as they did. The cat was away so the mice did play."

The reasoning made perfect sense, and mayhap the death of King Edward was why the Laird left early. The Bruce lifted his face. His brow was furrowed as if an ache thrummed behind his eyes. James understood that sensation well — he'd experienced something similar upon watching his own home burn.

"Shall we ride for the MacCanns? Find the bastard Dungal there?"

Robert stared into the distance, his eyes glazed in thought.

"I do. I want to ride for that fool and make him weep blood at my feet. Yet my vengeance must again wait. We have a larger need to take the lowlands from the grip of the English, and we can take advantage of the weak king's distractions. If we come upon Dungal along the way, the mores the better. But for now, we return to Auchinleck and plan our next round of attacks." The Bruce twisted where he stood to study James with his deep, sullen eyes. "I would have the lowlands returned to my control before the leaves change."

James held the King's gaze, trying not to notice how deep the lines ran from his eyes, how sallow his skin, the shadows haunting his cheeks. As he adjusted his sword and walked back toward the woods with several other men, a disconcerting notion crossed James's mind — if this war killed the Hammer of the Scots, how long would their own king last before this war destroyed him?

Chapter Sixteen: Are Ye Mine?

ONE ASPECT OF battle that remained constant was the fire it ignited in the blood, an explosive blaze that men could only quench between the thighs of a woman.

Vengeance makes a man's sword strike with greater ferocity, and the slain MacDoualls had no chance against the vendetta of the king and his loyal knights.

They returned the next day, their tunics and plaids still stained with the blood of the king's vengeance on those who executed his brothers, and James didn't wait for a dismissal from the king. His sole intent was to find Tosia. And their bed. Now.

And after the bloody battle with the MacDoualls, James's mind and veins burned with vitriol. The soundness of Robert and Shabib's desire for James to have a calming foundation, something to prevent him from losing the last of his humanity, became truly understandable at the prospect of taking his wife to bed. In sinking into Tosia, he'd reclaim his soul, his humanity.

The kitchen maid, Brigid, pointed to the gardens when James burst into the kitchen, bellowing Tosia's name.

She was pulling weeds from the pea plants, her hands and skirts encrusted with dirt.

Perfect, we shall be well met, sharing in the dirt of our tasks.

With all the will power he could muster, he gripped her upper arm. She balked, turning to look up at him.

"Ye must come with me now. I have need of ye," he commanded.

All the color washed from her face, and he cursed his tone.

"As my wife. I need ye as my wife," he clarified. She dipped her head silently and rose, letting herself be led by him.

He all but ran to their chambers, dragging her with him. Before they were in their quarters, his lips were on hers, slanting and aggressive, his bold hands twining in her hair and crushing against her backside.

"I should wash," she tried to say as his lips slipped to her jaw. He kicked the door shut behind him.

"Nay, I long to have ye as ye are. I need ye, Tosia. I've needed ye since we left."

His hands were rough, tugging at the neckline of her gown so her breasts popped from the thin fabric, ready for his eager mouth that found a nipple and sucked greedily. Tosia gasped, and James lifted his head, his bleary gaze barely able to focus. The grinding pull of his cock consumed him, like a beast he couldn't control.

"My apologies, wife, but I canna be gentle this time," he growled into her neck as he yanked her gown down to her waist, snapping her laces. "This is a driving need, one I canna tame, but know that it comes from a place of love for ye as my wife. I come to ye for this release."

He wasn't making sense — his mind couldn't form the words, and as he spoke, he drove her backwards to the bed, his lips scoring her skin as his hand lifted her skirts.

James rose up over her and loosened his braies, freeing that part of him that drove him mad with need.

"Forgive me this aggression, love. I'll be gentle with ye next time. Part your legs for me, aye?"

He didn't want to force his wife — God save him, he was already marked as a beast and he'd vowed never to be one with Tosia, but here he was, demanding that she tame that side of him. What if she didn't agree? What if —?

His thoughts were cut off when her gaze, steady and unafraid, bore into him and she dropped her knees, giving him full access to the one part of her that could give him succor.

James didn't hesitate. He drove forward, sinking himself into her warm welcoming sheath, grounding himself, pouring out the vitriol and regaining his humanity.

"Were ye satisfied, lass?" James asked as he huffed his breath, standing above her with his braies yet unlaced and manhood exposed. "I fear I took ye far too quickly. Hurt ye when I could no' think clearly."

Tosia shifted over to look up at him, letting her skirts fall where they may. The sheer force of his need, his desire driving him like an animal, should have frightened her, shocked her. Instead, his ferocious, beastly lust thrilled her, the burst of pleasure she'd experienced arising from his rough hands and pounding hips as much as from any joining they'd had.

Until this moment, James had been the pinnacle of gentle lover, guiding her to find her moments of pleasure with him.

This, today, had been all James, a raging hunger that thundered from him. Her skin was branded from his calloused hands and the rough scrub of his beard. He was blind with his need, possessed and driven to claim her, even if he hurt her doing so.

He hadn't. The sight of his rippling arms, his clenched jaw and his eyes, *oh*, tormented and predatory as he stared her down. She was his prey. His only prey.

And she was the lone person who might calm that beast and bring James back from the brink.

That knowledge set her entire body ablaze with her own passion. Such power in the control of that animalistic need.

"Ye did no' hurt me," she assured him in a languorous voice, one of a satisfied woman.

James's chin clipped to the side, and his gaze dropped to the length of pale thigh that extended beyond her hiked-up skirt. His eyes blazed wolfishly again.

"Nay?" Ignoring his own state of undress, he trailed a finger along her thigh.

"Ye have been a gentle, cautious man until today. Whilst ye have shown me my own pleasure, I had no' known that coupling between a man and woman could be so —"

"Rough? Carnal?"

"Urgent. Torrid," she answered.

James tucked himself in his braies and sat next to her on the bed. Blood yet stained his hands and tunic, and he dropped his head into his hands as if he were trying to hold his skull together lest it break apart.

"I've wanted ye like that since our first night. But 'tis no way to take a lass, a wife. Yet, seeing ye, knowing ye were yet safe, knowing I found vengeance for ye, set my head on fire. Knowing that ye are mine and no one else's, and that I can have ye when and where I may, can make a man ragged. And I was burning with blood lust. Those three can change any man into an animal."

Tosia had rested her hand on his back and now pressed against it to sit upright.

"I am yours? I belong to ye? As your wife, aye?"

Her curious tone was not lost on James, who shifted to face her, dropping his hands to his lap. With one finger, he traced the line of her jaw. Now that the beast inside him was tamed, he was again the gentle husband.

"We belong to each other, but aye. With men, we have a sense of ownership with our wives, with the women we love, or our children and kin. Ye are mine. And if someone were to take ye from me, I would fight every demon from hell to get ye back or find vengeance if ye were harmed. Men are no' as rational as we like to believe in that way."

Tosia was silent for a moment, studying the lines of his face. Whenever he opened his heart this way, she was awe-struck. It didn't fit the image of the Black Douglas. Yet more, it helped her understand the king and his motives, and the men of Scotland as a whole.

"'Tis why the king has ye as his second in command. Someone took his wife and child, who belonged to him. And his country, too. So he's fevered with getting them back."

James nodded. "Men might find solace for a night, but ye'd be surprised how they pine for the woman they love."

Tosia's lips quivered to suppress a smile. Oh, but she was learning much about the ways of men from one of the most hardened men of them all! Then her smile dropped, and her face grew serious.

"Would ye pine for me?"

He had said he owned her, but much of his words spoke of love. Did he love her enough to pine for her if she were no longer here? Or just seek vengeance for the loss of something that was no longer his? A girlish fancy, but she'd come to care for this man, more deeply than she let on or was ready to show to those outside their chambers. Was that emotion one sided?

James moved his hand to clasp hers, threading her slender fingers through his much thicker ones.

"I would no' say it outside this chamber for fear 'twould be used against me. Please always keep that in mind. Look what happened to the Bruce when his wife and child were imprisoned. They are using the lasses against him, and it eats away at him body and soul, like a disease. I would no' survive if I were the cause of your abduction, or worse." He kissed her forehead before returning his gaze to her eyes. "I had no' thought it possible, Tosia Douglas, but ye are the one single good thing I have in my life. And I adore ye for having the strength to be wed to the Black Douglas. Ye have trusted me in a way no other has, and your willingness to be so open to me, the monstrous, broken man that I am, has scarred my heart as much as my battles have scarred my body. I want ye and no other, my dear Tosia."

If his rough loving earlier had set her body aflame, then the strange tone of his heartfelt words scarred her heart, and she had to blink back the emotional tears that filled her eyes.

James cleared his throat and made to rise, obviously unsettled by his sudden, affectionate words. Clenching her fingers so he couldn't slip away, Tosia tugged him back to the bedding. She placed a tender hand on his lightly-furred cheek.

"Thank ye for those words. Ye are a man of war, no' sweet speech, and they could no' have come to your tongue easily. And I well understand how ye have taken strides to keep me safe, to ease my move here with ye. I'll have ye know, I no longer see the Black Douglas when I look upon ye. I see James, a man, my husband whom I am eager to have in my bed. And if anyone took ye from me, I, too, would pine and fight with the same vengeance as the king to have my retribution."

The side of his lips curled. "Bold words from such a tiny lass, but seeing as how ye tamed the king's beast, I'd quiver in my boots if ye sought vengeance upon me." Then he lifted her fingertips to his lips and kissed them. "'Twould seem we are well met, wife. Much to my surprise."

Tosia's lips also curled as she gazed upon her husband. "Well met indeed," she whispered.

James finally stood and assessed the mess of his arms and tunic. "I must wash. The king will want to discuss our next steps, and the next time I come to ye, I should be much more presentable."

His gaze lingered on hers for several more heartbeats, then he turned and left in search of a water bucket.

Tosia leaned back on her elbows and admired the man as he left. This crazed, violent man who was her dear husband. Then she adjusted her skirts and bodice, trying to salvage what remained of her laces, and rose as well to make herself useful in the kitchens.

Chapter Seventeen: Private Trysts

TAVISH HEALED QUICKLY, and all too soon he was back out in the bailey, training with the king's men and their squires. James took his vow to Tavish to heart, and when he wasn't with Tosia or in attendance with the king, he was outside, his practice sword raining blows upon Tavish without mercy.

Tosia was pleased that her brother was coming into his own, finding his place with James and the other soldiers. Yet, at the same time, the sight made her stomach tighten in a hard knot.

He didn't need her anymore, and she'd miss the adoring brother he'd been.

"Are ye ready, lad? If ye are, then we will make certain ye are more than ready for the next time we ride for battle."

James had stripped to nothing but the plaid that swirled around his thighs as he circled the yard adjacent to the stables. Several of the men abandoned their duties to watch and offer advice to and tease Tavish. The kitchen maids who'd fawned over Tavish for the past sennight also gathered around, their faces alighted at the excitement of watching their present love interest exert his manliness in mock battle.

Tosia stood behind the lassies and cast a cursory glance at her brother who seemed somehow larger and more vibrant after his injury. A crooked smile pulled at her lips — it was obvious to Tosia what the cause of his radiance, and they stood before her, sighing. She bit back a giggle as her gaze shifted from her brother to the powerful dark man striding half-naked around the yard.

"Come on, ye laddie. Ye've lazed about the keep long enough. Do ye even recall how to hold a sword?" James taunted, and Tosia bit back another laugh.

The sky was overcast and warm, and a thin sheen of sweat coated James's back and chest. The dark hair on his head had started to grow back where he'd had it shorn, and the hair on his chest was rich, trailing across his sculpted chest and down the flat planes of his belly. He lifted his sword over his head, and the muscles in his arms flexed and bulged. So much power and strength that he contained, and a dizzying tremor engulfed her. The memory of his words, of belonging to someone, rang in her head and she smiled to herself. This mighty warrior, he belonged to her.

As much as she wanted to keep her eyes fixated on James, it was more his sword, his movements and those of her brother that interested in her. Having been kept busy in the keep and with her own sudden marriage, she hadn't seen any of her brother's training. A bit selfish, she hated to admit to herself, but she was here now.

Had she even known that he was receiving any training? What exactly did squires do after all? And in truth, what did James do when he left with the king to do battle with the English? How did he manage to return every time, when so many men had given blood and life for the Scottish cause?

Her interest piqued, Tosia pressed her way into the throng of onlookers to observe the training in action.

Neither James nor Tavish moved right away, which Tosia found odd. Wouldn't one want to defeat their opponent swiftly?

Tavish took small steps to his right, moving in a slow circle, with James following his steps. Then, in a shocking burst of frenzied moves, James launched an attack. His muscles bunched and clenched with smooth precision in his explosive movements. The flurry of overhead and underhand swipes at Tavish left Tosia gasping for breath at her only recently recovered brother. And Tosia had held a sword before — no wonder

James's back and chest were corded with muscle. How much strength it took to keep up those sweeping moves with so heavy a weapon!

She shifted her gaze to Tavish, whose own lean muscle had increased since their arrival, but appeared naught more than boyish when compared to James's thick chest and arms.

A sudden shiver overtook her as she continued to look upon her husband. Such power, indeed — a power that was, as James told her nightly, at her complete disposal. The space between her thighs grew damp as she recalled those heated moments.

She cleared her throat, certain that those nearby must feel the flush of her heated skin and see her pinked cheeks, but no eyes were on her. Everyone's attention focused on poor Tavish and how he might combat James's attack.

"Do ye see where ye were weak, lad?" James asked, his breath calming as he rested his sword tip in the dirt. The way he handled the weapon, 'twas a natural extension of his body. Tavish, on the other hand, had yet to grow so comfortable with his broadsword, and still held it awkwardly in his hand.

"I was no' ready," Tavish admitted sheepishly.

Tosia knew it couldn't be easy to train and admit one's failures in front of an audience. She hoped her encouraging face might give him a measure of comfort.

"Aye, 'twas obvious. What did ye miss because ye weren't ready?"

"Weel, ye could have killed me easy with that overhand strike."

James nodded. "How might ye have known I was ready to make my move? I knew the most opportune moment to unleash hell upon ye. How might ye know the same of me?"

Tavish dropped his gaze, his face scrunched up as he pondered the question. The audience of lasses held their collective breaths in hopes that their champion might know the answer.

Then his face smoothed and brightened. "Your jaw," Tavish answered. "With ye being clean-shaven, I could see your jaw clench before ye lifted your sword. Ye had to clench those muscles in your shoulders to lift your weapon."

He spoke as though he amazed himself for having an answer, and pride welled in Tosia's chest for her brother. *Smart lad,* she said to herself. Then again, Tavish had always been a deep thinker.

"Aye, well done. And if I was no' clean shaven? If I was as bearded as our king?"

Tavish studied James for a moment. To help him answer, James moved slowly, lifting his sword over his head again, this time in an exaggerated manner.

Tavish's eyes lit up like a torch. "Your shoulders! I can see those muscles shift under your tunic!"

James smiled widely. "Good lad. Even if your opponent is wearing armor or mail, the plates or links will shift. So ye have more than one way to read your enemy afore he gives attack.

Read your enemy well enough, and he will tell you what his actions will be. All ye must do is respond."

The girls watching tittered at James's words and Tavish's accomplishments. At least her brother had the good sense to blush under their attentions.

And James's lecture told her much of what she had wanted to know about him and his military accomplishments. He must be able to read his enemies very well — then used that knowledge to frame a battle strategy. It explained why he was heavily scarred yet alive when many lay dead in a field under his sword.

Tosia gave one more glance at her husband's strapping, hardened body, then left him to Tavish's lesson.

One lingering thought did rise in her mind as she lifted her skirts to step through the soft dirt. Would the day come when he didn't read his enemy as he should, or worse, when his enemy read him first? Would he come home with scars? Or not at all?

James had been gone from her too long, too many days and nights training or riding into battle with the king, and if it weren't for the generous company of Lady Elayne, Caitrin, and Caitrin's mother Davina, Tosia would have been positively alone. Brigid worked well as a chambermaid, but her duties kept her far too busy to be a companion to a lonely new wife. Tavish, too, had his duties to attend. He was no longer the bumbling lad shadowing her throughout the day.

Tosia threw herself into any tasks she might find at the king's stronghold. She wasn't one who found joy in boredom. Her mother had often cautioned her about idle hands and what the devil might do with them. Moreover, Tosia enjoyed busyness. Milking cows and goats, scattering feed for chickens and collecting their eggs, preparing meals in the kitchens, and sewing clothes — these solitary duties provided a sense of calm and solace in her new life as the wife of the Black Douglas. The more peace she could find, the better she could provide a sense of solace to salve the emotional wounds of the beast himself, if not his physical wounds.

Yet too much solitude surely wore on a person. A woman needed the company of other women, and Tosia was fortunate in the ladies of the keep. They made sure she was never too alone, where her mind might wreak havoc from all-encompassing loneliness. In fact, one misty summer morn, she had folded her mother's shift and placed at the bottom of her trunk. Between the ladies of the keep and James himself, she no longer needed that linen memory of her mother where she might see it daily. Rather, she'd keep it safe and sound, taking it out only when she felt the need.

She didn't mention any lingering sense of loneliness to James, however. His own duties to the king wore plainly on his face — deep lines etched into the hard planes of his face. From worry, from over-thinking, from battle. He slept little, fought much, and it wore on him like the ocean against stone. Eventually, ocean would win out.

On nights when he did find her bed, she wrapped her arms and legs around him, touched every inch of his rough skin to hers, let him sink into her as one would a warm, welcoming bath. Tosia was the balm to James, ensuring he didn't lose himself over to the violence he thought on and participated in almost daily.

So on a bright summer morning, Tosia was surprised when James didn't leave their marriage bed early to find a sunrise meal with the king. Instead, he rolled to her, curling around her in a protective embrace.

"Ye have been most patient, my wife. The ladies speak highly of your work ethic, how ye have found a place here, and I pride myself that ye have managed to do the impossible. Keeping me grounded when I'd play the Viking berserker against the world."

Licking her lips, she tasted the salty memory of his lips on hers from the night before. She turned her gaze to find his gray-green eyes, soft instead of flinty, searching every curve of her face, the swollen expanse of her breasts, down to her hip.

"I have done what the king asked, milord. 'Twas ye and your kind nature that ye hid from the world that has made being your wife and enjoying our bed what it is."

The edges of his eyes crinkled as a light smile crossed his lips.

"I thank you for your efforts."

Tosia grunted and patted his scruffy, black-furred cheek. "Methinks ye thanked me enough last night."

James shook his head. "Methinks much of our nightly loving is for me. Nay, something outside the bed. A joining of souls in conversation and affection, in addition to our joining of bodies."

Tosia half-sat, clutching the brown and green tartan blanket to her breast. "Outside? We are to walk the bailey? The gardens?"

James dipped his head with a chuckle. "Nay, more than that. Finish your duties for the morn. I will do the same. Then meet me outside the kitchens near the noontime meal. Inform the chatelaine that ye will no' be joining them in the hall."

Tosia's heart fluttered under her breast, then her smile faltered. "This surprise is no' what I'd expect of ye, James."

He levels his gaze at her. "Weel, lass, I've made a name for myself doing things that people did no' expect of me."

His lips curled into a knowing smirk, and Tosia found her lips mirroring his own. Then she scrambled over him to nab her kirtle, eager to start her day and prepare for James's surprise.

The woods covered them in a canopy of green, rich with the fragrances of fern and honeysuckle tucked amongst the trees.

"Why are we here? Is this the surprise?" Tosia asked as they walked through the vibrant fauna.

James reached a hand above his head to push away a low-lying branch.

"Aye. Most of our days have been spent in service to the king and his household. We should have some time to ourselves, in the fresh air, away from the bustle of the keep. I thought ye might prefer the calmer scenery here in the wood. Too much singular focus can drive a man, or woman, to the brink of madness."

Tosia's lips curled into a slight smile. He'd know about such things.

"I may be familiar with such conceits," he said with a touch of self-effacing humor in his voice. Tosia giggled.

"Whatever your intentions, I do appreciate the change in scenery. It reminds me a bit of our ride from my croft when you retrieved me for Auchinleck."

His shoulders twisted slightly against her. "'Tis the only time ye've seen the landscape of the lowlands? Have ye never been far from home, lass?"

She nodded, her eyes darting around the lush scenery, trying to take it all in at once. "Aye," she affirmed. "I was born and raised at my mother's croft. I only met my father a few times when I was a child, and 'twas at the croft. Until we rode for Auchinleck, I'd never been more than a few hours' walk from home, and that 'twas only to attend the village."

"The ride to Auchinleck must have been eye opening for ye, then."

In more ways than one, she thought. "Aye. Ye, though, 'twas naught more than a day's work?"

James nodded, stepping around a large stone that blocked their path, guiding Tosia to a more stable footing.

"Aye. I've been far from home, from Scotland, for a long time. Across much of France and back."

"Where ye met Shabib," she interjected.

James nodded. "He joined me, which made traveling less solitary."

"How long were ye gone?"

"Years. I had hoped to return to my homeland, claim my stronghold, but . . ." He trailed off with a shrug. Tosia patted his arm in understanding. Tales of the Douglas Larder left nothing to the imagination, and she didn't want him to revisit that painful memory.

"I'll admit, I was afeared of my journey to Auchinleck, of meeting the king and ye. Now, I can see it as an adventure."

"Are ye no longer afeared of me?" he asked, turning to take both of her hands in his. She smiled coyly at his face, one that shined with a happiness rarely seen on his features.

"Nay. Ye made a vow to me, one that I am certain ye will keep, under threat of your king and friend. Ye seem a man who keeps his vows."

James's smiled widened, becoming wolfish. "Och, ye have no idea, lass," he said as he bent low to kiss her.

She pulled away, her face a sultry mask marked with mirth. "Ye did make me an offer once."

His eyebrow lifted at her guile. "Och, lass, what offer was that?"

Tosia wrapped her hand around the back of his neck and pulled his face as close as he could be without touching her.

"Ye said ye didn't bite unless I asked ye to."

His sensuous face didn't shift. "And?"

"And I'm asking ye." She lifted her chin to expose the soft underneath of her milky neck. "Start here."

And he obeyed, his lips and teeth running a ragged path over her inviting skin as he lay her back onto the grass.

Chapter Eighteen: An Unexpected Encounter

A CRUNCHING SOUNDED from beyond the trees, and James froze mid-thrust, his head twisting to his side as he listened.

"Wha—" Tosia started to say, but James slapped his hand over her mouth.

He lifted a finger to his lips in a shushing gesture, then withdrew from her body. He fastened his braies with one hand as he lifted his sword with the other — all in absolute silence.

Tosia brushed her skirts down to cover her thighs, but otherwise didn't move. What was it he thought he'd heard?

When James stepped on light toes through the tree line, Tosia finally shifted onto her hands and knees to watch his trek through the wood, following far behind him, his body and the fragrant low bushes shielding her against the sounds he'd heard.

The first noise that disturbed the quiet majesty of the forest was a screech as James burst through the trees onto the unsuspecting English soldiers picking at a midday meal under a shady rowan tree. Tosia peeked through the brush to watch James do what he was best known for — finding vengeance and retribution in blood.

The first Englishman fell in an explosion of blood as James leapt down on him, his broadsword finding home in the crook of the man's neck. Wrenching his sword from the man's dead body, James turned as the other two English scrambled for their swords and out of James's way. Tosia's eyes flicked from the taller of the men to the shorter one.

The shorter one was also younger, with mussed blond hair, and his stained tunic hung on his frame. He wore no mail, no armor to speak of. He reminded Tosia of her brother. *So young!* What was he doing as a soldier?

James grappled with the taller soldier, who lifted his sword in a frontal attack. James spun and grabbed the man's wrist before he could bring the sword around and stuck him in the belly like a pig. He dragged his sword across the man's stomach as he removed his blade, and the man's guts poured from his belly. The solider dropped his sword and tried to catch his innards as they dropped in a pile of steaming bloody offal, and he fell atop them.

When James moved again, almost in a dance, the length of his sword was an extension of his arm. The lethal sword edge dripped thick with blood as the point of his blade caught on the thin tunic of the youth, and a shriek tore from Tosia's lips.

James paused, but kept his gaze fixed on the young man, whose own sword hung uselessly at his side.

"Tosia! What ails ye?"

She lifted her skirts as she climbed over the fallen log that, until moments ago, had been the English men's picnic seat, and stopped an arm's length from the panting James.

"Milord, please. Look at him. He's little more than a boy." Her pleading voice was low.

James's visage altered a bit, his eyes narrowing at the Englishman.

"A boy," he stated flatly. He wasn't impressed with her statement.

"A boy. No older than Tavish."

At this, James's jaw ground his teeth together, yet his muscled arm didn't move as it held the youth a breath from death.

"He is a soldier in the army that has cast its deathly shadow over the Scots for far too long. What will ye have me do with him?"

Tosia bit her lower lip and found her skirts suddenly interesting.

"Ye canna kill him. James, he's just a boy," she reasoned.

James inhaled, his broad chest expanding, and the lad quivered visibly, surely believing his young life to be cut short here in the Scottish wood.

"Ye canna mean for me to let him go. He's a bloody English soldier!"

"He's a lad," Tosia pleaded.

James's jaw worked even harder, and his stony eyes glanced to her then back at the lad.

His shoulders slumped and the tip of his blade lowered an inch. He flicked the tip of his blade to the fallen log and Tosia moved to stand behind James. In a moment of bravery that surprised herself, she rested her hand on his free arm. If James noticed, he didn't show it.

The lad stumbled onto the log, sitting down hard. Every last bit of color drained from his face, and he was as pale as a day-old corpse as his frightened brown eyes fixated on James.

"My wife has a heart too large for this world. What's to stop ye from scuttling back to your barracks and bringing the full weight of your contingent down upon us?"

The lad's blond brow crinkled. "Contingent?"

James shook his head. "Ye dinna mean to have me believe ye dinna have a bloody army camped nearby?"

The lad's head moved slowly back and forth, his eyes never leaving James's threatening sword.

"I'm scouting, but we are just a few, living out of a tent near Locherbie."

"And the king? He's right behind ye?"

The boy's brow crinkled more. "Edward the second? I don't know the king's whereabouts. In England I'd suppose?"

"Ye are lying." He brought the sword tip to the boy's chin where nary a whisker protruded.

So young! Tosia's hand squeezed James's arm where his muscle bulged under his sleeve.

The boy's head whipped from side to side. "No! No! They don't tell me anything! I've only just arrived here. I don't know where I'm at, and I don't know how I will even find my way back!"

His voice cracked as he protested, and James dropped the sword tip. Tosia was certain he tried to hide the tight smile that tugged at his cheek upon hearing the lad's voice.

"See?" Tosia stood on her toes to whisper into his ear. "A lad."

"Could be a lying lad," James threw over his shoulder. His hard gaze landed on the boy again.

"What's your name, laddie?"

The young man's frightened eyes flicked between James and Tosia. "Simon," he squeaked out.

James let his shoulders drop but kept the blade tip on the lad.

"Out of deference to my wife, and against my better judgment, I'll send ye off into the wood and ye can try to find your way back. If ye bring your army here, I'll cut it down in a thrice. If it comes back that ye said a word of this to anyone, ye'll find yourself at the end of my sword again, your bloody gullet hanging from the tip like your kinsman over yonder. Aye?"

The lad straightened and nodded furiously.

James set his sword by his side and shifted his head to speak over his shoulder to Tosia.

"Dinna let it be known that James Douglas has a soft spot for his wife. I'll no' hear the end of it."

"Douglas?" the boy squeaked. "Black James Douglas?"

James didn't hesitate and lifted his sword to the boy's neck again.

"My reputation precedes me. Consider yourself fortunate and thank God above for your good fortune. Few enemies cross my path and live. And ye never saw me, do ye understand my meaning?"

Again, the boy's head nodded. James's sword flicked toward the wood. "Go. Get ye gone. Find your own way through the wood and ye never saw us. A random group of Highlanders came upon your group, and ye managed to escape with your life. And ye canna recall where in the wood. Aye?"

More nodding. A surge of warmth flushed through Tosia, and her shoulders relaxed. The boy would live, for now. At least she wouldn't have this lad's death on her hands. Nor would James.

James waved his hand at the boy who scrambled to his feet and ran into the trees as if every demons of hell chased him. Perchance one did.

They stared after the lad as he disappeared into the forest.

"I fear I might regret this, wife. And we dinna tell the king. 'Twere but two men, aye?"

Tosia smiled into her husband's broad back. "Aye, husband."

Now he'd have to hedge the truth with his king, a feat James dreaded. He'd have to alert the king as to the English scouts and admit one got away. Would the Bruce believe such a tale? Mayhap he could use Tosia as his excuse, that he was focused on her safety and didn't give chase . . .

They retrieved the rest of their belongings on the west side of the tree line, and James kept a protective arm around Tosia's waist as they walked back to Auchinleck. They were silent for most of the walk.

James worried for his wife. She was too silent. Was she in shock? Had she seen a man die before? She certainly hadn't seen her husband slay a man before — was she horrified at the true man that lived in the skin of the loving man she presumed her husband to be? He was a beast at his core, and today she saw the reckoning of that beast. Would she turn from him now that she witnessed him firsthand?

"Are ye well, lass?" James asked in a low voice. Christ knew he didn't need to scare her more than he already had.

"Ye have my gratitude for no' killing the boy," she told him, keeping her face forward as they walked. James did the same, studying the horizon.

"Your gratitude?" he asked.

"Aye. Ye could have killed him. Ye probably should have. But ye didn't. Ye stilled your sword. Thank ye for that."

James cleared his throat. Whatever he expected her to say, it wasn't that.

"Ye aren't distressed over my slaying the other men?"

"The other men who would have slain ye and ravished me before killing me? I may have experienced little in my life, but my mam raised me to be smart enough to know danger when it presents itself. Nay, I know we are at war and what monsters the English can be."

James tilted his head toward her and flexed his arm so her body pressed closer to his.

"But no' your husband."

Finally, her delicate face and those wide, amber eyes looked up at him. "No' my husband? What do ye mean?"

James stopped walking and turned her to face him, her body tight against his. She curved into him, as though she were made for him, and he had yet to stop his wonder at that.

"Your husband as a monster."

There it was. They might have discussed his military strategies, his violence in war, but this was personal, killing men right before her eyes where she could see the beast instead of only hearing rumors.

Was he holding his breath? Was he worried at what she thought of him? Bloody hell — he was. Shabib would laugh his deep rumbling laugh and call James smitten.

The Black Douglas, smitten. Wonder never ceased.

"If ye are a monster," Tosia said as she rested her palms against the broad planes of his chest, "'Tis only because circumstance has demanded it. What I saw today was a man, a fair man, who slayed when necessary and gave a young man a lesson and the gift of life. One he will no' forget. That is what I saw today."

James cupped her cheek, her smooth skin a moment of softness in his hard, hard world. And he knew one thing for certain — he was the most fortunate of men to have that softness.

"I made a vow to ye, that ye could ask anything of me and I'd deliver it to ye. Today ye asked much, and I could no' say nay. That ye must know, I can deny ye nothing."

Tosia turned her head, her rosy lips puckering to kiss the rough skin on his hand. Too rough to deserve a kiss from the rose that was Tosia.

"Aye. Ye have more than shown me. And I vow the same. I'd lay my life down for ye."

The mere thought drove a knife in his chest, and he clenched his arm to crush her against him, as if he might fend off the thought by shielding her from it with his body.

"Dinna speak such a thing," he said hoarsely. "Dinna ever speak it."

Tosia rested her head against his chest, nestling into him. Exactly where she should always be, he thought.

"Yet I make the vow. Because I have managed to fall in love with the beast of a man known as Black Douglas," she admitted in a trembling voice.

Was it possible for his heart to wrench from his body? James grazed his lips over the top of her brunette hair, warm under his lips even in the cool air of the late day.

"And I, ye, lass. The king indeed gave me a gift, one I have come to adore, one that resides in my heart."

Tosia sighed into his chest. "Och, who would have thought the Black Douglas so have such romantic sensibilities?" she teased lightly as she wrapped her arms around his waist.

"Dinna tell anyone. 'Twould ruin my reputation," he teased back before lifting her chin to press a light kiss on her welcoming lips.

Aye. He'd never admit it to Robert, but Tosia was a gift indeed.

Shabib leaned against the cool limestone wall, his head lowered under his blue hood so only the tip of his nose and his rough black beard peeked through, when James entered the stairwell with Tosia.

James noted his presence right away. He wanted something, that James knew well enough. Whether it was something serious or not, he couldn't discern, but better to not take the chance. James kissed Tosia's forehead and patted her backside as she ascended the stair to clean up and ready herself to help serve the evening meal.

Her fingernail trailed along his wrist as Tosia glided up the steps, and she gave Shabib a small smile before stepping around the curve in the stair.

"You have accomplished no small feat," Shabib commented with an air of authority.

"What do you mean by that, oh sage one?"

Shabib tipped his head to the stairwell as he pushed himself off the wall. "The lass, your coppery wife. You have managed to make her love the beast."

James's jaw clenched involuntarily. That beast hadn't been well tamed today, and worry of Tosia's safety only made his fury toward the English worse. The idea that she might suffer for his sins hadn't fully occurred to him until this day. James drew his shoulders in and turned to Shabib.

His face was touched with a shadow of joy — something James hadn't truly seen on his friend before. That Shabib found joy in James's happiness reinforced James's commitment that one day, Shabib, too, might find his own joy.

And that joy was never found in vengeance. James had seen the look in the Bruce's dark eyes when they attacked the MacDouall's — he felt a sense release, but no joy. Vengeance didn't bring back family, it didn't restore love to a bereaved heart.

Only love could do that. Robert was confident that he'd be reunited with his wife soon, and that hope was the last thread of humanity that remained in the Bruce. That and his love and admiration for his men.

Shabib had none of that. Nor had he expressed any interested in trying to mend his heart after the loss of his own family in Spain. The dark Moor had been a ghost to himself, a shell of a man. James had pulled him from the precipice of decay, and though his friendship with Shabib and Shabib's rediscovery of his faith had given the man a semblance of himself back, the emptiness in Shabib was discernible to any who knew him well.

"Och, mayhap the beast was ready to be tamed. I can only hope that she finds peace in the wake of my monstrous ways."

James clapped his hand on the lean man's shoulder. "And mayhap we must find a woman for ye, one who can bring ye a measure of peace. A long time has passed, man."

Shabib's smile tightened, and he dropped his face under his hood.

"James, you well know my peace awaits me after my death, when I join my family in the afterlife."

James shook Shabib. "Aye, that is most assuredly true. But would your wife want ye to pine away while ye still walk the earth? Or would she desire that ye find peace here while ye may?"

Shabib grew stiff under James's hand. He'd struck a chord, one Shabib wasn't ready to release. Now was not the time to continue that train of thought.

"Did ye have a need of me?" James asked, changing the subject. "Were ye waiting on me?"

"Aye. The Bruce desires to meet before the eve tide meal, to study your next moves on the English. I'd ask that I might be able to attend?"

James nodded. "Of course, as ye will. The invitation is always open to ye. Let us go."

Shabib's eyes lifted back to James, and he shook his head. "Not until ye wash the blood and grime from your clothes. I dinna know what you do with your wife in the wood, but perchance make it a little less aggressive?"

James's jaw clenched again as his hand went to his tunic. Was it that obvious? Shabib chuckled under his breath as he walked away, leaving James to his ablutions before he attended the king.

Chapter Nineteen: A Plan for Scotland

THE SUMMER DREW nigh as did the Scot's trampling the English south of the Great Glen. Asper Sinclair announced to the Bruce and his men that he was to travel north to retrieve his brothers and spread word that they were going to start the king's conquest of the Highlands. Robert embraced him warmly, and James noted the king's reticence. Sinclair had been by the king's side since he'd returned from the isles last winter. Sinclair's absence would create a hole that needed to be filled.

After Sinclair departed, the Bruce turned to the men who crowded the room. MacCollough and his man, Torin, stood to the King's left as James sat to his right, with Shabib standing behind him, between James and the door. Several other lairds and their representatives had made their way to Auchinleck, MacMillans and MacKenzies having recently arrived, with more riding through the port gate daily. A few of those men sat at this important table as well.

Robert recounted their present successes at beating back the English swarm, which had resulted in a surge of Scotsmen joining to swell the Bruce's ranks. As James had been present at most of those skirmishes, he only half paid attention. His eyes focused on his sword that he held in between his hands, the tip balanced on the floor. He spun it between his hands, the steel glinting and ringing softly as it rotated.

He kept spinning his sword but lifted his eyes at the Bruce's next words.

"Which brings me to the message I've received on behalf of Edward the Second."

At this, this entire room fell deathly silent, with only the ringing of James's sword breaking the thick atmosphere.

"What message?" James asked.

The Bruce's hooded gaze swept the room, looking pointedly at each man present.

"They want to speak on terms. His representative, Hugh Despenser the Younger, has asked for a meeting at Locherbie to see if a resolution might be reached."

The words hung in the room, adding to the already thick air. Several of the men shifted in their seats, uncomfortable with any olive branch offered by the weak king, while others smiled, proud of the Scots' success.

"So our work over the past summer had netted results, and the foppish king now quakes in fear of the Scots drum that beats to the north. None too soon, I might add," Laird MacMillan announced. Heads nodded in agreement, followed by grumbles.

"I'd nay say as much," Torin's deep voice resonated in the cramped chambers. "I dinna trust an Englishman as far as I can throw him."

"'Tis no' saying much," his Laird, Declan, countered with a sharp grin. "Ye could throw a man rather far, ye ken."

The grumbling became low guffaws at the giant Torin's expense, and the man reveled in it. James glanced around the chambers, taking the measure of the men and the value they put on the missive. James, for one, had no faith in the message at all. Too often, the English have reached out, only to turn on the Scots at the last minute. This could readily be the same.

The Bruce waved his hand to garner the men's attention. "Aye, I tend to agree with Torin. I want to move cautiously. Yet, we have struck hard into the heart of the English encroachment in Scotland, and with how weak the new king seems to be, I'd err on the side that they desire to settle this once and for all. To control Scotland was Longshanks' great desire, no' necessarily his son's, after all."

The men grunted and nodded in agreement. What man didn't prefer to lay his sword to the side and sleep in his own bed with his wife? James thought. They were tired — tired of battle, tired of the English, tired of death. An opportunity to end all that? Even James was enticed. He spun his sword again.

"Douglas?" the king interrupted his reverie.

James flicked his gaze over his shoulder to Shabib who nodded enigmatically. Shabib would follow James's lead, as he had thus far. Had any man had a companion as loyal as Shabib? James returned his eyes to the Bruce.

Mayhap a man had.

"What do ye think of this missive?" Robert asked.

James stopped spinning his sword, and gripping the worn hilt in a steady grip, he flipped it up, admiring the weapon that had kept him and those he loved alive to this day.

"Aye, it could be the boy-king wants to end his father's war. That he's taken full measure of his recent losses and desires for it to end. But we dinna know what his advisers, some of whom also served his father, have whispered in his ear." He dropped his sword tip to the stone floor again. "I think as long as we take every precaution, set the time and place, come well prepared for a sneak attack, then we should at least listen to what the emissary has to say."

The Bruce stared at James, as if weighing his captain's words. From the look on the other men's faces, James spoke what the others were thinking, and the Bruce took note of this. He nodded slowly.

"Aye, I believe we are all in agreement. I'll respond to this missive, and perchance, by the time the leaves change, this war might be at an end."

At the eventide meal, the Bruce introduced James, Declan, Torin, and the rest of his advisers to the Lairds and chieftains who had arrived over the past several days. The keep and nearby crofts were filled to bursting with men and their kin eager to join the Bruce in the Scots victorious army.

Of the new arrivals, it wasn't the MacMillan laird or his men who drew James's attention, rather 'twas the dark-eyed lass wrapped in a burgundy cape standing shyly with the two other women who'd arrived with the MacMillans. Full, ebony curls escaped from her hood and danced in the setting light of day.

It wasn't so much what the woman looked like, but what she didn't look like. The MacMillans were a fair bunch, mostly blonde and tawny hair, light eyes, and pasty skin. This lass with darker hair and shifting, nervous eyes stood out under James's astute assessment.

More importantly, James didn't miss the change in Shabib's stance when the woman appeared outside with the rest of her kin. He stood straighter and patted his cobalt blue robe, brushing away any lingering mud or dust. James struggled to stop the grin that formed on his lips. Shabib didn't know James watched him.

Like James, Shabib had been without family, a solitary man with a haunted soul, for too long. James raised an eyebrow at his friend. If the Black Douglas found a lass to give him the solace he needed, body and soul, then so might his mysterious companion. And after all the ribbing he'd received from Shabib about his marriage, James wasn't going to pass on his own opportunity for a tease. He leaned over to Shabib's stiff form.

"Och, the dark-haired lass seems a bit unnerved. Ye thinks she kens my name? I should introduce her to the Black Douglas. How fast do ye thinks she will run in the opposite direction?"

Then James took a wide step in the woman's direction. Shabib stayed him with a long-fingered hand.

"Do not cause the woman any more fretfulness. Can you not see she is petrified? She is as a lost doe, trying to find her way in a strange wood."

James bit the inside of his lip, trying to hide the smile that threatened to burst forth. "Such poesy from so hard a man. I did no' think ye had it in ye, old friend. Is there something about this lass that I should know?"

Shabib's face hardened, his lips pursed in irritation at James's tease.

"Nothing like that," Shabib grumbled. "I'd say the same of any frightened looking woman in your presence."

"Och, would ye now?" James's eyebrow rose high on his forehead, and he barked out a rough laugh, drawing the attention of several nearby men. James merely laughed harder as Shabib's jaw clenched. "I did no' see ye doing that for any other lass arriving at the keep. Ye did no' such thing for Tosia. In fact, ye threw that lass at me, convincing her into the arms of the Black Douglas."

"She was already claimed for ye by the king . . ." Shabib protested weakly, his voice trailing off. James clapped a heavy hand on his friend's shoulder, knocking Shabib forward.

"As much as I needed a woman to keep me from losing myself to a life of violence and vengeance, so ye need one too. I'll inquire if the lass is attached or betrothed. Robert will no' pass up the opportunity to play matchmaker again."

James strode off. Shabib grasped for James's plaid, trying to yank the man back, only to have the wool escape his grip.

Shabib would protest, James thought, smiling. Protest heavily. Claim his vow to his dead wife as the reason for why he could not find love, or at least a willing woman, again. But no God, not even Shabib's Allah, wanted a man to live a life consumed by vengeance. Shabib's soul, much like James's, was at stake, and James would not suffer his friend to such a fate.

If he could find a woman to be the balm to Shabib's own broken soul, then by God, both his and Shabib's, James would make sure she ended up in Shabib's arms.

A day later, as they prepared to leave for the meeting with the English emissary, James came around the side of the stables, covered in a layer of horsehair and hay, only to jerk back out of sight.

Shabib walked the side of the keep toward the bailey, the quiet Frenchwoman by his side. Shabib carried a basket over his arm, but his face, glowing bronze, peered down at the diminutive woman.

Once they reached the edge of the Bailey, where several men and woman labored with stock, worked hides, or sharpened their broadswords, the Frenchwoman reclaimed her basket with a tender hand. She took a moment to turn her refined face and sparkling eyes to the stoic Shabib, whose face belied a softer emotion.

James grinned to himself. Oh, the man who'd lectured James regarding the value of a wife but hesitated to find a way to mend his own heart now appeared enamored by this woman. His grin widened as he peered around the stables again.

The Frenchwoman had departed Shabib's side, and his friend approached with, was that a smile on his face?

James strolled around the corner of the stables and leaned casually against the dark wooden wall, pretending to be interested in his *sgian-dubh* dagger. Shabib slowed as he neared James.

"Weel, my old friend. Look what has caught your interest."

"James," Shabib said sharply. "You should have more respect for Lena."

A bold look of awe marked James's face. "Lena, is it?"

Shabib's eyes narrowed at the jest. "You overstep. It is nothing as you assume. She is kin to one of the MacMillan women. I was only offering a sympathetic ear to a woman who, like me, has left her home and finds herself fighting a war for people she's come to call her own."

Another tease rose to James's lips, but he silenced it as Shabib's words permeated his brain.

"Ye call me your own?" James asked.

Shabib dipped his head respectfully. "You are the only family I have now, James. You have been since France. I followed you to this far reach of the world, didn't I? I consider you my brother."

James swallowed the lump that formed in his throat. He wasn't one for emotions — much less comfortable discussing them than Shabib was.

"Ye are a shoulder for Lena to lean on then?" James asked, refocusing their conversation on Shabib's present interest in the Frenchwoman.

"Yes."

James clapped his friend, nay, his brother, on his back and walked with him to the stables.

"Well, I know ye dinna want to hear it, but ye need someone to ground ye, just as I did. Perchance this woman, Lena, is a start. The MacMillan laird says she is no' yet claimed."

"I've had my loves, James," Shabib said in a tight voice. "My scars run far too deep to find another."

"The world, the heart, I dinna believe works like that. 'Tis no' like bread, where once the pieces are gone, they're gone. With affairs of the heart, it can only increase. And would your wife want ye to live in solitude for the rest of your days?"

Referencing Shabib's slain wife again was a risk — the man never spoke of her unless it was absolutely necessary. And from the grim look in Shabib's face, a risk indeed.

"Dinna look at me like that. Ye know I speak the truth. A harsh truth, but a truth nonetheless."

They stopped at the doorway to the stables and Shabib had regained his stoic temperament. "An odd sentiment, coming from you, Black Douglas, but one I am pleased ye have found," he intoned before leaving James to the horses.

Chapter Twenty: Payback

JAMES HAD KISSED Tosia wildly before the small entourage of men mounted their horses. Excitement sizzled on his skin, and she could smell that heat from him as he pulled her close. The possibility of a free Scotland, finally, made them feel drunk, and James's excitement was contagious.

"I vow to ye, Tosia, I will return. We have not yet lived the fullness of our life together. Yet, we are not fully confident of the English king's intentions. If they are laying a trap, I want to have ye safe. Shabib?" James raised his hand to his friend. Shabib stepped around James's steed, where he stood with Tavish. "My faithful friend, I'll assign ye here, to guard the keep, our kin, and my wife, against any possible English incursions. We dinna know if this is nothing more than a plan to remove the warriors from the keep."

Shabib's black eyebrows furrowed on his brow. "Milord, I do not ride with you?"

His voice was strained, disbelieving. James shook his head and clasped Shabib's shoulder.

"Nay. We dinna trust this missive, and we dinna want to risk this stronghold. Only a small company of men will ride with the king, to keep him safe. I must have ye do the same here. Tavish, ye are to remain as well. Again, to keep your sister and the king's stronghold secure."

His eyes flicked to Tosia, and a surge of heat rose inside her. Once again, James's focus was on her and her safety while he put his own life at risk, no matter how sweet his goodbye.

Tavish bobbed his head eagerly, his face shining with pride at his lord's talks. Shabib, however, pursed his lips, but nodded tightly.

"I will guard the stronghold and those within it with my life." He made his own vow and bowed low.

James cleared his throat and turned back to Tosia.

"We dinna meet the boy-king's emissaries until the morrow. We are investigating the lands and locations today and preparing for the meeting. If all goes well, I should return within three days. Then we can discuss our move to Threave."

Tosia's chest fluttered — Threave, the stony keep that the king had promised to Douglas in return for marrying her, to replace the keep he'd decimated out of deference to Scotland. They had been waiting until the king's goal of subduing the lowlands before they moved to Threave, and now it was happening. She grasped his hand and twined his fingers with hers.

"My heart beats only for ye and will be still until ye return to my arms," she whispered in a tremulous voice.

Then James stole the rest of her words, and her breath, in a deep kiss that worked her lips, probed her tongue, and promised that his greatest desire was to return to her.

He released her as suddenly as he kissed her and mounted up, joining the king without a look back.

Shabib stepped up to stand right behind her.

"You have given him much to live for, milady. That is something he'd not had in years, if ever. And he will come back to claim all that ye have given him."

Shabib's rich voice and insightful words covered her in a cloak, warming her, and she sent up a prayer that James's man was right.

Autumn arrived well before summer was ready to depart, chasing the warmer day away in a rush of sunburst leaves and chilly breezes. And the cusp of autumn also signaled more work in Auchinleck. The inhabitants were uncertain of how long they were to remain, especially as rumor of the potential military excursion to the Highlands if the meeting with the emissary didn't go well.

Lady Elayne, a woman who waited for naught and left nothing to chance, dictated that the household begin to prepare for winter at Auchinleck, and with a presence and force of nature that rivaled the Bruce himself, set the house maids and the sisters, daughters, and wives who'd accompanied their men to the king's banner, to work.

Gathering eggs, cleaning the chambers, boiling linens and clothes, scrubbing the chambers and kitchens, and preparing food for the winter sent the women scurrying to please the iron-willed Lady Elayne. Even when softened by the sweet voice of her sister-by-law, Caitrin, none dared to fall behind in their work.

To avoid mucking up the gardens and tracking mud into the clean kitchens (and invoke the wrath of the chatelaine!) Tosia dragged each heavy bucket of murky water to the far end to the gardens where the grasses waved in the breeze. It was a long, laborious process, and Tosia's arms were beginning to ache from her exertions.

The king and his men had left that morning, and Lady Elayne had wasted no time. Tosia had toiled for hours and by late afternoon, her arms and back throbbed in agony.

She set the bucket on the ground and wiped her damp, chestnut locks from her face. Tightening her kerchief to hold the rogue strands in place, she grimaced as she bent to grasp the bucket again. A crunching sounded in the trees, and Tosia froze where she was.

Had James been correct? Were the English attacking the Bruce's stronghold in his absence?

She opened her mouth to scream when a young man appeared at the tree line, his finger to his lips.

A *very* young man, a young Englishman with frightened brown eyes, and Tosia stumbled back when she realized who stood before her.

"Simon!" she squealed and shifted her gaze around the gardens to make sure no one saw the lad. "What are ye doing here? If any of the king's men find ye, my words will no' be enough to keep your head upon your shoulders!"

He dipped his tawny blond head, as if registering the danger he presented, then lifted his youthful face to hers. His fair eyes were shadowed, as if haunted.

"Yes, I know. But I cannot let this lie, and if it means my life, so be it."

Tosia pursed her lips at his attempt at bravado.

"What can ye no' let lie?" she asked, stepping closer to the trees. Better to keep *this* peculiar interlude hidden.

"I've overheard information that does not sit well with me, not as a good Catholic or as a moral man. My mam raised me better than that. Your king, he's had a missive to meet with the King Edward's representative, yes?"

Tosia froze, a creeping, icy sensation reaching to her neck. How did this lad know of that meeting? What did he know?

"Aye. They left this day to prepare."

The lad cursed under his breath. "Can you find them? Send someone to warn them?"

"Warn them?" Tosia said in hushed voice. "Of what?"

"Your king, or better, your own man, might already have an idea that the English plan to lay a trap. But 'tis worse than you realize. The king's advisers are willing to sacrifice their own for this ploy."

Tosia clutched at her chest. "What do ye mean?"

Simon flicked his eyes back and forth in the trees. "They plan to burn them in the Locherbie estate house. The outside of is made mostly of clay and stone, but they have tucked wood and peat and the like around the edges and hidden it in wooden crucks of the building. Once they are all inside."

Tosia recalled what James had said about the previous events where the English previously burned unsuspecting Scots in churches and manses. "But my husband, the king, and his men won't enter until the emissaries are present and in the manse. They are no' fools."

"No," Simon said, shaking his head sadly, "but they are more honorable, even the man with the reputation — the Black Douglas, your husband? Even his most dire actions are naught compared to what King Edward's advisers deign to do."

"Nay, they are taking precautions . . ."

The lad waved her protestations away. "The King Edward is willing to kill his own men. The emissary? His coterie? They are not the only English headed to Locherbie. The first group is the sacrifice, the lure. And they have no knowledge of the second group that even now preparing to lie in wait until your king's men arrive."

All of Tosia's blood left her head, and she swooned. The English lad grasped her arm to hold her upright.

"How do ye know all this?" she whispered.

His eyes *were* haunted — sad and haunted and the windows to a soul trying to do what was right.

"I am with the party that is laying the trap," Simon told her in a terse voice.

Tosia swallowed, trying to dislodge the tightness in her throat. Her whole body wanted to shut down in shock, and she willed herself to focus.

A chime of laughter rose from the kitchens as several young women spilled into the gardens, and Simon slipped silently back into the wood.

"I have to go. My absence will be noted, and as I don't plan to rejoin them, I will have much to account for."

Tosia grabbed his sleeve. "Wait! Why are you telling me this?" she asked in a rushed whisper.

The lad dropped his eyes again. "You saved me, milady, when your husband, and truly anyone else in your position, would have seen me dead. I knew it to be providence, the grace of God and your kind hand that kept me alive. I vowed that I'd do whatever I could to repay that miracle. You are too kind a woman to be caught up in this, and many of my fellow soldiers are more violent and immoral than I care to admit. This kindness, to save your husband and perchance your king from a vile ambush, 'twas the best way I could conjure to repay what you did for me. For my family."

Tosia's heart went out to the lad — in this moment, he reminded her again of her brother so strongly, her chest throbbed. Oh, this poor youth, too young to be a party to such darkness.

"Ye did no' have to pay me back," she told him.

A slight smile played on his lips. "Perchance, but my mam would have my head if I had done anything less. Best of luck to you, milady."

Then he turned and disappeared into the misty shadows of the woods.

Tosia stayed a moment, watching his lithe form melt into the trees, and once she was certain he was safely away, she lifted her skirts and raced for the stables.

She had no idea where Shabib or Tavish were, and someone needed to find the king and let him know.

If it needed to be her, then she'd ride as she'd never ridden a horse before.

She vowed to save James even if she had to sacrifice her own safety, her own life, to do it.

Tosia gripped her rough woolen skirt as she rounded the side of the stables. She didn't see Tavish standing inside the door on a scattering of hay. He dropped his pitchfork and caught her as she slammed into him. He was more muscled than she'd remembered, his body showing the results of his sparring and sword practice with James.

"Tosia! What has ye so distressed?" he asked as he steadied her.

She stared at his face and gripped his tunic.

"'Tis James! And the king! 'Tis a trap!"

Tavish clicked his tongue at her. "O' course 'tis a trap. They know what they are walking into and will no' be the first in manse. If the emissary is no' there, they will no' go in. If the English arrive with an army, they will fight. Sir James has crafted a fine plan."

Tosia whipped her head from side to side, panic rising in a sour ball to her throat.

"Nay! The English have learned from James's brilliant ways! The emissary will be there! Inside. They will draw the king and his men in under a guise, but another army awaits, will come behind, enclose them all and burn it down. With their own men inside, Tavish. They plan to sacrifice their own men!"

Tavish's face paled as his brow creased. He stiffened under her grasp. "How have ye come to learn this, Tosia?"

The sour ball in her throat was choking her.

How can I tell him? Will he believe me? She and James had never mentioned the English lad they had sent off without a mark. Now that untimely cock had come home to roost.

"'Tis of no consequence," she said, trying to push past him. Tavish gripped her upper arms.

"'Tis of consequence. I want to know how my sister came to know of these devious English plans. Plans that no' even the king's most staunch adviser knows."

His eyes leveled against her, and his shoulders squared. He'd become the king's man, James's man, and was now ready to guard them with everything he had.

"Tell me," his voice was inflexible. "How have ye come to know this?"

She swallowed, trying unsuccessfully to dislodge that sour ball.

"A while ago," she began in a low voice, averting her eyes, "James and I came upon a scouting party of English soldiers in the woods. He slayed two of them right away, before I could blink. But the third . . ." She stopped and looked up at Tavish, cupping his face. "He was a lad, as young as you. He reminded me of ye so much, too much, and I begged James to give the lad mercy. James sent him off blindly into the woods."

Tavish hissed out a deep breath, blowing the loose strands of her russet hair from her face.

"Whilst I can see ye doing so foolish an act, I canna bring myself to envision James permitting an English soldier to leave alive. No' from what I have learned of him, what I *know* of him."

She dropped her head, her hair hampering her view of her brother. What she had asked of James seemed much more innocent than how Tavish was making is sound. The lad was just that, a scared boy fighting in a battle that wasn't his and was so much larger than himself.

At least, 'twas how it appeared to Tosia.

Tavish's tone, however, showed her something much larger was at stake, that she had asked much, perchance too much of James. Why had he done something so dangerous when she had asked?

A warm sensation of realization washed over her, dislodging the sour ball sticking in her throat.

He'd done it *because* she had asked.

"We have to go! Now, Tavish!" she screamed, pushing to move past him. "He's set to burn if we dinna leave now!"

"Tosia!" Tavish shook her, hard enough to make her neck ache. "Why do ye believe this Englishman? Ye could be walking into a trap! It could be to use ye against James!"

"Nay!" She screamed, stamping her foot. Frustration, worry, anger welled up in her, eking out as despondent tears. "He said 'twas to pay it back for his life. That he did no' agree with the English entanglements in Scotland and wanted to go home. And I trust him, Tav. As I would trust ye if ye said the same. And if 'tis a trap for me, then by God I'm willing to take that chance it 'twill save James!"

Tavish stilled his hands, the hard lines on his face softening. Stepping away, he nodded slowly with understanding.

"What if I dinna want to take that chance? Nor would James." His voice was flat, but his gaze roved over Tosia's face, and her determination won out.

"Och aye. Well, then we will need horses. These here are ready —"

"Ready for what, young Tavish?"

A resonating voice boomed from the door, and they whirled around to find James's Moorish companion standing in the doorway. Back lit and in his rich blue robes, he loomed even larger.

"Shabib!" Tosia cried out and grasped the neckline of her tunic. She probably appeared as guilty as she felt, sneaking out on the horses with Tavish.

"What did ye hear, Shabib?" Tavish asked.

Shabib's ability to overhear the most secret of conversations was a well-rumored trait. Tavish shared a look with Tosia. They had no doubt he'd overheard much, if not all, of their heated discussion.

"That there's a trap, and our dear Tosia desires to stop it to save Sir James?" Shabib moved, nay, *glided* into the stables.

Tavish moved in front of Tosia. "Aye. She's had information from a rogue English lad with questionable loyalties that the English army is laying a vile trap. Something Sir James himself might construe. I'd ride to alert Sir James of such a possibility."

"With the lass?" Shabib flicked his chin at Tosia. Tavish returned it with a half-hearted shrug.

"I prefer to leave the lass here, but she would no' agree and would follow me regardless. I erred on the side of no' wasting time in a fight with my sister."

"Then saddle three mounts. For I'd no sooner have James's wife enter the mouth of the beast than I would lead James there myself. You and I, young Tavish, have quite a task ahead of us, keeping Sir James's wife safe as we find the king and share this development with him. If we do not succeed in keeping her from harm, then we will fall under James's heavy hand. Two will accomplish the task better than one, aye?" Shabib ended his question with an eyebrow high on his forehead.

Tavish pursed his lips and nodded. Tosia's entire body sagged at Shabib's offer. Truly, they'd be more successful, and more secure, with a riding party of three. Strength in numbers.

The men check their weapons, then Tavish boosted her onto the horse. "Are ye sure ye want to ride with us? Shabib and I can do this for ye."

"James will listen to me. I was there with the lad when we found him. He'll know that I speak the truth. Certainty or pride in the Scots' cause and his own planning might cloud his mind otherwise. I will keep up with ye and Shabib, this I vow."

Tavish nodded at the unmistakable conviction in her voice. Shabib swept his robes to the side and mounted his horse in a smooth, practiced movement. He settled in and checked his own weapons — his knives and his curved scimitar which had traveled with him from northern Spain. Tavish grunted as he settled into his saddle and shook his shoulders to settle his broadsword on his back.

Then they galloped from the yard, Shabib in the lead and Tavish guarding the rear, each praying to God that they reached the king's army in time.

Chapter Twenty-One: Sharing the News

THE TRAIL THEY followed was well traversed and clear, and they made great time across Dumfries, veering southward toward Locherbie where the supposed meeting was to take place.

James had informed Shabib of their plan to camp in Lochmaben wood northwest of the manse. As they approached, the red dragon banner peeked through the lush green oaks and rowan trees, guiding the trio to the king's small encampment.

Thomas and one of MacCollough's men approached them as they neared, grabbing at Shabib's and Tosia's reins to control the horses.

Shabib bowed low at the men and slid off his steed. Though these men might not know him directly, the Moorish kin of Black Douglas held his own renown, and they asked no questions about who Shabib desired to see.

Tosia followed behind Shabib, hiding in the flapping folds of his robes. Visiting a military encampment, even a small one of only five tents as this one was, unnerved Tosia. The sheer number of gruff Highlanders with their swords nearly as long as she was daunting. Tavish fell in line right behind her, and some of the rigid tension left her shoulders being buttressed by both men.

James's dark head poked out of a tent near the center of the camp, one he assuredly shared with the Bruce. Her assumption proved correct, as the Bruce's own burnished head followed out of the tent.

"Shabib?" James exclaimed, his shock only evidenced by a slight elevation of his thick black brows. Those brows rose higher when he noted who hid behind his man. "Tosia!"

James pushed past the tent flap and rushed for her, his powerful hand seizing her upper arms with such vehemence as to bruise her fair skin. She grimaced at his grip, but he didn't loosen his hold.

"What are ye doing here?" Then, keeping his fierce grasp on her arm, he whipped his head to Shabib. "Why did ye bring her here? Do ye no' know the danger ye've put her in?"

His voice, normally gruff to begin with, took on a more hostile tone, one that made her cringe from him in fear. Tavish puffed up his chest and stood next to Tosia, trying to place himself between Tosia and her husband.

The James she'd come to know and love was gone, abandoned back at Auchinleck. The Black Douglas stood in his place, the full monster of reputation. She feared him in a way she hadn't experienced since they'd first wed, and even with her brother, Shabib, and the King of Scotland surrounding her, the fury that burned off him sent waves of shuddering panic through her entire being. He'd just as soon kill her as he'd listen to anything she had to say.

Shabib, however, didn't seem to fear the snarling beast and placed a sinewy hand on James's shoulder.

"Sir James. You assume much. Temper yourself and permit the lass to share her tale. Do you think me so lack-witted I'd risk bringing her if I didn't believe it was absolutely necessary?"

James's eyes were naught but slits, and his furious gaze shifted between among the three of them. The Bruce joined Shabib and offered his own counsel.

"James, it would behoove us to hear what your wife has to say. She did ride all this way."

The mocking tone of the Bruce's final words forced James to tilt his face sidelong at his king.

"'Twould appear I am outnumbered," he said, dropping his crushing grip from Tosia's slender arms.

He didn't move from her, rather he wrapped his arm around her waist, keeping her close to his side. James led her to a tree stump for use as a seat and settled her on it. Robert sat on another tree stump next to her. James elected to stand above them, his arms crossed over his rigid chest.

Shabib and Tavish moved behind her, serving to support her as she shared her news with her infuriated husband and her king. Shabib flapped his hand at her. *Go ahead,* he gestured.

"James, I was working in the garden, near the wood, and I heard a sound. I ventured in to find a man." She lifted her golden-amber eyes, pleading. "'Twas Simon, dear husband."

At that name, he stiffened, the hardness in his face shifting into something akin to interest.

"Simon, the soldier lad?" he asked with meaning.

Tosia nodded.

"What soldier lad, James?" the Bruce asked. James cut his king a treasonous look, then turned his face back to Tosia.

"What did Simon tell ye?"

"That he owed us, me, a debt, and 'twas time to repay. He detailed the trap the English are setting for ye as we speak."

Several men who'd been eavesdropping glanced around the wood, as if the English were trapping them right there.

"We know 'tis likely a trap, lass," the Bruce told her in a tight voice. "We have already investigated the manse. Naught is amiss. And we will no' enter the church until the entirety of Edward's emissary have entered."

Tosia shook her head. The ride across Dumfries had caused her to lose her kerchief, and her hair flew wildly around her shoulders.

"Nay, *that* is the trap!" She leaned to James and reached up to grasp his crossed arms. "They dinna plan on killing only ye. The English ye've seen in the emissary's camp? 'Tis only one army. The king has another army on the way. His plan is to wait until the emissary and his men are in the manse, and all of ye, then they will entomb ye and set the edifice ablaze, slaying ye all."

James swallowed loudly in the shuttering silence that followed her harrowing words.

"Nay, lass," Robert said in a low voice. "The new boy king might be susceptible to the words of his advisers, but even that inexperienced king would no' kill an entire contingent of his own men, and his representative to boot! I decline to believe even Longshanks, the dark soul he was, would have sacrificed his own men thusly."

James lifted his hand and held it up to the Bruce.

"I dinna agree with ye, my king," he said slowly. Tosia could see his brilliant strategist mind working over her words. "In fact, given the boy king's reputation as weak and foppish, it makes strong sense. What other way might a weak king gain the upper hand than through such vile subterfuge? And with the king's own representative in attendance, we'd never see the trap until we were caught in it."

The Bruce lifted his expressionless face to James.

"Am I to presume this soldier is no' Scots?" the Bruce asked James directly. James tipped his head. A muscle in the Bruce's jaw twitched. "Can we trust this soldier, James? How are we to know that he speaks the truth? What if his conversation with Tosia is part of the English's trap?"

James's gaze caught Tosia's, and James pursed his lips before speaking.

"Aye. We can trust it. This lad owes his life to Tosia, and he seemed earnest to me. Tosia?"

She nodded wildly, her husband's supportive words sending a burst of warmth to replace her icy fear. "Aye. I'd trust my life on this lad's words. More importantly," she said, her face softening to her husband, "I would trust his life. And yours, my king."

Their shared endorsement of the English soldier seemed to appease the king and he nodded once. He looked over his shoulder at the eavesdropping MacCollough. "Declan, gather the men. A change of plans."

Then he glanced at James.

"Sir James, a word, if ye may?"

The Bruce waved James to the narrow clearing where the kindling sat ready for the fire. Though his expression was indifferent, composed, James knew that under his guise, the king was fuming at James's treasonous deception.

"Do ye care to tell me about how ye and your wife are known to an English soldier? One that somehow owed ye a debt?"

The king's tenebrous voice carried with it a veiled threat. James might be the king's most staunch and loyal supporter, but no treason, or even the suggestion of treason, would be tolerated among his men.

James was abashed, feeling scolded by his king, yet his face remained firm and focused on Robert's.

"We came upon a small scouting party in the woods to the east of Auchinleck. I dispatched two of the men right away. The third soldier," James huffed, scoffing at the memory. "He was a lad, no' even old enough to shave, it seemed. Tosia saw something more in him. He reminded her of her brother and begged for his life. How could I no' grant my wife this small grace? So I sent him back the way he came, qualms and all."

"It appears that your kindness was rewarded. If the lad's no' lying, then he might have saved us all."

James dipped his head at his King.

"Or rather, your wife has saved us. Who would have thought your taking a wife could have such beneficent repercussions, eh?"

The king's tease was not lost on James, who ground his jaw at the jest. Then he bowed low, a mocking bow, Robert well knew.

"Och, your intervention served me well, my king."

At this, Robert cracked a smile, a thin white line amid his thick beard.

"Aye, now, serve your wife well afore we send her back, away from any of the fighting that will assuredly ensue and to the safety of Auchinleck. Then join the MacCollough and the rest of the men so we might decide our next course of action."

"Shabib, Tavish, thank ye for bringing Tosia and this news to our attention." James had to temper his voice — he certainly was *not* thankful they'd brought her at all. "'Twill enable us to change our tactics. And keep the king alive. But I dinna want her here, regardless."

"Sir James, I'd prefer to stay here with you. Another warrior, another sword, surely is needed?" Shabib's eyes lowered, and a wretchedness filled James. He grasped Shabib's shoulder in a powerful grip.

"Aye, 'twould. But Tavish is yet a lad, and I canna have anything happen to Tosia. Nothing, Shabib. Do ye understand?"

Shabib raised his liquid brown gaze to James. His lips pursed, then he nodded. Aye, of course Shabib understood James's desperate request.

"Very well, James. I will guard her with my life."

"Thank you, Shabib. As you save her life, ye save mine, aye?"

Shabib's pursed lips pressed into a tight smile. Aye, the man did know.

Robert approached the campfire near his tent, and James tilted his head at the King.

"I have to attend the Bruce," he told Shabib. "I will bring Tosia to her horse, then ye see her safely back to Auchinleck."

Shabib bowed low as James spun on his heel to Tosia who stood by her horse with Thomas. James caressed her cheek with a calloused finger.

"Thank ye, wife. I dinna relish that ye came out here and put your life in danger, but your efforts may have saved the king."

"And ye," she whispered as she laid her hand on his chest. The thrum of his heart under her hand appeared to soothe her. "'Twould save ye."

He dipped his head, a slight smile tugging at his lips. "Yet, Shabib might have relayed your message."

"I could no' risk it."

"And I'd no' risk *your* life!" James's thundering voice rose. Instead of shirking away, she jutted her chin at him.

"And why no'? 'Tis acceptable for ye to vow to lay down your life for mine. Should I no' do the same as your wife? Is the value of your life no less than mine? My heart, my life, would be devastated if your life was forfeit."

James, for once, had no words. He leaned into her, capturing her lips with his. His arms wrapped around her waist and crushed her to him, plunging his tongue deep between her lips. He poured all his desire, all his love for this woman into that kiss, and hoped it was enough to send her back to Auchinleck.

Or, if their chanced tactics with the English failed, enough for the rest of her life.

Chapter Twenty-Two: A New Plan

JAMES JOINED ROBERT the Bruce and the Highlanders gathered in front of the king's tent.

"We have an idea, James," the Bruce intoned, and James inclined his head, ready to listen. "MacCollough's man, Torin, has pointed out that there are two means by which the second contingent might arrive."

The giant Torin held a stick in his immense hand and drew in the dirt with it.

"Here, on the road. We've seen naught of the soldiers, which means they are hiding or still traveling from the south.

They will want to strike when we meet with the emissary at sunrise. That gives us time tonight to work. The trees thicken, here." Torin scratched lines in the dirt. "We can halt them from the north, then ride in from the south, blocking them in. We can assume 'tis a small contingent. They anticipate doing naught but lighting a fire, no' fighting, aye?"

James nodded. "Any idea of how to trap them?"

"The trees are the most obvious," MacCollough commented. "But if they see it from far off, then the trap won't work."

James crouched in the dirt, dragging his fingers over the lines. He narrowed his eyes in the pastel light pageant of the setting sun. The shadows of the trees cast long, purple shadows on the tents. James lifted his eyes to those trees, squinting at the dimming light that filtered through the leaves. Then he looked over at the king.

"I know how we can block them in. But there's more. They may anticipate something, the Scots guarding the road at the very least, so we also want to prepare the meadow to the east. Fire would work best there, methinks. And we can have a scout at each place, signaling an alarm when we know for certain which path the English shall ride."

The men had closed in on James and the king. Robert nodded sagely, his deep brown eyes blazing.

"Aye. 'Tis sound, James. What is your plan to block them in?"

They worked throughout the night, following James's instructions. One group of men rode for the easterly glen, pots of vitriol strapped to their horses. What they had intended to use on the manse with the emissary if needed would now be put to a better use.

The larger group of men had a grander challenge. James pointed at several thickening saplings that lined the road.

"We dinna need to cut them down, just make it impassable. Create chaos. If we cut the trees here, but no' all the way through, we can use ropes to pull them to the ground as the English clear that brush there." He pointed several yards down the trail. "Then do the same for the trees south of the brush, and they are trapped on the road. Once the horses are trapped, we can ambush them. Bowmen then can take out the men on horses. They will be the greatest threat if they can manage around the trees. At the same time, our warriors shall rush in and slay any men on foot, or horsemen who are injured but no' dead. Or we can let panicked horses do the work and trample them where they lay."

The Bruce stared at James, as though he'd never seen the man before. Then a sly smile tucked up the side of the Bruce's beard.

"Och, Sir James. What ye will no' conceive for a battle."

Stout men who were built like barns hacked at the tree trunks with swords and battle axes until the trees sagged under their own weight. Then other men climbed or sat high on horses, fastening ropes nearer the tops of the trees. Even as the sun set completely, the dark of night made their task more difficult, and their bellies growled in protest, they worked non-stop until the complex trap was laid.

Only then did they rest their weary heads, dozing lightly with their weapons at the ready and praying to God beyond the stars. When their lookouts signaled, the Bruce's army would be prepared.

Sunlight had not yet kissed the earth when a cawing sound woke James. He was immediately awake and rolling out of his plaid blankets with his sword in hand. The king had offered him a horse to ride in a place of command, but James preferred to have his feet on the ground, broadsword in hand.

The Bruce's men melted into the trees as the night turned from black to gray, their tunics and plaids blending into the flora as they laid in wait. James played with the leather-bound hilt of his sword absently as his eyes scanned the trail. His heavy breathing helped him focus, helped his body adjust to the battle set before him. A confident man, James rarely feared a battle.

This time, though, he had something to lose, and his chest clenched every time his thoughts wandered to his bold wife who waited for him back at Auchinleck, the woman he was going to build a life with once Scotland had her freedom.

Sending up a silent vow to the Heavens, James used his desire to return to Tosia to steel himself for this conflict ahead.

The high-pitched whistle of a lark broke the early morning quiet. The signal meant the English were on the trail, riding north on the road. James flicked his eyes to the Bruce who crouched near him in the brush, his own broadsword in hand. They nodded at each other, and the light sound of leaves on the wind accompanied the men who grabbed the ropes hidden in the bushes and grass. With unerring focus, they readied themselves to move.

The gray sky lightened as the sun broke the horizon, welcomed the earth with the clopping echo of horses' hooves. James's muscles shifted and his eyes narrowed as he waited and watched for the soldiers to clear the curve by the bush.

A sharp whistle sounded from the men to the south, and James's arms moved without thought. He jumped up and yanked his ropes downward as hard as he could. The trees cracked and moaned as they collapsed into the road, forming a type of horizontally threaded wall blocking the soldiers' path to the manse.

Neighing horses and clamoring men announced the first part of their plan was successful. The creaking sound of the trees to the south followed, and bowmen went to work on the trapped English regiment. Set back in the woods on horseback, the bowmen sent arrows whizzing overhead, and the shouts and screams that ensued heralded James, his King, and the rest of the men to break from their hiding spots.

Only a few men remained on their horses. The rest had either fallen to the ground as a result of panicked horses or the cruel hand of death from an arrow. James stepped over a dead man, assessing the enemy as he lifted his sword. Ten men that he could count.

Such a paltry number. Edward the Second had truly underestimated the Scots.

His sword swept the air with authority and skill, finding the soft belly of a soldier who was trying to pull his sword from its sheath. He died with a look of shock on his face.

The shouts of men surrounded him, and James spun on his toes, his broadsword before him, ready for the next man.

In less time than it took for the sun to spread its light on God's earth, the English's secret continent littered the dirt road in blood and fallen weapons. The Bruce signaled for his squires to collect the weapons and remaining horses, which now became property of the Scottish Army.

Robert spat on the bloody ground. "How arrogant are these English. Hugh Despenser's contingent at the manse is larger than this. We can leave them here, but what do we do with the emissary? Leave him? Confront him as to what happened? Slay him and his men, anyway? They will be looking for us, and we dinna look like those who are on their way to a meeting." He glanced at his blood-stained tunic and boots.

MacCollough approached, wiping his sword against his braies. "'Twould seem that Hugh and his men are no' as innocent as they seem. They'd have to know of a secret plan to murder the king, even if they didn't know they were part of the sacrifice."

James rubbed his black scruff of beard that had thickened as of late and itched.

"Declan has the right of it. Even if they didn't know the depth to which their involvement might be, they had to know that the offer of a treaty was false, that 'twas part of a larger ploy to assassinate the Bruce."

"What are we to do about it?" Declan inquired as he sheathed his broadsword on his back.

The king's face turned to the misty morning sunlight, bathing his skin in the new light of day. He took a deep breath, inhaling the fresh aroma of the late summer morn.

"We shall turn their ploy against them. We might trick them as they strove to trick us."

Then Robert's eyes caught James's and flicked to the slain men in the road. James returned the King's gaze, understanding the king's intentions.

"There's but a dozen, and we can have them lead the entry with the rest of us to follow."

"Entry?" Declan asked, his golden face a mask of confusion. "What?"

James pointed to the dead men in the road. "Strip the English of their clothing and gear. It turns out the second contingent will arrive right after sunrise for the meeting with the emissary after all."

"What if we are still walking into a trap? If they have figured out we dinna plan on any sort of accord?" Declan's questioning voice sounded apprehensive.

James's flinty eyes flashed. "Weel, then 'tis out of the pot and into the fire. Did ye really want to live forever, my lads?"

Chapter Twenty-Three: Waiting

TOSIA BARELY FOCUSED on the ride back. The fields and brush were buttressed by trees, backed by gray and purple-hued mountains rising in the distance. The sun was finalizing its afternoon descent, casting long shadows on the path behind them as if putting the arduous day behind them. All this beauty, and she didn't see it.

Tavish prattled on for most of the ride, his endless chatter filling the void in her chest since leaving James. She had done what she could, risked her well-being to bring him a message that might save his life.

Now she had to trust that they were able to make it out of that trap alive? How did she do that? What if they weren't able to come up with a counter plan to the English? What if they failed, and James burned inside a decrepit manse beside his king?

What if he didn't come home?

Her heart shuddered under her breast and a ball of knotted snakes sat in the pit of her stomach. Shabib had ridden behind them for most of the ride, giving Tosia the privacy she needed to work through her fear and trepidation. But as the forest thinned and they neared Auchinleck, he trotted up to ride next to her.

"Milady, you seem to have a weight upon you. What causes you such distress?" His deep voice rumbled in her ears.

"Och, Shabib. Aye. I know that James has fought for much of the past year, one battle after the next here in the lowlands. He is a powerful warrior, and the tales of his ferocity are the stuff of legends. But he's still a man. What if he's not able to thwart the English? What if they can no' escape the trap that's been laid?"

Her throat clenched on her final words, as if speaking them aloud would bring the action into existence. She'd never had a father, had lost her mother, and even Tavish was beginning to mature on his own. Her heart couldn't handle another loss. Definitely not the loss of James. He may have been a monster when they'd met, but she had tempered the beast and fallen in love with the man. She couldn't lose him.

Shabib nodded sagely at her queries. "Your concerns are not without merit, I'll admit. But may I tell you something about James?"

Tosia turned her face to Shabib, who sat tall and confident on his steed. "Please."

"Beast, monster, or man, there is something about James that seems to be touched by Allah. God. When other men might fall under the sword, blades bounce off him. When other men tire in battle, James becomes invigorated. When other men lose their concentration, James's mind focuses ever sharper. Believe me when I tell you not only will James survive this, he may well outlive us all."

Tosia's lips pursed at Shabib's pronouncement. He knew James better than anyone, even more than his kinsman, Thomas. They had walked through the fires of hell together and made it through with their scars to attest to their survival.

Yet, Shabib always tried to see the best in James. Perchance he wouldn't permit his own mind, his heart, to think on James not returning.

As she studied the man, she realized that he, too, loved James as a man loved a brother. Maybe even more.

James was a fortunate man. Did he know how loved he was? Shabib, Tosia, his kinsmen, the very King of Scotland.

Never was a man more loved.

And perchance Shabib needed to believe his words concerning James to soothe his own worries.

Tosia gave him a tight smile.

"I believe ye are correct, Shabib. He will come home with the king by his side, as if he'd done naught more than visit the merchants in the village."

Shabib didn't answer, but emitted a low rumble in his throat.

Tosia shifted to face forward again. Auchinleck rose in the graying horizon.

She spoke the words, yet she didn't believe them.

She wouldn't believe them until James was back in her arms.

Tosia slept little that night, even after further assurances from Tavish and Shabib that the men would return hale and jubilant the following day.

When she did wake and rubbed the sleep from her eyes, the women of the keep busied themselves. Lady Elayne had put several of the newly arrived women to work around the castle grounds, tending gardens, sewing and needlework repair, and tending the milking cattle for cheese. This included the MacMillan lasses and the comely, agreeable Lena, whom James claimed had attracted the amorous attentions of Shabib. Tosia grinned like a wee lassie whenever she thought on the stoic Shabib ogling Lena like a simpering puppy.

Caitrin invited Tosia to collect the dried rushes for weaving. Elayne took advantage of the sunlight and warmer weather to sit on a stone bench against the wall of the keep and nurse Gabriel. The sun shone on that fine woman, creating a sunlit halo atop her head. Truly, but for the missing men, Tosia thought it was quite a domestic scene.

"The Lady Elayne seems verra content with her life, the babe in her arms. She's a natural mother," Tosia commented.

Caitrin pushed a lock of her own golden tresses behind her ear as she worked. Her eyes blazed with focus.

"Aye," she said in her lilted tone. "She was no' certain she'd even bear a babe. Her mother only had her, the one, and died shortly after. Elayne had told me that her mother had lost a bairn or two before she was born. Lady Elayne fretted over ever having children. Yet she bore a braw laddie to Declan. My mother flits about the babe like a nervous hummingbird, scarcely believing she's got a grandchild. She missed much of Declan's youth, and I believe she's trying to give this babe all that she lost with Declan."

Caitrin spoke easily as she worked, her long, thin fingers separating the dried rushes, her own kirtle well-fitted against her body. Tosia dared another question.

"What of ye? Do ye have bairns with your husband?"

Turning her chin only slightly, Caitrin acknowledged the question as she kept her attention on her task.

"Och, we have no' yet been blessed. Torin is a bit apprehensive, having lost a hand-fast wife in child bed." She paused, peering down that her hands, and her cheeks pinked.

Tosia exhaled. Mayhap she'd treaded too far into private matters.

"Yet, we are hopeful to be blessed soon. I'm excited to have strong, mighty lads with Torin."

Her interest in Caitrin's desire for babes piqued, Tosia's mind returned to the presently absent husbands.

"But," she stuttered out, privacy be damned, "we are in the midst of war! Why would ye risk bringing a babe into the world now?"

It seemed a silly question as Tosia spoke it. One could not really prevent children, not if a husband was as virile as James, and unless Tosia missed her mark, she believed Torin to be as virile as her own husband.

Caitrin smiled, as if to herself, and lifted her sanguine face to where Elayne sat with baby Gabriel.

"I dinna have much of a choice, unless I deny Torin, which I am no' about to do. Even more than out of wifely duties, aye? 'Tis the same with ye and James, I presume?"

Tosia's hot blush burned her cheeks at Caitrin's frank assessment of her marriage bed, and she nodded quickly. A light bubble of laughter rose from Caitrin's throat, reminding her of a chirping of a small bird.

"Och, what I mean to say is, men desire children as women do. They might show it differently, no' carrying the babe themselves, aye? And I love Torin more than anything. I would no' deny him, or myself, the joys of a child. I'll just keep praying that Torin stays alive so he might know his bairns, and that he is successful in his war for a free Scotland, so our babes grow and thrive without the English yoke upon them. Why do these men fight as they do if no' for the future of Scotland? For the future of their own laddies and lasses? What is the point otherwise?"

Tosia's hands stilled against the slender rushes as she considered Caitrin's words. Her gaze drifted to the Lady Elayne, who had finished nursing her son and was adjusting the neckline of her kirtle against the lad's fair head. Then she regarded the rest of the women working at the around keep with that same pensive consideration, bustling in preparation for the king. Many of them, like herself, waited for their men to return with the Bruce.

Caitrin's words struck as a knife of truth in her head.

Of course, what would be the point for fighting for freedom otherwise? James fought for his king, aye, and for his kinsmen, but he also fought for something greater. For his king's children, for the children of the Douglas clan, and for the children, or future children, of every man who fought by his side.

A flash of warm pride filled her chest. While she still worried for her husband, she was more proud of what he had accomplished thus far, dark deeds though they might have been, and what he hoped to accomplish in the future.

The sun crested in the sky, and Tosia returned to her duties, her mind still working in pensive contemplation.

And if James managed to achieve a free Scotland under the Bruce, the future they would have, with possible bairns at the hearth, was as bright as the sun overhead indeed.

The few women who were in the keep for the evening meal broke bread together in the stifling main hall. The king's table was left empty as the women decided to share a meager meal of oat bread and thin broth together at a table closer to the open hall doors. Day had stretched into gloaming, and they had an unstated, shared yearning to be as close to the bailey as possible for when the men arrived.

Though Elayne and Caitrin maintained pleasant facades throughout the day, Tosia's discerning eye didn't miss the strained lines of Elayne's neck or Caitrin's furtive glances toward the main doors. Tosia had decided to err on the side of caution and not mention the trap Simon had revealed. They were on edge as it was — learning of King Edward's potential deceit wouldn't make them feel any better. The chatter might have been idle and light-hearted, but their thoughts were on much heavier matters.

And the thread that stitched together their concerns was one singular question.

When would the men return?

An anxious air settled into the hall, into the entire keep and surrounding crofts, as the day began its descent into darkness and the king and his men had not returned.

The low din of manly chatter in the bailey seeped into the hall like a snake, and the clansmen who'd remained at the keep at the king's behest grumbled that the King had perchance been foolish not to take more men with him. For such an audacious meeting, surely an entire army provided a measure of security for the king that a handful of men did not?

Tosia worked to push her fretting to the side and focus on finishing her evening meal when the chatter lulled before exploding in a celebratory cacophony. Tosia's eyes widened and caught the same wide-eyed exuberance on Caitrin's face. On Elayne, the taut lines of her face softened into a relaxed look of authority.

Rising in a swift swishing of her skirts, Elayne raced past the main door to greet the returning Scottish warriors.

The rest of the women knocked over their benches, racing to follow Lady Elayne. By the time Tosia arrived on the top step outside the main doors, her heart threatening to pound a hole in her chest, Elayne had reached the yard, her determined silver eyes regarding the men.

The king rode at the front with Elayne's own Declan, and Tosia's heart ached at the look of sheer joy that crossed Elayne's features, only to be replaced by a wry smile that, to Tosia, seemed more mocking than angry.

"Weel, for a meeting with an emissary, ye took your time!" Elayne's commanding voice carried across the yard and to her husband's ears. The lion that was Declan grinned widely at his wife as he slid off his mount.

"Och, we debated riding to England to bring an end to all this shite, but the king was hungry, aye?"

Then he lifted his towering wife into his arms and swung her around, planting a bold kiss on her willing lips.

Tosia's own excitement rose from her belly to her throat as she searched the men who rode into the yard. The king had dismounted, received by the other men in the yard. Declan's warrior, Torin, the MacMillan . . .

Where was James?

Her breathing grew heavy. James was the right hand of the king. He should have been at the king's side when they rode through the gate. Instead, the fair Declan rode in that place of honor.

Where was James?

The rest of the men on horseback rode into the yard, appearing worn and weary, but not injured. Almost euphoric. Surely they wouldn't be jubilant if James hadn't made it home? They'd be downtrodden, carrying his corpse.

None of which was the case.

Where was —?

A pair of dark bay horses galloped through the gate, lagging behind the others.

Thomas, and next to him, the beast of Scotland himself, his green eyes shining as bright as the sun on a loch.

"James!" Tosia screeched, her head throbbing with a mix relief and joy.

Lifting her skirts so as not to trip on the stone steps, she ran for the yard to the man dismounting and tossing his reins to Tavish.

She slammed into his solid form. His strong arms caught her easily, crushing her tightly to him as if to make sure she was real.

Tosia did the same, trying to convince herself that, indeed, James stood before her — he wasn't a spirit or ghost who'd ridden in after everyone else.

James released his embrace enough to bend his head low and find Tosia's lips in an aggressive and claiming kiss. Her hands found the black locks at the back of his neck and curled her hands in them, returning the kiss with fervor.

He lifted his head when the king slapped his back and laughed at the randy scene of the hardened Black Douglas kissing his wife.

"James, I would no' have believed it if I didn't see it with mine own eyes. Black Douglas, ye might be the beast of Scotland in battle, but the lass has tamed ye well. Get ye some food and retire with your wife to your quarters."

James gave the Bruce a light bow and then threaded his arm around Tosia's waist to escort her back into the main hall.

James lifted the platter of meat, cheese, and fruit from Tosia's hands in the main hall and led her to their chambers on the second floor of the keep. Though his cock throbbed in anticipation of sliding into his wife's sheath to the hilt, his fatigue made him ache to the depth of his bones.

In truth, what he wanted was nothing more than to be comfortable in his bedding with Tosia in his arms.

He'd been reckless. For the past several years, with nothing to live for, his behavior in battle, in his strategies, put him in the grip of death. He was more than willing to risk his life for the greater cause. And with Shabib by his side, who was of a similar mindset, they risked much, too much, too often.

But he hadn't regarded those who fought with him — the king, Declan, Torin — who had more than just themselves. They had wives, families, and whilst they there fighting for Scotland, they were also fighting for the future of their families in Scotland. James's recklessness could have gotten them killed. What of the future for their wives and families then?

James hugged Tosia tightly as he shoved open the chamber door. Now, he too had something more, a wife and a future. Being reckless didn't only endanger him, but Tosia as well. Yet he'd still fight with all the passion in his soul for a free Scotland, a Scotland for himself, for Tosia, for their future together.

Before he did that, however, he needed a wash. In their rush to return to Auchinleck, they skipped scrubbing the foulness of their day's atrocities from their clothing and bodies. James had wiped his hands, face, and sword with his tunic — that had been the extent of him wiping away the mucky English remnants.

Tosia set to lighting candles against the deepening night and rekindled the fire as James set the platter on the narrow table by the window and sat on the stool to tug off his boots. His feet had been encased since the day before, and once freed, he wiggled and flexed his lightly furred toes against the rush mat, enjoying the sense of cool freedom on his weary feet.

Tosia came to him, reaching to remove his tunic over his head when her hand paused at the hem.

"What's all this?" she inquired, peering closer. She scraped her finger at the dark brown, flaky stain on his tunic.

"Dried blood," James answered casually. "I tried to wipe away as much as I could, but we did no' stop for bathing, aye?"

Her hand recoiled as her eyes roved over the ruined tunic, to his stained braies, and even at the creases of his forearms, hands, and neck. He felt rather like a young child under the scrutiny of his mother.

"James, so much blood!" Tosia clutched at her neck.

He gave her a one-shouldered shrug and reached for Tosia's hip to draw her close. Even with her disdain at his bloodied clothes, she moved toward him.

"'Tis so much blood. How did ye survive?"

"'Tis no' mine! Here, help me remove this. We can burn it in the fire," James told her.

She did as James bid, yanking the soiled clothing from his shoulders. At the crackling hearth, she gave him a side-long look, and he nodded. Holding the tunic as she might hold a dead animal, Tosia tossed it into the fire which snapped and popped at the offending kindling.

Not that his bare chest was much better, and she grimaced as she examined him. James eyed his skin, and while he was accustomed to what he looked like immediately after a battle, Tosia did not.

He barely felt the bruises, and she was used to seeing those. Between battles and training, James was often bruised when he took her to bed. The dirt and caked blood, that he typically washed off in a loch or the horse trough before coming to her.

She was silent as she walked around him, studying his body with surprising intensity, as though she were seeing him for the first time though they had been wed for months. The wide swaths of scars across his arms and shoulders, were marred with scrapes and covered with blood, both his own but more that of his fallen enemies.

His back, he knew, had taken a few strong hits, and he could identify every place he was either scored or cut, for her fingertips caressed every wound, every mark as she slowly explored his body. Chills coursed over his skin, and he dropped his head. The weight of the day, the indelible fatigue, the worry of whether or not he'd return to Tosia — he felt a bit like Atlas, trying to support the world.

Her fingers didn't stop. Undeterred by the horrors of his body, her fingers moved up his neck to his hair and scraped against his scalp. His entire body relaxed under her ministrations.

"Let's get ye cleaned up," she said.

"Ye dinna have to tell me if ye dinna want to," Tosia told James as she began to wipe away the filth from his skin. "Ye've fought before and come home to me, but this, 'tis the first time I've seen ye so, weel . . ."

"Bloodied?"

Tosia dipped her head at the harsh reality of the word.

"Aye. Was it bad?" Her voice dropped low as she continued her ministrations, trying to wash every last drop of blood, every last bit of dirt, from his body.

He stilled under her hands, his skin taut against the rigid muscles.

"Bad enough. Bad because we'd entered under a banner of truce and were forced to rescind that truce. When a new strategy is made all of a sudden, the results are usually less clean than when a full set of tactics are embarked upon."

Her hands moved easily over his shoulders and back, lightly scrubbing with the rag. James dropped his chin to his chest and moaned deeply. She took advantage of his position to wipe the rag over the grime on his neck and he moaned again, a resonant rumbling that touched her at her core.

"So 'twas a trap? And ye had to account for that?"

He tipped his head to the side so she might scrub behind his ear.

"Aye. Your new ally Simon had spoken true. We set up a type of pit trap for the second regiment of men who rode in early that morn."

Tosia dipped the rag into the bowl and paused, the water rushing in rivulets over her hand.

"What did ye do to them? The Englishmen in the trap?"

He shifted to give her a sidelong gaze that was at once hard and shrewd. In that instant, and her stomach knotted.

"We dispatched them. They will no' have the opportunity to lay another trap again."

James and his men killed them, that's what he was telling her in his subtle way. Tosia resumed her scrubbing, moving in front of him to bathe his chest. James sat up tall on the stool and puffed out his chest, granting her full access to his body.

"What of the emissary?" she asked, keeping her eyes on her task. She was afraid to look into those granite eyes and bear what they might convey.

"If he did no' know himself and his men to be sacrifices," he told her in a tense voice, "then they at least knew a trap was to be set. Everything the emissary might have said would be a lie otherwise, and he had to know that."

Tosia's hand stilled. "What did ye do, then?"

James's own large hand rested atop hers, holding her close to him as if he feared she might pull away when he told her of what he did. That she'd pull away from the monster he oft had to become in battle.

"The English, they were scattered on the road. But the emissary was expecting them, one way or another. We didn't disappoint."

This time, Tosia did raise her eyes to his face. She didn't understand his implication. "What do ye mean? Ye said the men were killed. How —?"

James released her hand, and she was certain she noted his lips tug as if to smile, as if to flatter himself on what had transpired.

"They had no more use for their armor or weapons, so we donned their tunics, set our own plaids aside, and put on their armor. Thus, when we rode up to the manse, and the emissary welcomed us inside with open arms. He was expecting the English, ye ken, and the English he received. Or rather, their clothing. The men underneath, weel, he was no' expecting them so much."

Tosia clutched the damp cloth to her chest and gasped. "Ye used their own clothing against them? Like a costume?"

James nodded, his smug expression no longer hidden. "Aye, we did. The emissary and his men had no' notion of what happened until his own kinsmen appeared to turn on him. Before the Bruce ran the emissary through with his sword, he did remove his helmet, so that the emissary's final sight was of the King of Scotland. He thought it fitting, aye?"

Astonishment at James's casual words over so dire a deed stilled Tosia, as she stood stock-still before him. He leaned forward and wrapped his arms around her waist, pressing his head into her belly. Her hands had their own will and found his hair, threading through it, twisting and brushing the black locks.

How did he manage to find *any* peace after such a battle? To have hope crushed, to turn around and slay those who betrayed him, then ride home to find sanctuary her arms? To shed the skin of the beast and just be a man, a captain, a husband, took more mettle than Tosia could imagine. Perchance speaking those horrors aloud gave him a way to forget the events, move on with his life, until the life he lived was one of peace under an independent Scotland.

Tosia found it difficult not to judge him, but she wasn't there; she wasn't a soldier— at best she'd been the bearer of harrowing news. How could she judge him for the actions he deemed necessary once presented with that information?

She couldn't.

Instead, she finished wiping down his face, chest, and belly, helped him removed his stained braies (and tossed those in the fire as well), and then put him in the bed. Tosia shrugged her dampened kirtle from her shoulders where it fell in a creamy pool on the stone floor and joined him in bed.

There they lay, naked and skin on skin, but unmoving, holding each other as night closed in on them, guiding them to sleep where their minds might be cleansed of the horrors of James's battle, and where the world would be bright and new with the rising sun.

They did not make it to the hall to break their fast the next morning.

Chapter Twenty-Four: Shabib

LENA WASN'T IN the hall when they returned, or in the inner bailey. He shouldn't have hoped for her to be, and why should she?

Shabib left his horse in the hands of a stable lad, and rather than heading for the hall with the Bruce as most of the returning warriors did, he retreated back out of the palisade, searching for the MacMillan crofts.

Many of those who flocked to the Bruce's banner during the summer had been settled in small crofts around the keep with plenty of land for tents so the lairds and their men, and any women who traveled with them, might be well set whilst attending the king and fighting for Scotland.

Some women elected to work in the keep directly and sleep in the maid's quarters instead of sleeping in a drafty tent on the hard ground.

Lena was not one of those women. She kept close to her cousin and mistress, feeling a deep sense of obligation to her. And since where the king went, so did the MacMillan, they were destined to linger at Auchinleck, or wherever the women of the clan were assigned to be.

Shabib wrapped his blood-stained robes tight around his lean frame as he moved like the wind among the tents toward the croft. She wasn't outside, and he didn't think she'd sleep in one of the tents.

No, most likely she'd be by her cousin's side. Lena's sense of obligation and responsibility was unrivaled. It was one of the traits about her that he noticed.

And it made a stark impression on Shabib.

That, and her understated, dark-haired beauty. She reminded him of the all the good from his homeland, but her skin and dress were different enough to help him forget the bad. His heart had been locked away in iron since the slaughter of his betrayed wife and son, locked away so much that he didn't believe it could be revived again.

Then came Lena, in her russet kerchief tied over her lush blackish-brown waves, her soft voice and attention to detail, and Shabib lost himself in her.

He made it to the croft and froze, his hand aloft, ready to bang on the warped oaken door.

Aye, as Douglas would say, Shabib had lost his heart to her, but did Lena feel the same? She behaved properly around him, never getting too close or spending a scandalous amount of time with him. And he was a Moor, which brought a wealth of complications to the pale northern land.

Yet she wasn't of this land either. She was French, with hair as dark as the night and a bronze undertone to her skin, and a way of smiling at him where her lips barely moved but her eyes crinkled and narrowed and sparkled.

Shabib threw his shoulders back and pounded at the door.
Hesitation be damned!

There was only one way to find out if Lena's heart turned toward him, and that was to ask her.

The door whipped open faster than Shabib imagined, and he stepped back in surprise. The woman at the door was the MacMillan woman, Lena's cousin.

Stray locks of her honey-brown hair escaped her calf-colored kerchief from her labors of the day, but her silvery-blue eyes sparkled brightly with interest.

"Ye are Black Douglas's man, aye?" she asked with a raised eyebrow. Shabib clasped his hands before himself and gave a deep bow.

"Yes, milady. May I ask if your cousin, Lena, was in the house?"

The woman's chest inflated as she gazed at Shabib down her nose, licking her lips.

"Och, so 'tis like that, is it?"

Shabib couldn't stop the grin that tugged at his lips with her suggestive question. He dipped his head to her.

"Yes, it's like that. Do you think — I mean, would Lena be —?"

She held up her hand. *Thank Allah*. He felt like a green stable lad, unable to form the question to ask after Lena.

"Lena!" the woman hollered over her shoulder into the flickering depths of the croft. "Ye've a visitor. I think ye shall want to meet with him!"

Oh, but the MacMillan woman was enjoying this! Shabib kept the light smile on his face and tried to hide the embarrassment that burned under his skin.

Lena appeared behind the MacMillan woman, her rich, chestnut locks unfettered by a kerchief, and Shabib struggled to control his breathing. It was like seeing her completely undressed.

Her eyes widened at his appearance, but he didn't miss the roses that bloomed in her cheeks.

"Milady, might you join me here in the gardens this fine evening?"

Lena tilted her head, studying him, and Shabib froze so as not to squirm under her intense gaze. Then she dipped her head slightly.

"Oui, you might."

"It is refreshing to hear the French language again. I've missed it," Shabib told her as he walked with her toward the stables where men busied themselves with the horses. Better to stay within sight and not appear inappropriate with her. She was a woman who seemed to take stock in propriety.

She looked up at him, her eyes reflecting the sparse moonlight and flickering torches. "You have the French?"

His lips relaxed at her accented English. The sound was refreshing, a bit like coming home. He had pleasant memories of France, of meeting James and joining up with him, of forging a friendship that rivaled a brotherhood.

"Oui," he answered with a grin. "I lived in France for a while. It is where I met the Black Douglas. We had many good times there before he returned to join the Scottish cause."

"I, too, had good times in France, before most of my family died of a strange disease. A wasting away disease. My cousin here offered up the generosity of her clan, they call it? And her home. I am fortunate to have her. She makes me feel more welcome than I might have imagined."

"If you ever want to have a French conversation, you can search me out. I'd enjoy speaking with you."

She halted her steps and squinted her eyes up at him. "Why do they call him the Black Douglas? It's not just for his hair, is it?"

Shabib stiffened. Oh, what if James's reputation was too much for this fair woman, and she rejected Shabib for his affiliation with the Black Douglas? He took a deep breath before answering.

"You are right. It's not. Surely you've heard of some dark battle strategies that have led to Scottish success as of late?"

Lena shrugged. *"Oui,* but I try not to listen to gossip. Too much to misconstrue in rumor."

Ahh, beautiful and brilliant. Shabib's shoulders unclenched a bit.

"There is a bit of truth to a few of the rumors, and he's been dubbed such for his supposed black heart."

"But he can not have so black a heart, if his fair, dainty wife tempers him so well?"

So she *had* noticed how the mighty beast that was James became nothing more than a wee pup when his wife was about. The Bruce's plan had worked exactly as he, and Shabib, had hoped. Shabib smiled widely.

"Oui, but titles do stick."

"And he is to move to Threave soon. Are you to join him there?"

Shabib swallowed. Here was where the conversation grew murky.

"Well, that rather depends on you."

Lena's hand flew to her ample bosom. *"Moi?* What of me?"

Shabib's heart threatened to burst from his chest, beating as hard as it was. When had he last felt such heady sensations? Not since before his wife and son were slain, and he'd made the rash vow that his heart was dead. Allah indeed could perform miracles.

"I know it is much to ask, but we are both strangers in this land. I have found it to be a fine home, a place I would like to stay. Especially since you have arrived here. I have spent the past fortnight trying to garner the courage to ask if I might woo you?"

"I have heard rumors of you as well. Ones I tried to ignore. But they persist the same. Are you ready for such a thing? Despair doesn't cloud your judgment or your heart?"

Shabib understood her question, and his eyes scrunched up as he gazed upon her curious face.

"It did. For a long time. But by James's side, I saw how anger, despair, and vengeance can wreak havoc upon a man's soul, and how the love of another is the only healing balm. But then, I could ask you the same. You said you've experienced the death of your family. Am I asking too soon for you to consider opening your heart?"

Lena turned her face to the stables, losing herself in the steady work of the men. Her profile was strong, with a high, clear forehead, a sharply defined nose, and pouty lips. Shabib believed he could look upon her face and never tire of it.

"*Oui*, I lost family, but unlike you, not a spouse or a child. My mother and father, but *mon pere* was elderly. My younger brother who was ready to leave the house died, too. We weren't overly close. There is sadness in my heart, but it has not locked my heart away."

She turned to face him again. "But you are leaving, *oui*? Joining the Black Douglas when he removes his wife and household to Threave?" she repeated her question.

"Not if I might court you. The MacMillans are set to remain attached to Auchinleck for a time and will move only when the King's household moves. I have permission to become part of the King's household. I will always be loyal to James, but now that he has Tosia, I don't need to be his conscience anymore. And after seeing the joy and hope in these northern people, I am anxious to contribute to it, find the same for myself. I have been given leave by the Bruce to remain at Auchinleck before we travel to the Highlands."

"And you would stay here, *pour moi*?"

"*Oui*, for you. I'd not depart to Threave if there is something that might keep me here. My sword is sworn to the

Douglas and the King, but my heart, such as it is, is my own. I offer it to you."

Lena stilled, so quiet and motionless it seemed as if she stopped breathing.

"Yours is yet so fragile a heart, Shabib," Lena finally answered in a tender voice. "What if I can't hold it well and only bruise it more? And what of your beliefs? You know I do not share the same."

Shabib risked it all and reached for her hand. She let him take it, and another scar on his heart healed.

"First, we each must come to our Allah in our own way. I am not one to dictate that, and while it may cause a complication here or there, we don't live in a land where those complications might matter much. As for my fragile heart, I am a courageous man, a warrior. More importantly, I have faith, in both Allah and you, that you will tend to it with the utmost care. If you will take it."

His blood pounded in his head as he awaited her answer. Perchance it was too soon. Perchance he overstepped. Perchance his faith, his appearance, and his draping robes were too much for her. But if he didn't ask, he'd never know. And he'd rather take the risk than miss out on what could be a passionate, loving future.

Her hand warmed as he held it, and the fact she didn't pull her hand away made his heart soar with hope. After so long a dead, leaden thing in his chest, the light sensation was glorious.

Who knew that he'd find family, kin, and perchance even love in a cold northern country so far from his own?

Her hand moved, and he had a moment of panic that she was pulling away, that he had grossly missed his mark with her interest in him. Then she adjusted her hands so she was holding both of his. His massive dark hands swallowed her smooth ones, and his insides shivered at her touch.

"Then I will take and cherish your heart, *sa coeur*, Shabib."

Chapter Twenty-Five: Heeding the Call to Arms

AS THE GLORIOUS brilliance of autumn raged across the land, the Bruce's army grew by the day as word of his successes over the English. He gained control over much of the lowlands, spread farther throughout Scotland. His successes bred solidarity, and Auchinleck and the surrounding lands filled to bursting with MacKenzies, MacDonalds, and Cunninghams.

Asper Sinclair had sent word via messengers that his wedding was complete — Haleigh had finally made an honest man of him, and his brothers were presenting themselves in advance of his own return within a fortnight.

John Sinclair, in all his fiery charm, entered the hall with his brother Marcus, the red Sinclair giants ready to resume the Bruce's mantle.

Robert welcomed them with a bear-like embrace. "I hear that congratulations are in order for ye, John! That ye won the wager?"

Robert winked at the younger brother, Marcus, who shook his head in jest.

"Och, such a fair lass, to be sure, but I'm far too young to be wed. Let the old men that my brothers are be shackled to one woman. No' enough lasses have yet fallen to my charms for me to think of marriage!"

John's cutting gaze at his boisterous brother let Robert know what he thought of *that* inflated claim.

"Marcus, *haut yer wheest*!" John flapped his hand at his brother. "There be ladies present!"

Marcus waggled his eyebrows in an annoyingly suggestive manner. "That I know, and I want them to know I'm no' wed!"

John brushed off his brother's antics and focused his gaze on the Bruce.

"And how is Aislynn? She fares well?"

John gave the king a curt bow of his bright red head. "Aye. She has adapted well to the Highlands. She had designs to join me, but I thought it best for her to remain in the Highlands, for now."

Robert nodded at John's sage decision. The English-borne niece of an English earl might not be well received amid the sizable number of Scots under the Bruce's banner.

"And your brother, he will join us soon?"

John nodded. "Aye. After he spends a bit of time with Haleigh, aye?"

This time, it was John who waggled his eyebrows, and the king burst in a rich belly laugh, the smile driving away the deep worry lines on his face. He clapped John on the back.

"Och, then we should celebrate these nuptials with mead! Shall we?"

The Bruce gestured toward his study, and the sprightly Sinclair men followed.

Late the next day, a buzz of excitement rustled amongst the orange-tinted leaves and reached the ears of the Bruce. Following the sounds of the commotion, Robert made his way to the bailey where the sight of the well-built, raven-haired man made his eyes widen. The Bruce rushed to him before the man dismounted his horse.

"MacLeod! What are ye doing here? I sent orders that ye were to remain on the coast, to guard it against the English!"

Ewan swept his leg easily over his beast. The tawny hair-man who accompanied him, Gavin, followed suit, slipping from his steed. Several other MacLeod men had ridden in with Laird Ewan MacLeod, and the king regarded them with a drowning sense of shock.

"Dinna fret, ye old bugger!" Ewan teased as he clasped the Bruce's forearm. "I've no' disobeyed my king. I left my brothers in charge with a contingent of men as ye directed. Your shores are well protected. Gavin here," Ewan flicked his thumb to the other man, "could no' well wait any longer to fight by your side. Our swords were rusting from lack of use."

A slow smiled worked its way across Robert's face. "Well, 'tis good to have ye. We are forming our plan to reclaim all of the Highlands. Ye and the Sinclairs are most welcome, as ye can provide information as to the movements and allies in the north and west."

"What of the eastern Highlands?" Ewan asked, as he waved at his men to care for the horses as he and Gavin entered the hall with the king.

"The MacColloughs were kind enough to relive me of the Ross and his machinations, so that helped secure it a bit. But the Gordons and Frasers have worked tirelessly to keep some control. The Fraser Laird and clansmen should be joining us within the next few days." As they walked through the cavernous hall, the

Bruce cut his eyes to the left and right. "But, I must warn ye, Ewan, that MacCollough is here and he did no' come alone —"

The Bruce was interrupted by a high-pitched shrill of command. Ewan blanched at the voice, recognizing it immediately.

"Nay," he said breathlessly.

The king strode toward the kitchens. "Elayne, Caitrin, are ye within? Might I have a word with ye?"

Elayne glided out, her milky skin and chestnut hair a brilliantly stark contrast to the deep blue gown she wore, and to the green and black plaid that held a bundle to her chest.

"Elayne, I believe ye recall Ewan MacLeod?"

She had the good graces to blush a bit before she clutched at the bundle and curtsied. "Of course, Laird MacLeod, how fare ye? And your wife?"

Ewan's jaw dropped at her light banter, and he flicked his gaze to Gavin, whose expression conveyed the same question. What had happened to the Harpy of the Highlands? Ewan stepped cautiously forward to greet her when the bundle squawked, and he jumped backward. Elayne's laugh echoed in the hall.

"Och, Ewan. I know ye've seen a babe before. Ye have a daughter of your own, no?"

His mouth opened and closed like a landed fish. Elayne smiled widely at his discomfort and patted his arm.

"Dinna fret. All is well between us, is it no'?"

Before he could respond, Elayne swept to the side and held her arm out to the other woman who had entered the hall with Elayne.

The woman was, in a word, stunning. Only one woman had looks of such renown, with hair more brilliant than sunlight and her face in perfect, beautiful symmetry.

"May I present my sister-by-law and Torin Dunnuck's wife, Caitrin MacCollough Dunnuck?"

Ewan had no words and bowed to both women. Robert waved them back into the kitchen as his ferocious gazed turned to the Bruce, his eyes sparkling with mirth.

"Quite a bit has changed in the past year, aye?" Robert asked, dragging Ewan and Gavin from the hall.

The buzz of the previous day became a full cacophony of activity as the king solidified his plans to head north in his quest to reclaim the Highlands. Many Highlanders had rallied to his call and poured in droves to the keep. And Robert met every laird and chieftain as they arrived.

The Frasers of Broch Invershin rode in from the northeast shortly after midday, their horses frothy with sweat and the men more worse for wear. The Fraser laird was known to be ill, so his brother Robert Fraser, called Rob when in the presence of the king, had claimed that title and stood in his stead. Rob and his men dismounted, rough-and-ready men, with one smaller lad in attendance. The Bruce eyed the lad warily as Rob and his men approached.

Surely no' a warrior? The Bruce asked himself as he opened his thick arms in greeting.

"King Robert!" Robert Fraser called out and gripped the Bruce's forearm. "We have rallied to your call. Half of my men are here, the rest await ye in Beauly as we press forth." The Bruce nodded at Rob, then flicked his eyes to the lad who pressed close to a tall Highlander with unruly raven hair.

"A squire?" the Bruce inquired.

Fraser glanced at the clean-shaved lad who blushed a bright pink, then caught the side smile on the wild-haired man. All three erupted with laughter.

"No' quite. May I introduce my niece, Brenna Fraser?" He gave Brenna a scowl. "And remove the bonnet, lass. Let the king see ye are a woman with copper hair."

The small Fraser removed the bonnet, and a cascade of lush waves unrolled across her shoulders. The king's eyebrows rose high on his forehead.

"And her husband, Rafe Fraser?" Rob continued.

The wild-haired man bowed low.

"Your niece, eh?" the Bruce asked in a bantering tone.

Rob Fraser shrugged as if this behavior were familiar. "Brenna's more comfortable with the men. Fighting and hunting and the like. Her husband did promise to make sure she stayed out of the way, though." From his terse words and cutting glare, the Bruce had the idea that bringing the lass had not been an agreeable idea by *all* parties involved.

"No' much place for her with the men here," the Bruce spoke honestly, "but if the lass is amenable, we can always use extra hands in the keep and gardens. I am sure Lady Elayne can find a use for her."

Rob Fraser dipped his head and gestured to the rest of Fraser's men.

Robert the Bruce sighed heavily. What he wanted was a nap, but he put a wide smile on his face and stepped toward them.

***

His desired nap was not forthcoming. Robert the Bruce had hoped to sneak away later in the afternoon when a lull in the activity meant he could duck into his chambers and find some much needed rest.

It wasn't to be. Just as he started to sneak away to the stairs, Lady Elayne joined her husband, Declan, with Torin and Caitrin in the hall. Torin informed the king that boats had arrived from the isles to the west, and those men could be seen on the horizon.

Finally, reinforcements from the wavering MacRuaidhrís and stout MacDonalds. Men flooded into the bailey like water from the Minch flooding the shoreline in the spring. Another fake smile, and more salutations.

James stepped into the hall with Tosia as Rudy MacRuaidhrí bowed low to the king. The Bruce stepped close to the man and bent his head so Rudy's words were heard by his ears alone.

"Christina has been delivered of a boy," Rudy commented, then straightened and smiled faintly at the rest of those in the hall.

The news came as a bittersweet relief. Christina had been swollen with child by Robert when he'd left North Uist at the end of winter. He'd told her he'd stay until the bairn was born, but Christina had waved him off, flippant as always.

"Lioslaith and Muira are close to care for me," she'd told him, "and will attend me in my time. There is naught for ye to do, Robbie, but return to the mainland and do what God has set before ye. Be king."

And he had obeyed, arriving with a small MacDonald party and a pack of hollow promises from the MacRuaidhrí's that they'd soon join in the fray.

Yet here they were, and none were more surprised than the Bruce. The blur of faces careened before him until one man in particular stepped hesitantly through the door. The chatter in the hall died down, and the heat of summer dissipated as if summer itself turned a cold shoulder to Auchinleck hall.

James noted the terse change in the air and moved to stand in front of Tosia, guarding her from any potential harm or violence this shift wrought. His hand drifted down to rest on his sword hilt, always at the ready. Shabib, too, had entered the hall with James and followed his lead, shifting to stand closer to Lena and resting his long, dark fingers on his scimitar.

Declan MacCollough, conversely, rushed the man, his face a mask of rabid fury.

"Alistair MacNally! What possess ye to set foot on Scottish soil again, ye wee bastard!"

The crowd pushed back, allowing Declan to approach the smaller, compact-muscled man.

Declan's tone was full of acerbic hatred, and Tosia cowered into James's backside. "Do something," she whispered to him. "Or 'twill be bloodshed in the king's hall."

James eyed the scene, shared a glance with Shabib, then crossed his arms over his chest and shook his head.

"Nay. I would see this unfold. Declan is no' a man to insult his king that way. Something else burns under the surface, and I think it must be revealed."

He leaned toward Tosia as she nestled closer, peeking from behind James and waiting for a fight in front of the king. The air in the room shifted again; now it sizzled, as if struck by cold lightening, and it seemed every hair on Tosia's body stood on end. Why didn't anyone else appear upset? Other than Declan, most faces appeared bemused, if wary, at what Declan might do.

Tosia looked to Lady Elayne to see what her reaction to her husband's fiery temper might be, but instead of commanding anger, Tosia saw surprise, the hard edge to Elayne's refined face softened at the humbled-appearing Alistair. Amongst the Highlanders and warriors, he seemed dwarfed, hiding among the MacRuaidhrí and MacDonalds.

Declan had reached the craven, wide-eyed man, and something in those eyes struck Tosia. The shape, the intensity . . . Elayne lifted her skirts and stepped quickly to her husband, laying a commanding hand on his upper arm.

Anger flared in Declan's whiskey-hued eyes, as if someone had lit them on fire, but he halted himself from finishing the assent of his fist into the man's face. Tosia was enthralled with the power Elayne wielded with a mere touch of her hand. What mysterious power did that woman contain? Even the most powerful men did her bidding without question.

"Lane, ye must let me." Declan's voice rolled like a low thunder to Tosia's ears. " I never had my retribution against him for what he did to ye."

What had this sorrowful man done? Tosia flicked her eyes back and forth from Elayne to the man and it struck her — their face shape, their eyes, the curve of their jaw, all shared. Was this man kin to Elayne? A cousin? A brother? What had he done to her that Declan might want to beat him bloody on the stones?

"Nay, Declan. Look at him." Her ferocious silver gaze remained fixed on Declan as she waved a hand at Alistair. "He's suffered his fair share, methinks. What say ye, Alistair? If I miss my mark, then I will unleash Declan and his men upon your person."

Tosia hadn't noticed until Elayne spoke that Torin and several other MacCollough men had appeared near Declan, a loose circle of vindication and plaid.

"Lane." Declan's voice was tinged with pleading desperation. He was a husband denied a right to dispense punishment, and Tosia leaned around James's solid form as she would a tree trunk. He moved his arm to lay it over Tosia's shoulders.

"Lane," Declan repeated. "Ye canna deny me this."

Lady Elayne's hand rose from his arm to cup his jaw, the most tender gesture Tosia could imagine.

"Let him speak. Then we will determine his fate." Her eyes shifted slightly to the Bruce who had the true final word on the matter, and he dipped his head almost imperceptibly.

Declan's jaw clenched as he bit back his fury but deferred to his wife's authority. He moved to her side, ready to step in if needed. Elayne lifted her face to Alistair, who stood apart from the other men with his head bowed. He looked so pathetic, Tosia's heart went out to the man.

"Alistair," Elayne's voice, as strong as the woman herself, carried across the hall. If Alistair heard it, he didn't react.

"Why are ye here? Ye were banished. And ye are fortunate my husband stayed his hand, otherwise he'd have your head for your attempt on my life."

Several in the hall who didn't know the rumored history of Elayne MacCollough sucked in harsh breaths, Tosia's included. Their thoughts had to mirror Tosia's — how did Elayne not let Declan cleave the man's head from his body?

Alistair was silent but raised his head and rushed toward her in a swift move that caused Declan and Torin to leap violently toward him. Even James stiffened against Tosia, his hand shifting back to his sword, preparing to leap into the fray.

Instead of attacking her, Alistair slid to his knees into Elayne's skirts, hugging her legs like a desperate child awaiting consolation.

Declan and Torin froze where they stood, as did Elayne. She held her arms aloft at her sides, her shock at Alistair's movements emanating from her body.

"I'm sorry, cousin," he wept — *wept!* — into Elayne's skirts. "I'm so verra, verra sorry. I was tainted, a man possessed. I dinna ken what I was doing and have no excuse for it. All I can do is apologize. And I do, with all of my soul, before these men and God Himself. I apologize for what I did to ye in my heated, misguided attempts. If ye canna forgive me, I understand. If ye want your man to have my head, then I will no' fight. So be it."

Tosia's hand flew to her mouth. Whatever the man had done to Elayne, he sounded as if he surely deserved this punishment, and now Elayne was the arbiter of his very life. Would she end it as she might step on a bug? Did Elayne harbor so much hatred for her cousin's actions that she'd forfeit his life?

For several heartbeats, Elayne didn't move, her hands upraised like an angel's wings. Her silvery eyes stared at the tawny head bent into her skirts. Then her fingers twitched, as if the decision she made needed time to flow through the blood in her body and make it move her dictates. One pale, long-fingered hand floated down inch by inch and came to rest on Alistair's head. She clenched her hand in his hair, threading her fingers through the unruly amber locks.

Alistair clenched as well, gripping her skirts forcibly in apologetic sobs. Elayne's other hand followed the first, and she hugged his head into her legs. Her chin dropped to her heaving chest. Waves of her dark, burnished hair fell to cover her face, which Tosia was certain was covered in tears.

Declan reached his hand to Elayne's back, a reassuring gesture meant to provide more comfort as she gave absolution to the most undeserving soul.

"Elayne?" His low voice was meant for her ears but echoed in the quiet of the hall.

She used her sleeve to wipe her hidden face before lifting it to him, then removed her other hand from Alistair's head. "He can stay with the MacDonalds."

Then Lady Elayne tugged her skirts from her prostate cousin and, with Declan and Torin, returned to Caitrin's side.

That poor woman was beyond the pale, holding her stomach as if she would be sick over the matter. Cut from a different cloth than her sister-by-law, Caitrin was.

As for Tosia, she again marveled at the Lady Elayne — her stoic nature belied a soft and forgiving woman. Would Tosia have been able to forgive someone for so grave a sin? She didn't know.

Chapter Twenty-Six: The Future of Scotland

JAMES HAD REQUESTED a conference with Robert, and as he entered the keep, heading for the king' study, Shabib appeared from the entryway to the stairs.

"Ah, Shabib, just the man I was searching for. I'm about to have counsel with the king. 'Tis time for us to set up our own place at Threave, as promised by the king when I wed Tosia. I want to do that before we leave for the Highlands so she might be settled. Come with me so we might learn when we can to begin our transition to that keep."

Shabib's stoic face hid in the royal blue of his hood. Instead of an eager reception and the prospect of a home, Shabib's hesitancy raised the hairs on the back of James's neck.

The reason Shabib had sought him out was not a good one.

"I do not believe I'll be leaving with you, my brother." Shabib's deep voice emanated with an air of sadness.

James inhaled, trying to take in Shabib's words. They had been together for so long. Why did his friend want to part ways now? James narrowed his eyes at Shabib.

"Why not? Have I, or the king, offended ye somehow?"

Shabib's blue hood shook. "No, my brother. Nothing of the sort. And I will yet travel with you to your northern lands. I am not leaving your king. At least, not yet."

James raised an eyebrow. "Your decision to remain at Auchinleck wouldn't have anything to do with the black-haired lass who arrived with the MacMillans, would it?"

Finally, Shabib's impassive visage broke, and he dipped his head low. James's lips split into a wide grin. "Och, so it does."

James clapped his friend on his shoulders hard enough to make Shabib stumble forward.

"Weel, then, my brother. Ye will be missed at Threave, but I applaud your desire to pursue this woman. I canna fault ye for affairs of the heart when I worried that ye had lost your heart altogether. And as long as ye fight by my side, I dinna have a care where ye lay your head at night."

"I could say the same of you, James. When you set your own keep on fire, decimating your own stronghold, I worried for your heart and soul. While I have to leave your soul to Allah, I'm pleased that you have yet retained your heart and gifted it to the care of your wife. She has grounded you in a way you didn't know you needed."

James's grin faltered a bit. "You as well. I hope this woman has a care for your heart and provides a salve for your wounds when you return from battle."

"Thank you, James. Your blessing makes this easier for me."

James rested his hand on Shabib's shoulder, gripping him tightly. "Your life has no' been easy. I could no' image having to reject my own people, my prior life, after so devastating a blow. Lands and castles, they are dirt and stone and can be replaced. Your loved ones can never be. But you can try to reclaim a measure of that in the future. I bid you the best life here with your woman in a free Scotland."

Shabib nodded his head. "And I will fight by your side until that day arrives."

The wee Brenna Fraser had joined the other women to help prepare and serve dinner to the swelling ranks of the Bruce's army. With the recent arrivals of the Sinclairs, the Frasers, the MacLeods, and the MacRuaidhrís and MacDonalds from the islands, the Bruce's army bordered on formidable. The English would surely tremble in fear. Yet it also meant much assistance was needed to help house and feed so many men. Even the help of the oddly dressed Brenna, with her perky smiles and easy manners, was more than welcome.

Caitrin was absent from the kitchens, much to Tosia's dismay. Over the past months, Tosia had grown fond of Caitrin and her austere sister-by-law, Lady Elayne. As Tosia arranged the meat on a platter, she decided to check on the fair woman if she didn't appear to evening meal. In the meantime, Tosia chatted with the pert Brenna, avoiding the obvious topic of her manly dress.

Once Tosia found a moment to sit at a table near the kitchens with Brenna, she craned her neck to see if Caitrin had appeared. Indeed, the lass reclined on a chair nearer to the Bruce, her normally milky skin wan and pale. Her husband, the mighty Torin who attended the table in front of the king's, never took his protective eyes from her form. Something about the woman worried him, just as it worried Tosia.

Davina wove her way through the tables to sit by her sallow daughter, fawning over her. A similar sense of concern tightened the lines of Caitrin's mother's face. Tosia forgot her own meal as she watched with overt curiosity the scene unfold between mother and daughter. Only Elayne seemed unworried, and Tosia noted a small smile tugging at the Lady's cheeks, as if she knew a secret none other did.

What does she know?

Then Caitrin's pasty lips formed their own slight smile as she leaned into her mother, speaking into her ear. Davina's face transformed into equal parts shock and joy as she screeched loud enough to garner the attention of those in the hall before clapping her hand over her mouth.

Attention turned to the women as Davina threw her arms around her daughter. Torin knocked over the bench he shared with MacCollough, who ended up on the floor as a result, as he barreled past the table to his wife. Caitrin's still pale face yet glowed as she smiled at the giant.

"Caitrin! What is it?" His large hands gently grabbed hers as she rose partially from her seat. Her mother rose with her, unable to stop patting her daughter's hair and shoulders.

Caitrin's hand snaked to her belly, and she dropped her gaze before speaking. More quiet than her mother or husband, Caitrin once again leaned in and spoke low to Torin. His bearded jaw dropped open.

"Are ye certain? Are ye well?" His eyes dropped to Caitrin's belly, and he covered her slender hand with his own.

That movement told everyone in the hall what ailed Caitrin. Tosia glanced at Elayne, who stayed seated and picked daintily at her meal. She'd known the whole time. Elayne could keep a secret, that was evident to Tosia.

Torin wrapped his bear-like arms around his wife before half-turning to those in the hall.

"Congratulate me! I am to be a father!"

Declan sprang up from the floor and rushed his friend, slapping his back before embracing his sister in an affectionate embrace.

Tosia fairly sighed as she watched the scene. So much love in one family, one kin, one clan. The Bruce, and Scotland as a whole, was all the better for Highlanders such as these living and fighting for it.

As cheers rose around her, drowning out other sounds in the hall, Tosia wrapped her arm around her own waist. James had been unending in his attentions toward her. Might she be carrying a babe now? And how would she birth it and raise it if she did find herself with child? Here at Auchinleck? James, under the command of the king, planned to situate her at Threave before they departed for the Highlands — would he even be here if she bore a babe? The uncertainty, the precariousness of their circumstance suddenly overwhelmed her.

"Are ye well?" Brenna asked, placing her hand on her arm. Tosia turned to her with a weak smile on her lips.

"Aye, thank ye. I got caught up in the joy of it all, aye?" She tipped her head toward the celebratory family.

"Och, aye. Babes bring such joy, do they no'?" Brenna agreed and turned her face to the activity at the front of the hall.

Tosia nodded absently at the lass's words, as she searched the hall for James. "Aye, that they do," she said more to herself than to Brenna.

Was James thinking the same as she? Did he even desire children? They had never spoken about it. What would he do if, *when*, she did find herself full with child?

James hunkered down next to his king and wondered, *what next, what next?* The past few weeks had been enough to try any man's soul, and he glanced at the Bruce. What of *that* man's soul? He was still separated from his wife and child, and the fate of his crown and country yet undecided. James knew he'd not fare as well, or with the same measure of composure, as the man seated beside him. The Bruce's eyes sparkled as he watched the tender scene of Torin learning he was to be a father.

James's own eyes shifted from his king to the women in the hall, searching for the russet-haired lass who'd stolen his heart. The idea of children was one that hadn't crossed James's mind when they first wed, but now that the past few days had been ones of reunion, of forgiveness, of family, and now of babes, his mind had turned to his wife and their procreating activities.

As he gazed upon her face from under hooded eyes, her expression changed from one of celebratory delight to one of furrowed brow and fretful lines. Perchance she'd been thinking the same as James, of the eventual results of their frequent coupling.

That expression of concern tore at his heart, and bowing to the Bruce to excuse himself, he made his way through the throng of lauding men and women toward Tosia. Cheers of *Slainte!* rang throughout the hall as he reached his wife. The strangely dressed Fraser woman perched next to her, but that lass's attention focused on the joyous MacColloughs. Tosia started when he placed his hand on her dainty shoulder. Her hair entwined in his scruffy beard as he leaned in to speak in her ear.

"A word, wife?" he asked. Tosia reached her hand up to cover his before rising.

She wiped the fretful look from her face and replaced it with a tender smile. "Of course, my husband," she answered as she stood.

James took her hand in his and tugged lightly as he led her past the tables to the main doors of the hall, flung wide to the only moderately cooler air outside.

He walked her to the low wall that buttressed the front steps, turning her so she faced the bailey, then stood behind her, his arms on either side of her hips as he rested his hands on the stone wall. She was cradled in his arms, protected.

A gentle breeze lifted flyaway locks of her hair, and he caught scents of grass, heather, and the oncoming autumn, lingering scents that spoke of her day. All that combined with an underlying scent that was uniquely Tosia, an aroma that drove his mind to a heated madness. His groin throbbed every time he caught the scent. Tonight, he forced himself to tamp that arousal down.

He had more important matters to discuss with Tosia.

"Lass," he spoke into the wind. "What was on your mind in the hall? Instead of celebrating with the new mother, ye appeared concerned."

His arms tightened against her, trying to be the solid foundation, the rock she needed to rely on, to ease her ability to voice what had her disheartened. She took his meaning and reclined back, her eyes on the darkened skies and slowly twinkling stars.

"I did celebrate for them, briefly. Caitrin, and the Lady Elayne, have been so kind to me here."

James waited. When she didn't continue, he urged her. "Yet?"

She whirled around in his arms, her eyes searching his face. "Yet we are naught but visitors here. Even after we move to Threave, ye are yet his man. Are we to be endless guests of the king? And what happens when I am with child? Are we to raise it here, amid an army? And what of ye?"

Her rush of panicked questions surprised him. James snapped his head back. "Me?"

"Ye are to leave with the king for the Highlands soon. What if ye dinna return?"

There it was. She feared for his life, for their future. His arms tightened around her, drawing her shaking body to his. The night was far too warm for her to shiver from cold — it was fear of an uncertain future that drove her shivering.

"Aye, lass. Ye speak the truth. At any time I might give my blood, my life, for the idea of freedom for Scotland. 'Tis a prospect I gladly took up when I swore my oath to the king. But I have his assurances that ye, and any babes we have, shall be cared for if I dinna return from battle. That being said," here he lifted her chin with his finger. "I plan on returning every time. To our home at Threave. If the English haven't been able to best me yet, and believe me, they've tried, I dinna think they will get to me at all. I will outlive them all, I vow."

Her arms flexed around his waist, clinging to him as though he was the single, solid thing to hold on to as they floated through the unknown of the world. James kissed the top of her cool hair, soft and comforting against his lips.

"More than that, I made a vow to ye. The day I wed ye, and every day I am with ye. Every time I share my body with ye. I vow to be here for ye, to love ye, to grow old with ye. I've no' forgotten that vow. I am no' ready to leave this earth yet. God willing, I will be here to love ye for a long time yet."

She melted into him at his words. He didn't often share the tender sentimentalities of his heart, but after the past few days, and with the conversation he'd had that afternoon with the Bruce, he needed her to know how deep his feelings were for her.

"And I ye," she whispered into the rough fabric covering his broad chest. "I was so afraid when I came here, was told to wed ye, but ye have given me a life I never imagined, a love I never knew possible. I thank ye for that gift of your heart."

James's chest throbbed at her words. At this moment he hadn't considered possible in his days before the Bruce. He lowered his lips to hers, brushing against their yielding softness with a light kiss.

Then he lifted his head and peered into her upturned face, as bright and glowing as the half-moon that had begun to shine above them.

"And with that, I spoke with the Bruce this day. I have asked that we be permitted to settle at Threave in a sennight's time. We lived there before we came to Auchinleck, so a household is already in place. And if ye have any maids here, Brigid, for instance, that ye want to join us, he's granted leave that they may come as well."

"We move to Threave?" Her eyes reflected the moonlight, shining up at him. James barked out a laugh.

"Dinna be too excited. 'Tis only the start of a keep. Right now, 'tis no more than a pile of rocks on a peat-covered island in the middle of a loch. There's much work to be done to put it to rights and finish the construction."

Tosia shook her head wildly, her chestnut tresses flowing around her shoulders.

"'Tis of no matter. A place that is ours, where we can put down our roots, where ye can rebuild your stronghold, one that is no' tainted by the English, 'tis all that matters to make it ours."

"And ye," James finished for her. "As long as I have ye there, by my side or waiting for me when I return, then 'twill truly be home. Though, I may have to take on the mantle of monster in the north to oust the English. I will always be Black Douglas, my love."

"Aye, and I may be his wife. But when you are here with me, I shall tame that beast so ye know how great of a man ye truly are."

"Ye are the light in my darkness, Tosia."

Her full, flashing eyes fixed on him. "Always."

He kissed her again, under the gentle moonlight, his lips searching hers with all the promise and hope that the heavens, watching from above, might grant them in this shared life in a freed Scotland, together.

The End

If you love this book, be sure to leave a review! Reviews are life blood for authors, and I appreciate every review I receive!

Want more from Michelle? Click below to receive Gavin, the free Glen Highland Romance short ebook, free books, updates, and more in your inbox

[Get your free copy by signing up here!](#)

An Excerpt From The Maiden of the Storm

This new series will take us back in time, to a place where the Ancient Celts, the Caledonii tribe, fought for their land and their people against the Romans in 209 AD

The Maiden of the Storm

Northern Scotland, north of Antoine's Wall, Caledonii Tribe, 209 AD

RUMORS OF ROMAN Centauriae extending their patrols beyond Hadrian's wall north beyond Antoine's wall, what they referred to disdainfully as *cnap-starra*. And to her father's tribe watched from their secluded positions as those soldiers behaved as stupid, overly confident ways. If they wouldn't have risked giving away their positions, the painted men might have laughed at the ill-mannered soldiering of these weighted-down men.

Ru was chieftain of his tribe, a remote relative of the great King Gartnaith Blogh who himself managed to run the

Roman fools from the land. 'Twas said the king laughed with zeal as the Latin devils, in their flaying and rusted Roman armor, scrambled over the low stone wall. As though a minor *cnapstarra* could stop the mighty Caledonii warriors from striking fear into the heart of their Centauriae. Fools.

But when rumors blossomed of rogue Roman soldiers venturing far north of the wall, a foolish endeavor if Ru's daughter, Riana, ever heard one, warriors from her father's tribe and other nearby tribes traveled across the mountainous countryside, through the wide glen to meet them.

Thus far, the soldiers had remained close to the wall, fearing to leave the false security it provided. Ru's warriors had struck down one or two that meandered away from that security, wounding them, perchance fatally, with a well-aimed throw of a spear. The diminutive Roman soldiers, even clad in their hopeful leather and metal armor, were no match for the powerful throw of a Caledonii spear.

This most recent Roman soldier, however, appeared less resilient, less aggressive than his previous counterparts. Though clad in full Roman military garb, he wasn't paying attention to his surroundings — distracted as he was. The Centauriae had traversed the low mountains and lochs to their hidden land. And he was alone. Ru noted his lean-muscled build and made an abrupt decision.

"Dinna kill this lad," he whispered to Dunbraith, his military adviser and old friend. "We should keep him, enslave him. Melt his iron and armor into weapons. And use his knowledge against these pissants. Give them a bit of their own medicine."

Dunbraith's face, blue woad paint lines mixed with blood red, was fearsome and thoughtful. "Severus is defeated," his growling voice responded. "The Roman lines are scattered. 'Tis a safe assumption they will not even try to retrieve the lad." A frightening smile crossed his face, one that Ru knew well. A cruel smile that didn't reach his eyes.

Ru nodded his agreement and waved his hand at his *Imannae*, a young Caledonii eager to prove his worth. The young man positioned himself just beyond the leaves of the scrub bush in which he hid, narrowed his eyes at his prey, and launched a strong-armed throw of his sharpened spear.

The *Imannae's* throw was perfect, catching the young Roman's upper arm in a sharp drive. The lad cried out and dropped to his knees in pain and shock. Ru and his warriors moved in as silent as nightfall.

The Maiden of the Storm
https://www.amazon.com/dp/B08DQY62JD

Historical Fevered Short Novella Series
~ The Highlander's Scarred Hearts ~

Looking for a palate cleanser? Something to read quickly when time is short? Give this short novella series a try –it's hot and fast, like a fever! All free in KU or get the box set for all the loosely connected stories.

Chapter One

Sean

Southern Highlands, 1335

WHEN SEAN WALKED into the village, he kept his head down, but he noticed the stares from under the edge of his hood, nonetheless. He tried to tug the worn leather down more, trying to hide his vicious scars that plagued his face, but a worn hood can only hide so much.

Drizzling rain helped him keep his cover — no one questioned a man wearing a hood in the rain. Yet, he still had to glance to the side, look over his wide shoulders to make sure he kept his distance, and with every movement of his hood, parts of his face peeked out.

And villagers were the worst. Nosy. Gossipy. Wary of strangers. None of which helped him as he ambled past sodden stalls and rain-soaked thatched coverings. His deep-set hazel eyes, more wary than any villager's eye could ever be, scanned the well-trod path before him.

Of course, he was more wary than any villager — no Highlander still living in the safety of their clan lands would ever know the horrors he'd seen. Sean MacDubh's caution was, if nothing else, well earned.

At the end of the pathway was the space he'd been searching for. A hooded plea to the local laird had elicited sympathy from the burly man and his dear wife. Ahh, wives . . . They were the one shining light for Sean. Their hearts were large and ready to aid those in need — the poor, the downtrodden — and they oft convinced their husbands to act with more goodwill than they might otherwise. And in this case, the comely, walnut haired lady used her womanly graces to encourage her husband to extend a small stall in the village to this artisan. Better than tithing for a beggar, she had pointed out. Disgruntled, the laird had agreed.

And here he was, walking in the rain to the stall at the end of the path, hoping that someone in this miserable village might have a need for brass buckles or a variety of beads, both of which were small enough for Sean to carry as he traversed all of Scotland, a lone journeyman with no prospects, no family, no hope for the future.

Check out this first book here: *The Highlander's Scarred Heart*

Then look for Michelle's newest series – The Glen Coe Highlanders – coming in 2022!

A Note on History —

The final book in my Glen Highland Romance series, sigh.

It was with nostalgic pain that I wrote those last few chapters. In those chapters, we go back to all of the books in the series, touching on them in some way, and brining the harrowing events of book 1, 2, and 3 to what I think is a beautiful close. Forgiveness is hard, and especially for Declan and Elayne, they also learn that you cannot forgive a person on behalf of someone else. Alistair better stay far from Declan for the rest of my imagination.

As usual, though I try to retain historical elements as much as possible, such as Robert the Bruce's army advancing and the clansmen flocking to his banner when they could, I do change elements as necessary to move the story. Though this is set in the middle ages, there is still brief mention of kilts (to help setting and just because I love the idea of all Highlanders in kilts!). Some things that actually happened? The Douglas Larder, James Douglas becoming a military strategist and right hand man to Robert, and the death of King Edward I of England in July of 1307.

This book focuses on more of the movements of Robert the Bruce and of the clans that joined him as he began his military movements full force, but the focus on James Douglas was something I'd been wanting to write for a long time. He's such an enigmatic character, and when I read about the Douglas Larder, I had to write a story about him.

I do hope the history seems as real for you as it does for me, regardless of any of the changes I made. And if there are any mistakes in the history, or from the first book to this one, those are completely mine – reconstructed for creative licensing, of course!

Thank you for reading this entire series. If you loved it, go back in time to Ancient Scotland (Alba) and give my Celtic Highland Maidens series a try. Then, look for a new Scottish Highlands series next year, focusing on the clan

A Thank You–

    Once again, Thank you to all my readers who keep coming back, digging into my stories, and asking for more! Without you, this would all be for nothing. You make every word worthwhile!

    I would like to thank those who helped this book come to life – the great people at Period Images for the cover art; to GermanCreative for help creating the cover, to my editors/beta readers Lordcoldemort and Mike; my proofreader Lizzie at Phoenix Proofreading and to all my ARC readers who are kind enough to leave reviews – some of which are so amazing I could just cry!

    I also want to thank the great community of writers I have found on social media who provide unending encouragement when it is needed most.

    And a final thanks to my family – my children and hubby – who are ever so forgiving to mommy when she has writing on deck and needs to lock herself away! I love you guys!

About the Author

Michelle Deerwester-Dalrymple is a professor of writing and an author. She started reading when she was three years old, writing when she was four and published her first poem at age sixteen. She has written articles and essays on a variety of topics, including several texts on writing for middle and high school students. She is also working on a novel inspired by actual events. She lives in California with her family of seven.

You can visit her web page, sign up for her newsletter, and follow all her socials at:

https://linktr.ee/mddalrympleauthor

Also by the Author:

Glen Highland Romance

The Courtship of the Glen – Prequel Short Novella
To Dance in the Glen – Book 1

The Lady of the Glen – Book 2

The Exile of the Glen – Book 3

The Jewel of the Glen – Book 4

The Seduction of the Glen – Book 5

The Warrior of the Glen – Book 6
An Echo in the Glen – Book 7
The Blackguard of the Glen – Book 8

The Celtic Highland Maidens

The Maiden of the Storm

The Maiden of the Grove
The Maiden of the Celts
The Maiden of the Stones – coming soon
The Maiden of the Loch – coming soon

Look for the Fairy Tale *Before* Series
Before the Glass Slipper
Before the Magic Mirror
Before the Cursed Beast
Before the Red Cloak
Before the Magic Lamp

Historical Fevered Series – short and steamy romance
The Highlander's Scarred Heart
The Highlander's Legacy
The Highlander's Return

Her Knight's Second Chance
The Highlander's Vow
Her Outlaw Highlander

Her Knight's Christmas Gift

As M. D. Dalrymple: Men in Uniform Series

Night Shift – Book 1
Day Shift – Book 2
Overtime – Book 3
Holiday Pay – Book 4
School Resource Officer -- Book 5
Holdover – Book 6 coming soon

Campus Heat Series

Charming – Book 1
Tempting – Book 2
Infatuated – Book 3
Craving – Book 4 – coming soon
Alluring – Book 5 -- coming soon

Printed in Great Britain
by Amazon